FEY IMPULSES

Penny Fairland

For Morgan and Tristan

Acknowledgements

This book couldn't have been written without the acts of selfless love and sacrifice from A.J. Fisher. Thanks goes out to Maxie Mae, who taught me the value of grace and patience, and to M.A. Trump, who persevered against adversity and showed that happiness is a choice that gifts the chooser.

Fey (from the Scottish/Gaelic), meaning doomed, mentally unbalanced or to affect an otherworldly demeanor.

Impulsivity: a form of manic behavior often characterized by impatience, short temper, perusal of risky activities and narcissism.

Contents

Chapter 1

It was Saturday and the women's clinic where Kiera Scruggs and her family worked was closed for the weekend. This was the day of the week Kiera usually set aside time to dust her home. She found the chore relaxing as it allowed her to transfer into her labor all the troubles and annoyances collected throughout her week. Once she was finished and the house furnishings stood clean and shining once again, the weight of the world usually felt a million miles away.

This Saturday was different. Kiera's thoughts had been troubled lately over a persistent and ever-increasing worry. It seemed impossible to put her mind to anything. She grew impatient with herself and fussed aloud and cursed as she worked, sometimes going back and again to sweep her micro-fiber duster over the same spot on a piece of furniture she'd hit only minutes before.

Kiera was in the dining room when she realized her efforts weren't going anywhere. She lowered her duster and looked around with an agitated sigh.

Although the large bay window here provided a breathtaking view of the evening sun, her family typically didn't use the dining room table except to entertain dinner guests or to celebrate a birthday supper. Her husband Wendell had his gun cabinet here as well, an oak one he had constructed himself. It had been made with a solid sliding door, which allowed him to keep his rifle and shotgun from prying eyes. Wendell's Glock pistol and the ammunition for all the weapons were stored in the bottom drawer.

The dining room was also used for showcasing a six-foot-tall weathered oak bookcase. Kiera didn't use it for storing books, though, but rather for photographs. Inside the bottom drawer were three thick albums of pictures. Above this drawer were five shelves, each lined with particularly cherished framed images. Several of these were of Kiera's husband and children. Others were photos of friends and people whom she and her husband had known and/or worked with throughout the years. On the fourth shelf down were a few photos of people Kiera had known when she was younger. One in particular she cared about was of an African-American man she had been in love with before ever meeting Wendell. The man's name was Anthony Leyton Johnson and he had died some years ago. Kiera had taken this picture of Anthony when they had been together.

Kiera had snapped the photo outdoors. Anthony had been posed leaning back on the white Renault 5 Turbo Kiera's dad had given her before she'd traveled to Kentucky. That day, Anthony had dressed in the Peter Christian moleskin trousers and silk Hawaiian shirt Kiera had bought for him. She'd always remembered how suave Anthony had looked in the ensemble. Every time she looked at the photo and saw his sly half-smile, she was reminded how very handsome a man he had been. No man had ever affected Kiera like Anthony. So easily had she lost herself to his resonant voice, so happily had she surrendered to his rapacious touch. Never before meeting

Anthony (and never once afterward) had a man exerted such a strong effect on Kiera. She had taken great pride in the fact Anthony had pursued her, and she'd taken just as much pride in showing him how much he meant to her.

To Wendell's credit—knowing how deeply Anthony's unfortunate death had been for Kiera—he had never once complained about her keeping the photo on display.

But this morning her attention was drawn to another picture on the second shelf from the top: the one of her and her son Rory. Wendell had snapped this photo. It had been taken one spring day while Kiera sat holding Rory on a metal rocking bench beneath the mimosa tree that once grew near the house. This was before the poor mimosa became infested by termites and had to be cut down.

Rory had been almost a month old at the time—plump and pink of complexion, his little head thatched with thick dark fuzz. He had been such a good baby, and Kiera –who had previously harbored doubts she would ever feel like an adoring mother—had fallen in love with him the moment he came into the world. Rory was her firstborn and the closest to a perfect child as she could ever want. Although Kiera and Wendell later saw the birth of two daughters, both of whom were dear to her, the secret truth was that neither of her daughters could hope to rival her affection for Rory.

Seeing the photograph now provoked the worry Kiera had felt over the past many days. An intense, nearly feral kind of worry. As much as she'd tried to believe it was also a needless worry, Kiera's maternal instinct worked to overwhelm her rationality.

This instinct warned that something terrible had befallen her Rory.

Kiera's eyes stung with tears as she stared at the photograph. She angrily wiped them away and reminded herself that strong women don't give in to silly, groundless fear.

This did nothing to calm the nagging instinct. She knew there had to be another way for her to deal with the situation. Something that could alleviate her anxiety. Something that would tell her with assurance whether Rory was well and safe or in some kind of danger.

****

Kiera would not ordinarily have set foot for more than ten minutes in a place like The Woodsman. The Scruggs family was as white by skin color as the average country bumpkins residing in the area—even as Kiera was sure she and hers were far more appreciative of the ethnic minorities of the community. At the same time, the Scruggs were keenly aware that the majority of those white neighbors were frequent customers of The Woodsman.

Situated by the side of the road, the establishment was a combination convenience store and hunting supplies shop. The owners, Sam and Doreen Downie, also sold crafts and jewelry and candies, all of which they made themselves. Kiera's family would often drive past and joke about the ramshackle woodboard exterior, the wrap-around porch with four big rocking chairs sitting there, and the metal sign beside the front door with the handwritten text that read: **Nightcrawlers For Sale** in peeling blue paint. To the Scruggs family, the humble establishment's appearance screamed redneck.

The Woodsman was also the only place for five miles around that still sold gasoline. Fortunately, the Downies had put in a small electric station for hybrid cars a couple of years back. Since then Kiera and her family had done business with them five or six times. The owners were indeed redneck in dress, manner and speech, but they were friendly enough. And to the surprise of everyone in the Scruggs family, the establishment's interior was, despite its consciously rustic design and hillbilly layout, immaculate. Sam and Doreen were both in their late thirties. Sam was a large, burly guy with a chatty disposition. He had decidedly Native American features and jet-black hair, which he kept in a single braid down his back and he always wore several strands of beads around his neck and silver cuffs at his wrists. Kiera and her family, being proud of their sensitivity to marginalized cultures, showed deference to this fact whenever they encountered Sam. Wendell in fact had done his best to engage Sam in conversations he thought might be of interest to the man. Sam didn't show much concern for these topics, however, though he always smiled politely while Wendell talked.

On the other hand, Kiera and Wendell felt Doreen was the epitome of lower-class white society. Kiera thought it was such a pity that Sam, for whatever reason, had married the woman. Doreen's arms were heavily tattooed and she was usually found wearing jeans and some spaghetti-strap tight blouse. If not for the silver chain with the gleaming jewel-encircled pentagram Doreen wore around her neck, Kiera would have mistaken her for an aging biker chick.

The couple had a daughter who looked to be in her early twenties. Kiera couldn't remember the daughter's name, but she sometimes worked the cash register and stocked the aisles. Sam and Doreen also had a couple of younger children. Kiera had never paid the children much mind, though they seemed to be always hanging around at The Woodsman.

It was during one of the stops to recharge her family's hybrid jeep that Kiera caught notice of a sign hanging over a door on the west interior wall. The sign was actually a small embroidery sampler—a remnant of cream-white cloth and set in a rough pinewood frame. The words **Fortunes**

Told Here had been embroidered in the cloth with thick indigo weave.

The sign had indeed surprised Kiera. It wasn't the kind of thing her many Baptist and Pentecostal neighbors would deign to display. She wondered at the time if the Downies caught hell from the local provincials over the display. Being that Kiera had never been very skillful in divination herself, she thought if the time ever arose when she needed that certain type of spiritual advice, she might come in and ask if there was an actual fortune teller on the premises or if the sampler was just some novel piece of handiwork?

Now it was Sunday and Kiera took advantage of the fair weather to make the trip from her secluded mountain home on Clanton Valley Hollow to The Woodsman. As she pulled the jeep into the gravel parking lot she saw Sam Downie and some other man seated in rockers on the wide wood porch. Sam's raven-haired little son and daughter were here as well, sitting cross-legged and engaged in some kind of play. Kiera turned off the engine and got out. As she stepped onto the porch, she saw the kids rolling little metal racing cars across the boards.

Kiera gave Sam a bright hello. He looked at her and smiled. "You doing alright today, Mrs. Scruggs?"

She said she was and he returned to his conversation with his companion. Their voices were loud enough that she managed to overhear they were talking about fishing and how the smallmouth bass were biting this year over at Gem Stone Creek. Kiera noticed the children were both looking at her.

"Hello there," she offered. They said nothing but went back to playing with their little cars.

Kiera entered the store to find Doreen and the older daughter sitting on stools behind the counter. When Kiera reached the counter she noticed the daughter was heavily pregnant. She was surprised not to have noticed it before, but then again, she knew she had always been in a hurry to get in and out of the place.

The two women were giggling about something. Doreen bit off her laughter as soon as she saw Kiera.

"Hi, Mrs. Scruggs. Need to recharge your hybrid?" Doreen asked.

"Not today," Kiera said. She looked toward the west interior wall and saw that the sampler still hung over the door. "I want to ask you something though."

"Sure."

"That sign back there, about fortunes told. Is it just a display sampler for sale?"

"Are you looking for a sampler like that?"

Kiera saw a tight-lipped grin come to the daughter's face.

"No," she told Doreen. "Just want to know if someone reads fortunes? Legitimately, that is."

"Legitimately?" Doreen asked. "Are you asking if there is a fortune teller in the store or do you want to know if the fortune teller knows what she's doing?"

Kiera got the distinct feeling the woman was poking fun at her. Never patient with jerks, Kiera felt her easy temper rise a little.

"Yes, and yes," she answered stiffly.

"Well, there is a fortune teller," Doreen retorted just as stiffly, "with many years of experience."

Doreen picked up an opened pack of cigarettes and a lighter from the counter. She eyed the pentagram that Kiera herself wore and a dubious smirk touched her face. Kiera wondered if the woman had not noticed it before. She often wore her pentagram, not because she believed the symbol held any power, but because she liked the look of horror it invoked from the religiously superstitious.

With a raise of an eyebrow, Doreen said, "Look, no offense intended, but some people like to come in here after church service and leave their pamphlets and shoot off their mouths off about the witch in the back room. And we've had our share of nosy Satanists and those tree-hugging Wiccans who drop by, too. Real pains."

Kiera understood about church zealots. And though the goddess she prayed to was the Celtic crone Cailleach, she did find it amusing whenever somebody assumed her pentagram meant she was a Satanist or fluff-headed Wiccan.

"I'm not a Satanist or Wiccan. And as I'm sure you can tell, not here on a mission for any church. Just a pagan, and I have the highest regard for those who are true practitioners of the arts."

"Okay," Doreen replied in a dull tone. "I'm a pagan, too. So let me ask: can't you do your own divination?"

"I can," Kiera said. "But I'd appreciate fresh eyes to look at a certain matter." It wasn't quite the truth. Kiera had just never possessed much patience for the divination arts. The few times she had tried her hand at reading the cards or consulting tea leaves, she had received exactly the answer she had hoped for and then, when these answers failed to manifest, she had ended up disappointed and enraged. This time the question on her mind was far too important to leave to her own handicapped skills.

She confessed, "It is rather important to me, Doreen."

Doreen tugged a cigarette out of the pack and put it to her lips, lit it and took a draw. Turning her head to one side, she exhaled a thin trail of smoke. Kiera saw empathy registered in her expression.

"The fortune teller is my mom," Doreen explained. "She's been doing this since, well gosh, for years before I was born. She doesn't charge a fee. She takes donations from those who can afford it and if not, for free. You want to see her?"

"Yes, please."

"Let me go ask."

Kiera watched as Doreen walked out from behind the counter and to the door under the sample. Doreen gave three light raps to the wood.

"Hey, Mom, you up for a consultation? One of our customers from down the road is asking. Mrs. Scruggs."

Kiera heard a feminine voice from the other side of the door, though she couldn't make out the words.

"Yes, we know her. A regular customer," Doreen answered.

A few more words from inside were uttered. Then Doreen gestured to Kiera. As Kiera walked over the door opened a bit from the inside. Cold conditioned air streamed out of the room and mixed with it was a heady floral scent.

Suddenly, the door opened fully and a woman appeared on the threshold. She certainly didn't have the look Kiera had half-expected. This woman was pleasantly plump, and dressed in casual pants and an off-the-rack peach blouse, little white sandals on her feet. Her hair was silvery gray (likely a professional wash, Kiera thought) and coiffed in a wavy shortcut. Her make-up was light yet meticulously done; the scant eyeliner and only wisp of mascara very flattering to her wide brown eyes. Kiera thought she could have been mistaken for any sixty-plus matron living in the area.

"I'm Doreen's mom," the woman introduced herself in a thick example of the local rural accent. Kiera accepted the hand extended in greeting. "Michelle's my first name, but everybody calls me Micky. Doreen says you need a consultation?"

The woman's demeanor, so like all the other country bumpkin women around the vicinity, gave Kiera a moment's hesitation.

"You're in good hands, Mrs. Scruggs," Doreen said. As she turned and headed back to the counter, Kiera felt Micky give her arm a welcoming pat.

"Come on in. Mrs. Scruggs, is it?"

Kiera nodded and stepped into the room. As Doreen closed the door Kiera realized that with its textured drop ceiling tiles, white roller window shades and flooring of buffed hazelwood, the room had likely been designed as an office space. A narrow wooden cabinet painted blue stood against one wall; on the opposite wall, there was a couch and a desk, on top of which stood a gleaming clean computer and monitor. The blinds were pulled up halfway, allowing Kiera to see the numerous flowerpots that lined the sill. These bedded a variety of thick ferns and herbs and mints. In the center of the room stood a small oval table draped by a clean black fabric cloth, with a chair to either side. In the center of the table was an earthenware bowl filled with sand. A stick of incense was staved in the center from which curls of billowy gray smoke wafted. This, Kiera recognized, was the source of the floral fragrance.

Micky invited her to take a seat in the chair nearest the door. As Kiera sat down she noticed a framed picture hanging on the opposite wall. It was a reprint of an old painting portraying a pregnant woman in medieval attire and standing beneath boughs of breeze-tossed willow. The woman's long, flaxen blonde hair cascaded to her feet and her hands were placed lovingly about her rounded womb. A brass placard in center of the frame's bottom portion displayed the title of the work: *Frig.*

Kiera couldn't help but feel disgusted. She considered herself a genuine pagan, but those of the Norse path elevated their gods to the same standing as their goddesses. Not something Kiera would ever accept from a religion. Besides, she detested this Frig's golden hair, the fair complexion, and the dumb, Madonna-like gaze on her face.

An empty-headed northern European breeding mare, Kiera thought disdainfully. *Real goddesses are dark, fierce and commanding!*

Micky observed her interest in the print. "Ah, you notice Frig. Lovely print, isn't it? I love her, the fecund Lady. She has well blessed my family and me."

Kiera summoned a tightly polite smile. "Yes?"

Micky—possibly picking up on Kiera's aversion to the print—shrugged. "Well, Frig is not everyone's goddess, of course." She turned the conversation to the reading, "Alright, before we begin: my preferred method is throwing the bones. Not human bones, of course, but those of my beloved pets who have passed on and chosen to help guide me. My bag also includes selections of stones, feathers, pieces of wood and other items that have called to me on a spiritual level. But if throwing the bones isn't for you, I can read the tarot or scry the crystal."

Kiera thought a moment. "If you are more experienced with throwing the bones, I think I'd like that."

"I am," Micky said with a modest smile. "It was the first sort of divination my grandmother taught me. And it is the most popular among those who regularly come for consultations."

Micky walked to the blue cabinet door. As she opened it Kiera got a quick glimpse at the inner shelves and saw there an assortment of objects. Many of these were things Kiera recognized as magical implements. But it was a white velvet pouch, stuffed full and cinched tight with a black silk ribbon that Micky drew out. She closed the cabinet door and returned to the table, where she set the stuffed pouch in front of Kiera.

She took the seat at the other side of the table. "Now, what I need you to do is hold the bag in your lap and between your palms. Concentrate on what it is you need advice or information on. Take your time, and do not allow other worries or concerns to intrude on your thoughts. Then tell me when you feel satisfied with the contents and know the situation you need addressed."

"Should I tell you what I want to know"?"

"No need, Mrs. Scruggs."

Kiera nodded and took the pouch. It was indeed heavier than she'd expected, but she nestled it over her thighs and gently cupped her palms and fingers around it.

"Close my eyes?"

"If it helps you concentrate."

Kiera closed her eyes. The unseen contents inside the pouch felt hard, bumpy and completely inanimate between her hands. She focused her thoughts on the matter that had brought her here. An image of her son Rory formed in her mind's eye. It was Rory as he was now, all of thirty-two, with his rich reddish-brown hair and beard, the becoming smile, the gentle glint of his green eyes. The image crumbled and drifted afar like grains of windblown wheat. She saw now Rory through her heart's eye: the tiny blithe child, with the mop of unruly curls that had been the color of crimson fall leaves. The Rory who adored her, who had found no greater joy than to be in her company. He had been hers once, utterly heart and soul.

The memory of the beautiful child kindled a gnawing panic. She needed to know if Rory had extended his stay in Kentucky for reasons she did not know. Over two months before Kiera had given him a few hundred dollars in cash and he'd got into the flatbed truck she and Wendell had given to him on his twenty-fifth birthday. To the truck was hitched the family's old horse trailer, which he needed for his drive to Raywick. This town was not one that Kiera particularly liked him visiting as she had bad memories from her own time spent there. However, Raywick was still a town full of experienced horse breeders, and Kiera was interested in a Dutch Warmblood she'd seen listed for sale through a classifieds website. Rory had volunteered to go check it out.

The plan had been for him to stay at the Duck Crossing Inn and meet with the breeder. If the horse proved to be pure pedigree, then Rory was to call Kiera and she would forward a money order for the horse. Along with this business the trip would be a little adventure for Rory, something he had looked forward to as it was the first time he'd ventured alone any farther than the next county.

After a few days into his trip Rory had called to let her know the horse proved to be only a mixed-breed. He also informed Kiera that he'd taken a job at a local stable. *"To make a little extra money, Mom,"* he'd explained, *"and to see a little more of the world. You can understand this, right?"*

Kiera had been young once. Of course, she understood. And Rory was now some years older than Kiera had been when she left the proverbial nest. But it'd been over two weeks since he had dumped the unexpected news on her. Oh, he had called every other evening or so. And during these calls he sounded very relaxed, very happy. Wendell had assured Kiera that nothing was awry.

"Rory just needs to sow his wild oats like any other young man or woman."

Even if Wendell was right about Rory's motives, Kiera felt her husband was being incredibly obtuse. It was all too possible Rory could meet up with somebody who would tempt him into questioning the principles they had worked so diligently to instill in their children. More disturbing for Kiera was the fear Rory might meet some woman who would entice him to stay for good. Some shallow bimbo who would hold her Rory hostage through frail, carnal substitutes for the love of a mother.

Kiera opened her eyes and stared at the pouch balanced over her lap. The questions she posed poured through her mind's eye: *Tell me, where is my Rory? Does he remain untainted by outside influence? When is my boy returning home?*

Kiera was aware the velvet pouch felt somewhat warmer. Though her hands were steady, she perceived a subtle yet distinct ruffling among the unseen objects within. She stifled the natural reaction to gasp and toss the pouch away and instead repeated her silent questions again and again. The objects gave one last stir and settled inside the cloth. At last Kiera was satisfied they knew exactly what she demanded of them to reveal.

"I am ready."

Micky stood up from her chair and gestured her to do the same. "Alright, Mrs. Scruggs. I want you to untie the ribbon. Then empty the contents of the pouch over the table. Let them spread as they will."

Kiera got to her feet and pulled the black ribbon free from the pouch. She turned it over and allowed the objects to pour over the table. Kiera marveled at the things that rolled out: several different kinds of tiny animal bones and stones. Feathers of all sorts. Colorful crystals. Little yew branches. Dried flower heads. Acorns and seeds of numerous varieties. Peels of bark. Strips of preserved animal skins. Freshwater shells. A small deer antler. What looked to be the tip from the horn of some domestic beast. Numerous nails and screws and shards of broken glass. All these things now lay strewn in a seemingly messy and meaningless pattern across the black fabric on the table.

They both sat down again. The fortune teller leaned forward to assess the objects. Micky's eyes grew large, her face glowed with a mystic otherworldliness. Kiera watched as she lifted a forefinger, which she glided in the air just above the items, every now and then touching an item ever so gingerly. As Micky continued it felt to Kiera that time itself was slowing down. The little room echoed with silence.

As patient as Kiera knew she should be, the urgency to get her answers grew. Frustrated beads of sweat oozed out of the pores of her skin, her gut pained from the strain of waiting. And just as she felt her mouth open to demand, *What the hell do you see?* Micky blinked and the otherworldly expression disappeared from her face.

"There is much activity in your life," Micky said. "You know what you want and you go after it. Since birth you have been blessed with material comforts most others can only envy. The home life is satisfactory, usually harmonious –at this time in your life at least. You protect yourself by prudently choosing companions who are of a like mind. This brings you much happiness and sense of purpose. Very driven, I see, and more than most people..." Micky pursed her lips a bit, "are skilled at getting your way."

Kiera ignored this last assessment. "What else?"

"I do see it is your son you are concerned about, Mrs. Scruggs."

Kiera nodded. "That's right. Is he alright?"

"Your son is fine."

Kiera felt her anxiety lessen a notch. "Tell me more, please."

"He is enjoying himself, his health is ideal. No danger where he is. His present circumstances augur well for a long and very happy life. And he has made arrangements to get the horse trailer back to you and your husband."

Kiera was impressed and hoped the elation she felt looming was justified. "Will he be home soon, then?"

"He enjoys what he is doing. I wish I could say his stay will be extended."

This struck Kiera as an odd statement. She was not completely opposed to Rory extending his stay. Just as long as she knew he would be back, and in the not-too-distant future.

"If that is best, I will be sure tell him."

"I believe he will return to you, though," Micky added.

Relief washed over Kiera. She hated to admit it, but for the first time, she thought she'd done right to come see Micky.

The fortune teller's attention was drawn now to something else on the table. She stretched a tentative hand to one corner and touched what Kiera thought looked like two slender knotty strands of rope coiled around one another. The fortune teller gingerly lifted the thing and deposited it over a palm. Now Kiera could see the coiled strands weren't rope, but rather two plant spikes. Snapdragon spikes in fact, and the things Kiera had mistaken for knots were actually the ripened and dried little dragon-head skull pods.

Micky lifted the spikes with the fingers of her other hand. Giving them a pinch, she shook them over her outstretched palm.

"Hm," she said. "These snapdragon pods have no seeds."

"What does this mean?"

"See the little holes that look like eyes forming a face? The seeds should spill out like pepper when shaken."

"Well, I do know a little about growing snapdragons," Kiera responded. "Though I'm sure sometimes not all flowers get properly fertilized. But what does this tell you?"

Micky frowned. "I will be frank, Mrs. Scruggs. I do not like this. These barren spikes wound about each other foretells dark and violent events."

The ominous statement threatened to chase away the relief Kiera had felt to hear Rory would be back.

"What dark and violent events?"

Micky held her gaze for several unblinking moments. At last she said, "All I can be sure of is that they will transpire out of ties that bind."

Ice slithered up Kiera's back. It took her a moment of reason before she could drive the ice back down. She succeeded, angrily, for now she was sure the fortune teller was trying to play her.

"Oh, you're good, Micky! You had me going there for a minute. I see now you believe by telling me something scary enough, I'll be in here throwing money at you every week!"

Micky arched an eyebrow, an expression Kiera took as an attempt at intimidation.

"Surprised to be spoken to like this, are you?" Kiera chortled.

"Why should I be?" Micky asked, making a gesture over the objects from her velvet pouch. "I see you for exactly what you are. And sad as it is to say, while you may recognize all your other talents and characteristics, the one thing you should see but don't is a lifelong proclivity for fooling yourself."

Kiera's temper snapped. "You are full of it, fortune teller!"

She pushed her chair back so roughly the wooden feet scraped against the hazel wood flooring. Standing up, she fished her wallet out of the front pocket of her pants. There were seven twenty-dollar bills and five tens folded inside. She plucked one of the twenties out and threw it toward the table. The bill missed the target and fell quietly to the floor. Kiera didn't stoop to pick it up; she was sure Micky would pounce on it as soon as she was out the door.

"There's your precious donation," she said. "And thanks for giving me an enlightening glimpse into your trade!"

Kiera stamped to the door and reached for the doorknob.

Behind her, Micky said in an urgent voice, "Whatever you think of me, Mrs. Scruggs, don't compel your son to come home. Do not compel him by any means!"

For one fretful moment, maybe for two, Kiera was tempted to demand of her *why*.

Instead, she turned with a glower at Micky. The gall of the woman! Kiera could almost feel sorry for the pudgy fortune teller. She sensed the woman actually believed all the rubbish she spoke, unable to see that she was only an unskilled, useless excuse for a human being...someone who had no problem making babies and spinning scary stories to gullible clients because she had nothing more worthwhile to give the world.

Micky seemed oblivious to the emotions on Kiera's face. The fortune teller's eyes widened and gleamed keener somehow. She seemed to be peering into Kiera, to someplace beyond the mortal shell. Then Micky abruptly recoiled and her expression went blank.

"You have been shielded for a very long time," Micky said in a faraway voice. "But even the threads of the darkest veil burn under illumination."

The look Micky now gave reminded Kiera of one she had encountered a few times in her life: a consummate mix of contempt and pity. Kiera had long ago vowed she'd never again tolerate having that look cast her way.

"So," Kiera sneered. "You've heard some old gossip about me from the local rednecks?"

"I have heard no gossip about you, Mrs. Scruggs."

Against her will, Kiera detected truthfulness in Micky's claim to have heard no gossip. And this was something Kiera found impossible to square with the look of near disgust burnishing vividly in the fortune teller's eyes.

"Take your money with you," Micky told her. "If you leave it here, I will just burn it."

Kiera's gut instinct was to refuse to retrieve the bill. But something about the fortune teller's tone aroused in her an unknown terror for what might possibly transpire if she didn't comply. Kiera bent forward and snatched the bill. Standing up, she opened the door and walked out. She didn't shut it behind her, nor did she speak a word to any of Micky's relatives on her way out of The Woodsman.

Kiera relaxed somewhat during the drive home. She was able to laugh about the experience and curse the cloying charlatan. Micky may have been right about fooling herself, Kiera conceded, in that she'd been gullible enough to have visited a roadside gypsy in the first place! Kiera remembered that she was educated in certain arcane arts, and had at least a little experience in bending the course of the natural world in order to get what she needed. It had only been out of motherly concern for her son that she had doubted herself. A fortune teller wasn't what she needed. She had simply fallen weak, and this was a mistake she was determined would not happen again.

Never again, she vowed.

Chapter 2

On the morning of the following Monday, Kiera removed a tofu and black bean casserole from her kitchen oven and placed the dish atop the laminate counter. There it would cool until she needed to put it into the refrigerator. That night, after she and her family returned from their usual tasks at the clinic, the casserole could be reheated in the microwave oven for their dinner. This was her usual routine, as Kiera would never let it be said she was too busy to cook for her kids or provide her husband with a healthy meal.

As she took the oven mitts off she heard a crack of thunder peal across the sky. The trail of the sound was odd to the ears, more like the mournful wail of a small dog than thunder. The entire peal lasted only a few seconds and Kiera was at once concerned about the irksome possibility of rain. She and her family had their usual work as escorts at the clinic to get to. On top of this, Wendell needed to inspect the damage at the utility shed located at the clinic's parking lot as a windy storm had blown off part of the roof just a couple of weeks earlier. Ordinarily, Rory ordinarily could be counted on to help his dad, but he was still in Kentucky.

Kiera stepped to the sink window and braced herself for dismal skies outside. But the sun shone brightly in an azure firmament with not a single cloud to be seen. There was a wind blowing outside, angrily rustling the limbs of the trees which stood about the house. Such weather conditions were not uncommon for the property set atop their little private mountain. Kiera's father, Ira Hambrick, had bought this piece of Krumme County property as a wedding gift for her and Wendell. Kiera had picked it out herself, as she knew the seclusion offered a refuge from prying eyes. Throughout the thirty-three years since moving here the family had grown accustomed to rough droughts of wind which blew up from the twisting road and valley. These droughts were so frequent it often seemed the wind was hell-bent to assault their land. It would have been easy for Kiera to attribute these droughts to nothing more than mere natural gusts. But that their neighbors were all either hillbilly types or dull American bourgeoisie, Kiera couldn't help but sometimes wonder if the ignorance of these people hadn't infused itself in the very fluctuations of the atmosphere.

But she remembered hearing the weather forecast over the radio earlier. It had been a prediction for sunny skies over Avonport, where the clinic was located. So she covered her casserole with aluminum foil and transferred the dish to a rattan trivet on the kitchen table.

She turned around, ready to call Wendell and their young adult daughters to tell them it was time to get into the family jeep. Only now did Kiera notice the quiet in the household. She remembered now her daughter Skylar had mentioned earlier Wendell had something to attend to at *the shades*. This was what Skylar and her older sister Tallulah—or Tally, as was her nickname—both referred to when talking about the northern area of their property where a grove of elm and juniper trees stood. At the time Skylar had mentioned it Kiera had been enjoying her first cup of coffee for the morning. Her mind had been occupied with the throbbing in her head from the half bottle of wine finished off the night before. Skylar's words had quickly been forgotten, and along with the words, the significance. But as she recalled the incident now, Kiera remembered the way Skylar had mouthed the words *the shades*. There had been a distinct ring of disapproval in her daughter's voice. A ring which, to Kiera's exasperation, was becoming more and more familiar when it came to Skylar.

Although Kiera didn't want to, she expected the worst. She had told Wendell some months ago he needed to stop shooting dogs. As much as she understood how aggravating it was when some mongrel came around – whether an abandoned dog or one of their neighbors' habitually roaming pets—Kiera knew the shadowy grove was replete with canine carcasses. Exactly how many dogs over the years had Wendell killed and stuck in that ground? Thirty? Forty? Maybe fifty?

Kiera was also aware their neighbors probably suspected what had happened to their missing dogs. She'd overheard their whispered rumors when she passed them in the aisles of the farmer's market and those times she had encountered them down at The Woodsman. She'd seen the baleful glares from inside their vehicles as they passed her on the road. Not that Kiera could forgive these people for allowing their unchained dogs to roam the countryside. Their precious beasts had certainly shown no compunction about entering her family's chicken coop and attacking the hens and helping themselves to the eggs. One of the damnable dogs had even ventured into the pen where they kept their goats. If Wendell hadn't heard it that night and gone for his rifle, the dog might have attacked one of the nanny's kids.

The possibility of further riling up neighbor suspicion wasn't the only reason Kiera was averse to Wendell burying more dogs out there. There was also Skylar's sensitive reaction to the practice to consider. Kiera felt frustrated now to remember all the warnings she'd given Wendell.

"Skylar doesn't need to see another dead dog!" she hissed aloud.

It was a mantra she had voiced many times throughout the years. Skylar was twenty-five years old and had always been more squeamish than their twenty-seven-year-old Tally. Skylar was also much more pitying of dumb animals. The entire family knew that Skylar's witnessing of the dog burials had left her with a deep-seated repugnance for the shades. Such behavior seemed weak to Kiera and she'd often teased Skylar about her *wimpiness*. And yet Kiera reminded herself that a good mother doesn't let their child be subjected to needless grisly visuals.

Oh, how she wished Wendell had the common sense to just leave the ground in peace! If it weren't too late, perhaps she could convince him to just burn the remains of whatever dog he was trying to dispose of.

Kiera stepped to the front door and grabbed her jacket from the wall coat rack. Hastily, she pulled it on and opened the front door. She went out, slamming the door behind her, and tramped down the three plank steps to the yard. Onto the well-beaten path leading north she trod and passed the lengthy herb garden to her left. Up ahead on her right was the horse barn with its pen. Her two riding horses, Little Crest and Felicity, stood with their heads over the wooden fence. She'd gone out right after waking to feed them and to make sure they had clean water. But she'd put off grooming them as she had the casserole to make.

Now as she passed, Felicity let out a piteous whinny. The thought passed that perhaps she should stop to pet the horses and talk to them for a few moments. But no, her suspicion about Wendell compelled her to hurry on.

Wendell loved having company when he did anything. Nothing satisfied him quite like having an audience. He loved to give verbose dissertations on his agricultural knowledge and his sociological views, to deliver sermons on his latest spin of some spiritual doctrine. To give his interpretations of some literary work. To discuss his theories about race relations and socialist doctrine, the impact of free enterprise for the lower classes, even the price of ham in Canada. Whatever subject preoccupied his studious thoughts at any given moment. When there wasn't a friend or neighbor around to hear Wendell flaunt an opinion their children made for a convenient audience. Skylar and Tally, more so than even Rory, were too admiring of their father to ever remind him they'd heard it all before. Never would they just get up and walk away when their dad was speaking. And Kiera knew it would be just like her husband to have both young women plunked right there on the grass at his heels while he yammered away in the midst of shoveling a new dog grave.

A few yards past the herb garden and horse pen, the ground beneath Kiera's feet began its gentle ascent. The path continued for about thirty yards to a stretch of grass. The grass there was short, as it was one of the favorite spots for their goats to graze. There was also a picnic table with flanking benches. At the far side of the stretch jutted the summit of their property. The summit looked over the valley below, with its little roadside trailers, old farmhouses and fields of corn and tobacco. White trash in all its glory, Kiera deemed the entire scene. And growing at this summit were the trees that made up the shades.

Kiera reached the grassy stretch and saw her husband and daughters. Wendell stood at one end of the picnic table, shovel indeed in hand. But it appeared he had taken a break from whatever task he'd come for as the shovel blade was rested on the ground between his feet. Tally sat on the bench closest to him and Kiera could hear her familiar ebullient, high-pitched voice. It took Kiera a few moments to catch sight of Skylar. At length she saw her youngest daughter standing against a tree trunk at the perimeter of the shades.

Wendell acknowledged Kiera with a smile as she approached. Sweat dripped from the strands of his nearly white beard and his fair complexion was rosy and glistened from exertion. There were heavy perspiration marks under the pits of his short-sleeved red and white striped work shirt. Kiera could only imagine how this work had fatigued him.

Kiera's suspicion as to what he'd been doing was confirmed when she saw his rifle lying across one end of the table. Tally, dressed in shorts and an old tee shirt, looked fresh as a daisy sitting on the edge of the table with her legs draped over. Kiera knew, dismally, that Tally would have happily helped her father kill or bury a dog if he allowed it. But Wendell was ornery about doing things for himself, especially when it came to the canines, which he almost seemed to take pleasure in hating.

Wendell wiped his brow with the back of a hand. "Good morning, my brunette queen. I dare say you quite enjoyed my latest batch of dandelion wine last night."

Kiera nodded but didn't feel like making cheerful small talk. Her eyes were drawn to the freshly packed soil close to Wendell's feet. Just the right size to cover a large dog's grave. This one wasn't even in the shades itself, but out close to the picnic table where the family often enjoyed summer dinners!

"And what the hell's this, dear husband?" she demanded.

Tally piped up sarcastically, "Well, Mom, I can assure you it isn't dinner."

Kiera had always been proud of Tally's acerbic sense of humor, but right now she wanted to hear from Wendell. She arched an eyebrow and asked him, "Please Wendell, tell me this is something besides another dog?"

With a little scoff, her husband answered matter-of-factly, "Had to be done, Kiera. American Pit Bull."

Kiera didn't realize Skylar had walked down from the shades until she heard her voice close by, "*Mother* pit bull. Still nursing, by the look of the full teats."

"Oh, who cares," Tally said. "The damned thing could have hurt our livestock. But you couldn't care less about that, could you?"

Skylar turned her eyes coolly toward her sister. "A big statement from somebody who does so little for our livestock."

Tally's hands arched into claws at her side. "Oh shut up, you idiot!"

Kiera had no patience to hear the two argue, even if they were discussing the ethics of shooting a nursing mama dog. So she changed the subject, "I need you girls to go put my casserole in the fridge and get ready to load up in the jeep."

Tally hopped off the table and declared, "My turn to drive!"

Kiera noticed the alarmed reaction that came to Skylar's face. The truth was they all feared Tally's manic driving. But at least now Skylar was distracted from the matter of the dog. Her two daughters turned and started walking toward the house, quarreling while they went along.

It was apparent by her aging husband's appearance he needed to sit down and have something cold to drink or at least catch his breath before they made the drive into Avonport. Wendell was almost seventy years old after all. But Kiera had to know first, "Why Wendell? We agreed you'd bury no more."

"We agreed no more buried in the shades, Kiera." He gave the earth several hearty taps with the shovel blade. "And I wouldn't have had cause to bury one today if the damned thing hadn't come up to our property. You know that. We got baby goats and chicks to think about."

Kiera drew a deep breath and tried to quiet the aggravation scraping at her gut. "Are you sure? Sure it was only a pit bull?"

Wendell heaved the shovel over one shoulder and stepped over to her. He laid a reassuring hand on her shoulder. "Of course. Why do you ask?"

Kiera couldn't forget the canine wail she'd heard earlier. If there was one thing she wanted to avoid today was giving Wendell an excuse to go hunting for a second dog.

She feigned a light laugh. "I just hope you don't plan on cramming the soil here like you have in the shades. We'd end up having to find a new place to hold our picnics."

"That will be up to our neighbors," he replied, "and whether they decide to keep their mutts at home."

Kiera wasn't very hopeful. "I don't see that happening. Most dogs tend to escape their leash or wander out of their own yard every now and then."

Wendell grunted. "And I think they especially tend to escape when their owners are our congenitally defective neighbors."

Kiera shuddered. *Congenitally defective.* It was a label Kiera often used to describe other people. People she considered low-class or who held the wrong political convictions or those who simply didn't belong to hers and Wendell's circle of carefully selected like-minded friends and associates. But somehow, to hear her husband use the term sounded ugly to her ears.

Yet she also realized how weak her reaction probably was. People like she and Wendell needed emotional fortitude to carry out their altruistic objectives. Sensitivity to germane and unfair descriptions threatened to weaken their resolve.

Wendell handed her the shovel and reached for his rifle. Carrying the tool over one shoulder, Kiera accompanied him away from the shades.

Chapter 3

The Scruggs family changed into the dark blue scrubs they wore for their jobs as Pink Escorts and headed out. Tally got her way and did the driving. To everyone's relief, she managed not to weave the family's jeep across a center line this time. And she made the highway turns with only a single momentary bump against an asphalt shoulder.

When Tally reached the Tri-Cities Women's Health clinic she pulled the jeep into a spot in the lot adjacent to Lader Avenue. This was the designated parking area for patients and the escorts (the winding thru-drive that led around the building to the secluded two-story parking garage was reserved for physicians, clinic staff and corporate members). The escorts' sheltering pink canopy tent –with its prominent Campaign Parenthood logo—was located on a strip of grassy area just outside the eastern part of the lot. Beside this tent stood their equipment shed.

Kiera had come up with the escort group's official name: Pro-Choice Krumme County. Often going by the abbreviation PCKC, the group had a Facebook page as well as fans and followers on several internet social platforms. They were also provided free promotion at the county's Democratic Party headquarters website. It hadn't taken long for their little group to go from a volunteer organization to a regional cause célèbre. Those who provided sympathetic moral support (along with private donations) included the city and county public defender's office, several city aldermen, the owners of two of the local newspapers and the CEO of one of the regional television stations.

The tent flap doors had already been opened and zippered back for the day. A handful of other escorts were seen gathered inside. The Scruggs removed their vests from the cargo area of the jeep. They put these on, then Wendell headed to work on the damaged shed roof while Kiera and Skylar entered the tent.

Wanda Long, Kristen Cox and Jayelle Yancey occupied three of the fold-out chairs and were sharing a box of doughnuts. Near the back of the tent, Jeremy Dinks and Shaun Wilcox were smoking a joint and laughing over some joke. Both men were friends of Wendell. He and Jeremy had known each other since junior high school. Jeremy was officially on disability after severing a leg tendon during a boating incident. Shaun owned a vehicle recycling lot, and with numerous employees to do the actual labor, enjoyed a great deal of free time on his hands. Both men were glad for the opportunity to work as escorts as Kiera made sure their subsistence monies from Campaign Parenthood were paid under the table.

An old wooden table stood in the center of the activity. Here the escorts kept items needed during the day: boxes of snacks, a large dispenser pitcher of coffee, a dozen Campaign Parenthood-issued pink umbrellas and a couple of bullhorns. The metal tub that sat near the table had already been filled with ice and soda cans.

Kiera saw Felix Henner sitting on top of the table with his legs draped over the side. The hood of a gray jacket was pulled over his head and his nose was crammed into his phone. He appeared to be playing some game on it. Felix was the son of Felicia Henner, who sat on the clinic's Board of Directors. The young man had recently earned his B.A. in information technology and had started working as an escort only a few days after graduation. His plan, he'd told everyone, was to take work in the public sector. It had been Felicia's idea for her son to work here until he had secured a job.

"Hello ladies," Wanda greeted Kiera and Skylar. "Care for a doughnut?"

Skylar shook her head and proceeded straight to the table. Felix greeted her with a warm smile. Kiera saw that he even put his phone down to talk with her. She knew the two had been on a few dates and it was no secret that Skylar was very fond of Felix.

Kiera, however, was sure Felix did not return her daughter's affection. He came from an affluent family, of course, and his mother was a good, outspoken advocate of women's reproductive rights. All the same, Kiera wasn't impressed by this boy's seemingly blasé motive for working as an escort. He had never shown any of the zeal typical of clinic defenders, nor was he known to have even once confronted the antis (anti-choice protesters) or the so-called sidewalk counselors who regularly showed up. Felix didn't even attend the Pink Escorts bi-monthly meetings at the county Democrat headquarters. Kiera suspected Felix's motive for being here had nothing to do with supporting the cause of abortion. No, she had already concluded, his aim was simply to appease his mother while continuing to live under her roof.

Kiera had shared this opinion with Skylar. As was Skylar's habit, she had patiently listened to Kiera without either agreeing or raising an objection. But it was becoming evident to Kiera that polite listening was the most Skylar was willing to give her these days. Kiera found it annoying, too, that her own daughter could be attracted to someone as shallow as this boy.

Now Kiera attempted to eavesdrop on their conversation. However, this proved impossible as the other women were chattering so loudly.

She heard Wanda exclaim, "Kiera, Kiera!"

Kiera released a frustrated sigh and indulged Wanda with a patient look. Her frumpy colleague was licking white doughnut powder off her lips.

"Yeah," Wanda said. "I was just asking *where's Tally?*"

"Oh." Kiera shrugged. Curious now, she walked to the doorway and looked out. From here she could see over the gentle grassy slope separating the clinic's property edge from the sidewalk adjacent to Lader Avenue. As she expected, there stood Tally. It had become her eldest daughter's habit to take a position on this portion of the sidewalk just in case any anti-choicers with their stupid signs showed up. One group of the antis, the one from St. Gerard Catholic Church, liked to gather on the verge directly across the street. The property behind the verge belonged to a lawn supply shop, the owners of which apparently had no issue with their presence.

Kiera looked across the street and, sure enough, saw three of the Catholics standing out there. Two women and a male, each of them holding a sign. One of the signs had an image of the Virgin Mary on it while the other two displayed some saint holding an infant.

She squinted to read the message printed in light blue lettering beneath all the images: *Pray To End Abortion*.

These Catholic antis proved to be generally less aggressive in their methods than the Evangelical and Baptist ones. Rarely did any of the Catholics try crossing the street in order to invade the clinic parking lot with their pamphlets or to offer so-called pro-life counseling. No, the Catholics generally just stood by the highway with their signs. Even so, Kiera deemed them christofascists like all the others.

Kiera had trained Tally how to get under the skin of practically all these people, and her eldest daughter had proven to be an excellent student. Mornings would find Tally taunting them and mocking their signs as she went about her patrol. Tally would sometimes even get a megaphone bullhorn to shout at them or make obscene gestures that turned their provincial faces scarlet. This behavior –especially engaged on the clinic premises— wasn't officially condoned or encouraged by the Board of Directors. But these tactics were mild in comparison to past incidents that had landed Tally, Kiera, Wendell and fellow escort, Kerry Halker, in court. Those incidents had primarily involved antis who dared to pray or distribute their anti-choice leaflets on the sidewalk in front of the clinic. Having to show up in court had been a nuisance, of course, but the clinic fortunately retained an experienced legal department. These attorneys had made sure to get each case scheduled to be heard before Judge Percy Slaughter. Judge Slaughter was an old friend of Kiera's family and had been a staunch supporter of her father when he'd served as *Mayor Hambrick* decades before. In each incident with the antis, Slaughter had come through for the escorts by dismissing the cases.

Kiera was very proud of Tally's combativeness. She did sometimes wonder if Tally needed to tone down her enthusiasm, at least a little and at least for a while. Especially because it had only been a few weeks since Tally followed one of these antis all the way to the woman's car in the public parking lot up the street. Witnesses to the incident testified in court (and Tally admitted in amused details to her family) that she'd doused the woman with a cup full of hot tea. The case for assault against her had been dismissed (Judge Slaughter having cited a lack of evidence that it had been anything but an accident).

Since that dismissal Kiera herself had got into the habit of anonymously visiting that particular anti's social media pages. She knew the tea-splashed woman was being encouraged by online friends to file a civil lawsuit against Tally. Kiera also knew the anti had posted two or more years' worth of videos which cataloged incidents involving her Pink Escorts. These acts showed the responses of Kiera and other escorts when antis got too close to the clinic. All perfectly reasonable responses, Kiera believed. The tea-splashed anti, not surprisingly, complained that she was a victim of harassment and aggression. In her posts, however, the woman had told her friends she didn't believe in seeking revenge and so had no intention of filing charges. Kiera still couldn't help but wonder how seriously Ms. Tea-Splashed meant her turn-the-other-cheek words.

Kiera had to remind herself the woman probably didn't have the financial resources to hire a decent attorney. She knew, too, that if Judge Slaughter's dismissal of other cases was an indication of local judicial prudence then Ms. Tea-Splashed didn't stand much of a chance of proving in court that she'd been victimized.

The problem Kiera saw with any online boohooing from antis was that such things tended to exacerbate the bias already habored against abortion by many locals. Too much attention drawn to the Pink Escorts was likely to invite more controversy and, in turn, public scrutiny of the clinic itself. And this factor held the risky potential of convincing prospective patients to cancel appointments or worse, decide simply not to obtain an abortion.

Kiera's father had used his financial fortune to help found the clinic. Her younger brother Daniel, an attorney, held the position of CEO on the Board of Directors. Kiera had dedicated almost the last ten years of her life as a Pink

Escort. While youthful indiscretions prevented her from taking a seat on the clinic's Board she preferred being on the front lines for the cause of women's reproductive rights anyway. She was certain of the righteous cause (sometimes it even felt as if she'd been called to it by a higher power). In doing so, she saw her role as essential and indispensable in the proper functioning of the clinic. She acted as a correspondent between the clinic and Campaign Parenthood. She kept certain state lawmakers abreast of the clinic's importance to the region. She'd spent hundreds of hours on the internet in building and maintaining the escorts' social presence. It was she who had convinced the other escorts that their duties consisted of more than merely walking patients in and out of the front door or shielding them from public view of passersby. Under Kiera's leadership the other escorts embraced the idea they needed to be very visible and unafraid about confronting the opposition.

Tally's passionate commitment to pro-choice gave Kiera a great sense of pride. And that commitment was something Kiera certainly wasn't prepared to discourage.

Kiera noticed Kerry Halker's silver Toyota Avalon approaching the parking drive from the west end of the street. Kerry was driving a little faster than was probably safe. The turn signal wasn't on either, and as Kiera watched, Kerry brought the car to a near stop to make the turn. This caused the driver of the truck behind Kerry to hit the brakes. Apparently annoyed, the driver blasted his truck horn. Kerry responded to him by throwing back her arm and flashing a middle finger.

Kerry pulled into the lot and Kiera saw the truck driver shake his head. As he proceeded on his way Kerry rolled across the lot pavement to take a space just directly across from the tent. Actually, it was two spaces as she parked the Avalon directly over a division line.

If it had been anyone else Kiera might have thought to ask them to move their vehicle. But Kerry was seventy-six years old and her cognitive functions were erratic at best. Kiera deemed it was probably safer if the Avalon just stayed where it was.

Kerry had worked for the Hambrick family's pharmaceutical company before Kiera's father sold it to a large chain. During Kerry's long career, she had won several awards for chemical research and application. She and her husband Frank had remained friends with Kiera and Wendell ever since. She was retired from all research work now, but as a lifelong, vocal supporter of abortion Kerry fit right into the escort group. Kerry was educated, well-spoken and possessed a fiery temperament suited for confronting antis. She had a special fondness for Tally as well, and the two of them had grown quite chummy. This was a relationship Kiera didn't mind. For all of Kerry's grandmotherly fussing over the young woman, Tally had always been quick to tell people that Kiera was her hero. Not even the laurelled old chemist could compete with that.

Kerry emerged from the Avalon and slammed the door shut. For a senior she had a physically formidable appearance: stout, bow-legged and top-heavy, with meaty arms and large pendulous breasts, which because she didn't wear bras, sagged all the way to her navel. Today Kerry was dressed in her usual apparel of tie-dyed shirt, denim shorts (probably not the most becoming choice for a woman with legs covered with bulging blue varicose veins), and old rubber flip-flops. She'd also stuck a plastic rainbow-colored headband over the crown of her stringy light brown hair.

The other escorts agreed it was the epitome of feminist confidence that Kerry didn't give a whit about her appearance. But as she entered the tent and greeted everyone, Kiera caught a whiff of her body odor. The smell was so ripe that it Kiera's nostrils sting.

"Where's our Tally?" Kerry asked. "I made her some of my scrumptious Happy Hippie Brownies she likes so much. You know, the ones made with trail mix and carob flour?"

"Tally has already stationed herself on the sidewalk," Kiera informed her. "The Catholics were up bright and early to get on the other side of the street."

Kerry clapped her shoulder. "Kiera, have I ever told you the story behind how I came up with my recipe?"

Kiera braced herself. She knew the recipe story all too well: how Kerry and her husband had made a trip to Machu Picchu back in the eighties, how they'd enjoyed a Teonanacatl mushroom-induced trance while there, how Kerry had come out of the trance with the recipe for her *scrumptious* brownies formulated in her mind.

"Only a few dozen times, Kerry."

"Oh," Kerry said. "I am sorry. In that case...uh, where did you say Tally is?"

Kiera compelled her to go to the doorway and look toward the sidewalk.

"Oh good, there's Tally," Kerry chirped. "Looks like there's already a line of jackasses over there I can help her deal with!"

Kerry left the tent again and started for the sidewalk. Kiera heard Wanda click her tongue.

"That was harsh, Kiera. Poor old Kerry loves telling the story about her weed brownies."

Kiera couldn't help but roll her eyes. "And the story of how she got stoned with David Crosby. The story of chaining herself to a tree at a logging camp. And on and on. We can love our friend but admit it, Wanda, you get tired of hearing the same tale by the tenth time around."

Wanda laughed. "I suppose so."

Kiera pulled her phone from her pocket and sat down. She checked her messages, hoping to find a notification indicating Rory had texted or called. There was none. She pulled up his number from her contact list and typed in a short text: *We miss you, son. Give me a holler back when you get the chance!*

By eleven o'clock twenty-some patients had arrived for and were finished with their appointments. As there were no antis hanging around the perimeter, there wasn't a risk of patients being harassed (though the escorts were technically still obliged to offer to walk them to the front doors). By noon the parking lot had emptied altogether of morning patients. Clinic doctors and staff drove out of their secluded private parking area and headed into town for the usual hour-and-a-half lunch break. This was the time of day the escorts also took lunch. Today, Jeremy and Shaun left to walk to Hot Dog & More, a few blocks away. Skylar and Felix grabbed drinks out of the bucket and went outside to sit under a shade tree.

Kiera was sitting with the other women when Wendell walked in. He looked overheated and Kiera was concerned to see his face was so flushed that his cheeks almost glowed under the full white beard.

"Need something to drink?" she asked.

At Wendell's nod she got up and found him a bottle of soda from the pail. He unscrewed it and quaffed the contents down. His face was still scarlet, though, and he had to take a handkerchief from his pocket to wipe the perspiration off his brow.

"You know," she mentioned, "it wouldn't hurt to ask someone to help you repair that roof."

Wendell chuckled. "It's already repaired."

Kiera was tempted to rebuke him, to remind him he wasn't getting any younger and that accepting help might be appreciated by his knees, which were frequently plagued by stiffening arthritis. But the virile pride in his work was something Wendell held onto. Considering how obsequious he'd been about satisfying her desire for a quick repair of the roof, Kiera was reluctant to insist he let go of this last measure of male pride.

"But I won't be disappointed when Rory gets back," he admitted. "If I ever did want help, he's the only person who knows what tool I need without me even asking for it."

Kiera had an unpleasant flashback of her visit to Micky. She was still mad at herself for putting trust in the silly fortune teller and so had not mentioned the experience to either Wendell or their daughters. Since the visit, she'd prayed to Cailleach and performed spell work of her own creation. All rites intended to meld her thoughts into Rory's mind. To remind her son that he had a family waiting for him. To compel him to call. To make him desire to return home without any further delay.

These rites she also hadn't mentioned to her family. Magic worked best when not spoken of, and especially magic consecrated to the dark and tempestuous Cailleach.

Tally and Kerry walked into the tent. Kerry immediately found a chair and sank into it. She looked awful, Kiera thought, with her face glazed red, her lips pale, the perspiration so profuse that big drops of it rolled out of her hair and down her bullish neck. Tally found Kerry a bottle of iced tea from the bucket and brought it to her.

"Want something to eat, Kerry?" Tally asked.

Kerry replied in an out-of-breath voice, "Maybe later."

Tally stepped to the table and hopped up to sit. Fishing through the bowl of snacks, she found a sleeve of peanut butter sandwich crackers. She took one of the sandwiches out and crammed the whole thing into her mouth.

When Kiera thought her daughter was done chewing, she asked, "How's it going out there?"

The grin that came to Tally's face gave Kiera the distasteful sight of mashed cracker and peanut butter stuck between and across her daughter's teeth.

"You'd love it, Mom," Tally reported. "We have the Catholics blushing and making their dumb sign of the cross. Kerry even got one of them to cry!"

Kiera couldn't help but snicker. Then Tally mentioned the *Pro-Black Pro-Life* people –one of the so-called sidewalk counselor groups—had temporarily shown up. This bunch usually wore shirts with slogans such as *Black Pre-Born Lives Matter*. They had a tendency to call out patients visible from the sidewalk and offer them leaflets about adoption and maternity services. The Pink Escorts found them as troublesome as any anti-group, but since they were African Americans the escorts were reluctant to confront them. Anything that could be seen as racially motivated was always a sticky situation. So the escorts left them to their fantasies of being counselors. The exception to this was if they trespassed into the parking lot. On these occasions, the escorts had always succeeded in chasing them off with threats of calling the police.

"They didn't stay long, though," Tally told Kiera. "But unfortunately, a couple of patients decided to go talk with them. Even took some of their stupid leaflets. Then both the patients returned to their vehicles and drove off without going into the clinic."

"Pfft!" Kiera said. "It's so frustrating when patients fall for the propaganda."

Tally growled. "And to top it off, before the black antis even left another group showed up. Took base on *our* sidewalk." She yanked another cracker sandwich out of the sleeve. "Six of 'em. Reverend Pumpkin Head is among them."

Reverend Pumpkin Head was the epithet Kiera had dubbed upon the minister from Creek View Baptist

Church. He was a skinny, thirty-something-year-old preacher with a mop of orange-red hair.

Kiera felt her mouth water with excitement. In addition to the Creek View bunch's habit of catcalling incoming patients, they liked to hold prayer circles on the sidewalk. Few things were as entertaining for Kiera as to assemble the other escorts in a locked hand circle around prayer warriors and bleat out gibberish or to shout out bogus summons to Satan. The tactic acted on the group's superstitious fears. Some of them were known to start crying out for the protection of Jesus.

Kiera and Tally decided to use the long lunch break to stroll down to the sidewalk and see what Pumpkin Head and his band of protesters were doing. They found him and the other acolytes lined up in two separate groups of three, one to each side of the clinic entryway. They had brought signs which were displayed toward the street traffic. Although Kiera and Tally couldn't see what was on the fronts of these signs without moving down the walk, Kiera knew from experience that one or more of these were likely plastered with photos of dead fetuses. How despised these propagandic images were to the escorts and clinic personnel!

Kiera gave Tally a knowing look and together they walked quickly back into the tent. They each grabbed an umbrella from the table and returned to the end of the drive. There they split up, Tally walking down the portion of sidewalk where three antis occupied the west side, while Kiera did the same with the antis standing to the east. She saw Pumpkin Head was one of hers to deal with. He stood the farthest down the line of three, dressed in what appeared to be his Sunday best. The two antis with him were females, both wearing floral dresses that Kiera imagined had come off a rack at the dollar store.

The three avoided looking at her as she passed in front of them to assess their dumb signs. The first woman and Pumpkin Head had plain white signs, scrawled with the words, "Unborn Lives Matters" in blue paint. The woman standing between them clutched one of the dead fetus signs at her chest.

Kiera decided this was the sign to block. Positioning herself in front of the woman, she opened her umbrella and held the canopy of it against the sign. The fetus image was now blocked from view by anyone driving by.

The anti dared to ask, "Do you mind, ma'am?"

"Yes," Kiera replied, "I do mind. Very much."

The anti sighed and gave a pitying look. Kiera, resenting the expression, decided to level some of her weight behind the umbrella. She pushed the ferrule against the sign and gingerly exerted increasing pressure on the umbrella.

"Stop it," the anti complained. "You're pushing into me."

Kiera scoffed. "Oh, gosh. Better turn the other cheek, sweetheart."

The woman backed up a couple of inches. Just as Kiera was about to move forward in turn, she heard Tally's shrill voice echo down the sidewalk.

She looked and saw her daughter facing the three antis down there—two males and a female. Tally's umbrella was still folded and she was shouting at the male who stood in the center of the little group. He was a very tall guy with long, muscular arms. While his companions held their signs balanced on the ground in front of their legs, he just held his sign at his chest. It appeared to Kiera that Tally was able to stand there and block whatever image or words was printed on the guy's sign.

However, it seemed Tally was more interested in shouting at this particular anti. Whatever words she was flinging at the man apparently only amused him. In turn, his amusement further riled Tally. Her shouting soon erupted into a sharp squall. When this brought no response from the tall guy, Tally raised a shaking forefinger and jabbed it into his chin.

This move clearly infuriated his companions. The other male said something to Tally and gestured angrily toward the clinic. To Kiera's joy, her daughter responded by spitting on this one's canvas shoes.

Now the tall guy extended his arms over his head so that anyone coming up or down the street could see his sign above Tally's head. Tally glowered up at it and struggled furiously to open her umbrella. The canopy didn't open. As she tried again it was evident to Kiera that the open/close button was failing to work.

Tally pitched the uncooperative umbrella to the ground and screamed, full-throated, at the guy. Kiera deliberated about running over to see if she could offer help with the umbrella. But that might just embarrass Tally and allow the dead fetus sign woman to freely flash passersby.

Suddenly, Tally jumped up and slapped both palms against the bottom of the tall guy's sign. Her effort to knock it out of his hands was futile. Yet Tally continued to jump, again and again, letting out a scream each time her fists made contact with the sign. The female to the tall guy's immediate left lowered her own sign. She clasped the sign between her thighs and pulled a phone out of the back pocket of her denim capris. Kiera watched as this woman began to videotape Tally's continued efforts to dislodge the tall guy's sign.

Kiera was also aware the spectacle had caught the attention of her own antis.

"That poor deluded girl," Pumpkin Head muttered.

Kiera turned on him. "Oh, shut up!"

She looked over their shoulders toward the tent. She couldn't see Skylar or Felix under the nearby trees now. She could make out some figures moving inside the tent, but no one was walking out of the tent or even paying attention to the commotion on the sidewalk.

Don't they hear Tally's screams? she thought. *Why doesn't anyone come to offer some help?*

At last Kerry and Wendell peered out. Kerry darted back inside as Wendell shot forth toward the commotion. He reached the sidewalk and demanded to know what was going on. He and the tall guy exchanged some heated words while Tally continued to thrash at the sign. Kiera now saw Kerry running forward. She was carrying a bullhorn, which she raised to her lips upon reaching the sidewalk.

Kerry positioned herself right behind the tall guy. She let out a torrent of obscenities that boomed through the bullhorn. Tally continued to jump and beat his sign. Wendell stood there with his hands on hips, glaring at the guy and mouthing something. Sidewalk passersby stopped to watch, while drivers slowed in their vehicles to see what was going on. The clinic staff were returning from their lunch break. And the woman with the phone was videotaping it all!

Kiera was sure the doctors and nurses weren't likely to stop and place themselves in the middle of a conflict. But Kiera knew some nosy, disgruntled, lowly clerk or janitor, seeing what was transpiring, might be tempted to report the incident to the clinic Board or to the police. She was worried, too, that the afternoon patients were due to start arriving at any time. She decided she'd have to be the one to usher Tally, Wendell and Kerry back to the tent.

Propping her umbrella over a shoulder, she left her group of antis and briskly walked over. She could understand Tally's words now and they were as vulgar as they were enraged.

Kerry's amplified obscenities turned to pitched fever as she shouted at the tall through the bullhorn, "Get out of here, mother-"

Kiera grabbed Wendell's arm in an effort to pull him away. But his glare lock with the tall guy did not break.

She forced a civilized tone in her voice and opened her mouth to demand her husband explain exactly what was going on.

But it was at this moment she understood why Tally was so upset. The tall guy continued to level the sign over his head, his arms unflagging, his face betraying a mixture of pity and amusement over the pandemonium. Kiera had a good view now of his sign and knew the sign was the cause. Written in huge white lettering over an indigo background were the words: "MURDER FOR HIRE WORKS HERE."

The blood in Kiera's veins froze. She could hardly believe what she saw. These antis had come up with a lot of exaggerated slogans for their propaganda, but this was indeed a first.

It's a deliberate vilification of every escort here!

She blinked and released a palliating exhale. "Tally," she said beseechingly, "come to the tent with Dad and me."

Kerry lowered her bullhorn. "But Kiera, just look at the defamation on this bastard's sign!"

It took great restraint for Kiera not to comment on the horrible message. Instead, she gave Wendell a hard poke in the upper arm and spoke his name. This worked as she hoped as her husband finally turned his attention away from the tall guy.

"Tally," Kiera instructed her daughter, "I said, come with dad and me."

Tally finally stopped jumping. She was breathless, her hands quivered. With a final dirty look at the tall guy, she picked her umbrella off the ground and thrust it stiffly under an arm. Then she turned and began to stomp up the clinic drive. Kerry followed, with Wendell right behind.

Satisfied that all the yelling was over with, Kiera sneered at the tall guy. "I guess you think the lie on your sign is clever, huh?"

"It's not a lie," he replied. "And you know it."

The nape of Kiera's neck stiffened with anger. How she longed to kick the insolent jerk and his companions!

She threw his male buddy a contemptuous look when she noticed the swaddled newborn pictured in the center of his black sign. She read the words written in pink letters beneath the photo. It was an organization name. And in this shocking moment, she realized these three couldn't possibly be part of Pumpkin Head's church group.

Pagans And Secular People For Life.

The word *sacrilege* erupted in burning embers before Kiera's mind's eye. *How dare they!*

She wanted to scream at them just as Tally had, and in truth, do much, much more. She saw these people as apostates to pagandom and traitors to the feminist elements of modern secularism.

Evil, evil, evil!

A low growl escaped her trembling lips. These people deserved far more than mere profanity. They deserved to be genuinely cursed for their blasphemy!

At the moment, however, Kiera was too stunned to deal with them. She would need time to think up and commit herself to doling out a fitting and painful retaliation.

But she did think to do what Tally hadn't thought of; she hoisted her own umbrella off her shoulder and rammed the canopy, ferrule-first, into the tall guy's sign. It was knocked backward out of his grasp and fell to the ground behind him.

The tall guy responded with a shake of his head. "Not much a fan of free speech, are you lady?"

Kiera looked at the fallen sign. To her satisfaction, the punch she'd given it had created a dent in the center of the word "hire".

She snorted contemptuously at the woman still videotaping.

"Hope you caught that with your little camera!"

The woman warned sharply behind the phone, "You realize that's assault, right?"

Kiera shrugged. "The police won't do anything. They never do."

With a sneer, Kiera left the three of them to claim their precious portion of the sidewalk.

Chapter 4

Kiera found Tally sulking in the tent. At least she seemed to understand her mother's reason for pulling her off the tall guy. Kerry, on the other hand, was another matter. The day was getting late for the senior; it was the time of day when her patience started to wear thin and her temperament often grew testy. Now she was pacing inside the tent, ranting to everyone about other ways to chase the tall guy and his companions off the sidewalk.

"Let me take the bullhorn back down there, Kiera," she pleaded. "Or better yet, I'll use the super-soaker in my car on him. It's already filled with vinegar!"

The afternoon's arrival of numerous patients provided Kiera with something to make Kerry forget her plans for immediate retribution.

"The sidewalks are crawling with antis," she told both Kerry and Tally, "so you know the patients will need some aid getting in and out of their cars unmolested."

Tally and Kerry promised her they'd remain in the parking lot that afternoon. For the rest of the working day the two focused their attention on offering their umbrellas as shields for patients. The physical activity quickly tired Tally, which worked out well for the rest of the family. By the time they were ready to return home Tally was only too happy to let Kiera drive.

While the family ate dinner that evening, Kiera checked her phone. To her dismay, Rory had not replied to her earlier text. Nor had she received notification he had tried calling. She was frustrated, almost angry. It had been nearly two days since she'd last heard from her son. For a moment, Kiera was tempted to call him. But dinner was going nicely, with her daughters listening while Wendell told them about some series of social documentaries he had watched back in the 1990s. Kiera didn't want to risk ruining the peaceable mood by fussing about Rory.

So she waited.

After the table was cleared, Wendell went out to tend to the goats. Kiera set the leftovers in the fridge and then left Skylar and Tally to wash the dishes.

She made her way to the bedroom she shared with Wendell. A lavender beaded curtain separated the bedroom from a private den. She drew the curtain aside and entered. The daylight was dusky now as it drifted in between the pair of black shades at the single window. This room was furnished with a gray couch and other comfy furnishings. This was the room she and Wendell kept their desktop computer, their stereo system and speakers. The couple's bookcase was also in this room. The shelves of the case were loaded with volumes on Fabianism, Marxism and other social literature. A large framed poster of Che Guevara hung from the wall opposite the couch. And closely adorning the space around the poster were hung several photos of their children.

Kiera stepped to the end table beside the couch. There was a lamp here with a big gray globular ceramic base. Kiera flipped the knob switch so that the bulb came on. Then she took a seat on the couch and retrieved her phone from her pocket. Pulling up Rory's number from the contact list, she pressed the 'Call' button.

There were only two rings before she heard the electronic click that signaled someone was answering.

"Hi, Mom!"

"Thought I'd better call," she said in a light tone, "since it seems you've forgotten you have a mom."

He chuckled tenderly. "Gee Mom, you wouldn't exaggerate just a bit, would you? I have just been real busy the last couple of days. I'm sorry."

Kiera was so elated to hear his voice that she felt all the day's tensions slip away.

She asked him how he was. How did he like working at the stables? He responded he was good. The job was hard but he enjoyed it.

"How are you doing, Mom? Is everyone else alright?"

She assured him she was fine. His father was well, just tired. His sisters were good, too. But they all missed him and hoped he was coming home soon.

"About that," he said. There was a pause, long enough for Kiera to feel nervous again. "I'll be headed home soon. And when I do get back, I have a surprise."

The words *headed home soon* were soothing to Kiera. "What surprise, son?" she asked.

He explained a friend would be following him home in their car and might be staying as a house guest for a few days.

"If this is alright with you and Dad?"

Kiera never had reservations about Rory's friends. Not that he had cultivated many friendships over the years. She and Wendell had home-schooled their kids and carefully made sure they were only allowed to spend time with the children of their personal friends. As an adult, Rory stayed too busy helping out with the farming and the escort work to waste his time on frivolity or to develop relationships with questionable people. She couldn't imagine Rory's new acquaintance was anyone who wouldn't meet his parents' stamp of approval.

"Your friends have always been welcome here." Hopefully she added, "If they're driving themselves, does this mean you will be home for good then?"

"I don't intend to go traveling again any time soon," he told her. "But when I get back, I want to look for another job."

"But you don't need that," she said, confused. "Your grandfather left every one of us very comfortable. Why on earth would you look for some proletarian job once you're back?"

Rory sighed from the other end of the phone. It was a restrained sigh, one Kiera suspected he didn't mean for her to hear.

"Just maybe I enjoy having a job."

She snorted. "You have enough responsibilities here and at the clinic." A worrisome thought crossed her mind. "Does this friend of yours have something to do with your attitude? Because if he does, just forget bringing him here!"

A moment's silence crept heavily into the conversation.

"It's my idea, Mom. You can trust me on this."

Kiera felt her eyes roll. But she wanted to avoid saying anything that might cause Rory to change his mind about coming home. "Well, we can talk about this job thing once you're back. The most important thing is that you get home. You've had a lengthy adventure and I truly hope you have enjoyed it. But you have been very missed, sweetheart."

"I have no doubt, Mom."

"So we can expect you in just a few days?"

"I'm looking at no more than two weeks."

Kiera felt a little stab of disappointment. "Alright. But don't forget how to use your phone."

"I won't," Rory promised. "Okay then. I gotta get off here and clean up for the night. I love you, Mom."

"I love you, too."

Kiera was elated as she ended the call. Her prayers had been answered and her whole world was brighter now.

A tapping sounded from the bedroom door casing.

"Come on in," she called out.

The beaded curtain parted and Skylar walked in. Skylar had changed out of her escort scrubs and into shorts and a spaghetti-strap tee shirt. She'd also brushed out her long hair so that the dark waves fell softly about her shoulders.

Kiera shared with her the news Rory was to be home in a couple of weeks.

"That's great, Mom," Skylar said. "I know you've been worried."

Kiera detected a hint of criticism in her tone. "Well, haven't you been worried? I mean, he's been out of the state, you know?"

"I've missed him, of course. But Rory's a big boy now. And he has a level head on him. I can't imagine him getting himself into trouble."

Kiera couldn't disagree. Rory was very sensible. But it seemed Skylar didn't grasp the dangers that faced them in the world beyond their little mountain haven. But then again, how could Skylar have firsthand experience with such dangers? It wasn't like the girl had ever traveled more than a few miles away from home.

"Don't try making me out to be a fretful old hen, Sky." You just don't understand the dangers out there. You've never strayed."

"Nope, Mom, can't say as I have ever had that opportunity."

"Opportunity?" Kiera scoffed. "I could tell you all about the wonderful opportunities that wait for people in the glorious state of Kentucky."

"You already have. Many times."

Kiera raised an eyebrow. "And you resent me for it?"

Skylar sighed. "No, Mom. Don't get defensive."

Another thinly veiled insinuation! Kiera was getting impatient with her youngest. Over the last few months, Skylar had noticeably changed, going from the smiling, admiring girl she and Wendell had known so long into this passive-aggressive young woman.

"Don't turn this around on me, Sky!"

Skylar threw her hands up in a surrendering gesture. "Look, I just came in to let you know Braeden and a couple of his friends are outside. They came by and asked Tally and me to go with them. She's getting ready now."

Braeden was Shaun Wilcox's son by his first wife. He, Tally and Skylar had all been friends since they were kids. Kiera asked if Skylar was going too.

"Uh, that's a decided no."

Kiera was genuinely surprised. "Why?"

Skylar stared at her in disbelief. "Because, Mom, Braeden is on probation for making and dealing meth."

Kiera couldn't believe how insensitive her youngest sounded. "Well whatever, girl! It's not like your dad and I didn't have our wild young days, too. If we hadn't had the same parole officer, you may not even have been conceived."

"I can't really compare whatever minor drug stuff you and dad got into with Braeden selling meth to teenagers."

"Skylar, stop acting like such a priss! You've known Braeden your whole life. And he comes from a good family."

"Good family? Braeden's step-mom is a regular at the methadone clinic. His dad is in and out of jail for DUI. And god knows which of the two of them almost burned down their house last year!"

Kiera shook her head. How could one of her own children have turned out so judgmental? Skylar had always been so tender-hearted. Naturally, Kiera had presumed her youngest would grow up to be just as inclined to share her parents' values as did Tally. There was less than two years difference in her daughters' ages. Both had been taught better. Of course, Tally was more like Kiera in personality: an extrovert, never afraid to speak her mind. Unafraid to voice her opinions and fight for what she wanted.

But Kiera knew she wasn't really being fair. Skylar couldn't help it if she'd been born with her own individuality. It was often very frustrating as Skylar, with her sensitive nature and blithe personality, sometimes reminded Kiera of her own mother. Of course, in the case of her mother, Kiera felt the blithe personality was just a disguise for captiousness.

Kiera shuddered now to think she may have failed the girl. *I should have never let any of my children even meet Dorothy Schwann!*

"What has happened to you, Skylar?" she asked. "You used not to be so judgmental. Do you see your dad or me looking down our noses at Braeden's family? No, you don't. And this is because we extend compassion to the deserving."

Skylar looked bored. "And the two of you will continue to do so as long as those deserving share your every political view."

Kiera bristled and her voice raised, "Excuse me, young lady? I thought you shared our views, too. Are you trying to tell me something?"

Skylar flinched. "No, Mom."

Kiera felt secretly triumphant. "You work on that attitude, honey," she said calmly now. "And may I suggest you stay off the social media? There are too many alt-right views floating around those places. I don't want my girl contaminated."

"Sure." Skylar thrust her hands into the back pockets of her shorts. "I'm going out to water and feed the horses. Give them a grooming. Rasp their hooves, which really need it. Want to help?"

Kiera considered it. But she remembered she had planned to spend some time digging up whatever information she could about that Pagans and Secular People For Life group. But considering the advice about social media she'd just given Skylar, she couldn't just come out and say this. So she told her a white lie.

"I need to plan out tomorrow's dinner. Do you mind doing it alone?"

"It's alright," Skylar said, her mouth pursing a little. "But you should ride them soon, you know. It's been a while."

"I know. Though I am sure they don't mind if you take them out for a ride."

"Yes, but they are your horses."

If Skylar meant this as more criticism, it didn't register in her voice. In fact, the look on her face was that of the ingenuous girl Kiera remembered.

She reached for Skylar's hand and gave it a loving squeeze. "I know, Skylar. We will take them for a ride together one day this week, okay?"

"Alright," Skylar said sweetly.

Chapter 5

Kiera sat in the den listening for confirmation Skylar had left the house. Once she heard the front door open and shut, she moved from the couch to the computer table. Sitting down, she brought up the internet and typed *"Pagans And Secular People For Life"* into the search engine. A results page popped up. The group's web page was the second listing down. Kiera clicked on the link.

The front page was rather boring. The name of the group appeared in white text across a teal header. In the lower right-hand corner of the page was a link to their group on Facebook. At the bottom of the page was the organization's snail mail address. Kiera was surprised to see it was located in Wales, UK.

Kiera guided the cursor over the menu box in the upper left-hand corner. A few items dropped. She clicked on the About page. A page with the words "Welcome and About" came up. A little below this more text appeared.

The first paragraph read: *"We are an international volunteer organization of Secular minded and non-mainstream religious peoples working together to promote the preservation, safety and welfare of pre-born life."*

"Pre-born!" Kiera snorted. "What imbeciles!"

As she continued to read, she laughed spitefully at numerous passages:

"We seek to help others to see the opportunity each and every life has to offer mankind and world. In this effort, we encourage pregnant women of all ages and backgrounds to understand that each new life has promise."

"Even a child conceived under the worst of conditions is not the end of a woman's aspirations."

"No one has the right to claim you would be better off killing your unborn child. Such misanthropic claims are not based on any knowledge of your personal future. Furthermore, such claims are merely lies used by people who seek to control the population of peoples they believe are inferior."

"The abortion industry is a lucrative business. One that has for decades profited off the fears and doubts of pregnant women."

"If you are pregnant and are experiencing pressure to undergo an abortion, we are here to help. We have a team of discreet professionals ready to listen and help guide you through this difficult time. We also have contacts with several legitimate adoption organizations. We additionally have psychological and spiritual counselors ready to help. When contacting, be assured everything you tell us will be kept strictly confidential. Thanks to our anonymous donors, you will never be charged for any help or service."

Kiera found it all self-righteous and condescending. But it was the final statement on the page that perhaps made her the angriest:

"They will say: Your body, your choice. But what they fail to acknowledge is the tiny body growing inside yours also has rights. We hope you will choose to allow your baby the chance to fulfill its potential as a human being."

Kiera snarled at the monitor. She scrolled up and allowed the menu items to drop again. There were four more pages: Home, Contact, Get Involved and Resources.

She clicked on Resources and was taken to a page that provided links for such things as international adoption agencies, community social help centers, spiritual counselors and psychological services. There was also a lengthy list of wholesale suppliers of maternity and breastfeeding supplies.

Not wishing to give their Get Involved page even a single hit, Kiera clicked on the Contact link. The text that met her eyes explained, *"We offer both email and toll-free telephone numbers for contact. To email us, please click the sunflower icon below. You will be taken to a separate page where you will be asked to provide your information. Our toll-free numbers are located near the bottom of this page. *Please note that return contact via email generally takes between 6 and 24 hours."*

Below this text and in the center of the page was a large cheerful sunflower icon. Kiera scrolled a bit further and found two phone numbers. One appeared to be a US contact, the other for the UK.

And just below these was again a link to the *Pagans And Secular People For Life* Facebook page. Kiera wondered if the woman who had videotaped the incident with the tall guy had uploaded her footage to this page.

She couldn't recall if she was logged into Facebook already from the computer and didn't like the idea of visiting their page if she was logged under with her private FB login name. But her curiosity was strong enough that she decided it was worth the try.

She hit the link. In a moment she landed at the pro-life group's page and was relieved to see she was still signed in under her Pro-Choice Krumme County identity.

The group's FB page was, like their website, decorated by a teal header with the organization's name printed in white. Below this was a brief description of the group. She clicked on the videos icon, but there were only two archived, both of which were dated from earlier in the year. Kiera was disappointed. She would have enjoyed reposting the video taken at the clinic and sharing it with the two hundred and some followers on the PCKC pages. This would have allowed her the pleasure of adding her own commentary about the tall guy picking on Tally and also let her tell her followers how these so-called pagans and seculars were just as bad as the Christian antis.

She began scrolling through the posts. Many were commentaries written by the page owner/moderator and the majority were addressed to expectant mothers. Kiera immediately hated their uplifting and encouraging tone. Other posts were mere congratulations to unmarried women who had recently given birth. Kiera felt nauseated at the umpteen photos of newborns she came across. A few posts linked to what the moderator deemed as violent actions from Pro-Choice groups.

Kiera was intrigued to find several posts which discussed upcoming or previously held protests carried out by the organization's various chapters. She scrutinized these, looking for any mention of local branches in her area. At last she spotted the words *Avonport chapter* mentioned in one of the posts. She immediately clicked to read the entire thing.

The post had been made six weeks before and proved to be little more than a welcome-into-the-fold type of message about the Avonport chapter. In the replies was a short quote from some local member named Sandra. This Sandra said this new arm was small but all the members were eager to spread the message that "the unborn are our future" and "there is inherent good in protecting the most vulnerable among the human race."

Kiera was galled. She wanted photos of the Avonport chapter members and full names to go along with the photos! With names Kiera could—as she'd done with other anti-groups—track the individual members down. Kiera had succeeded in having such people stalked by other Pink Escorts. Having names also made it easy to buy home addresses and phone numbers from online tracer services, all information which could lead to the doxing of an anti. Her most ardent fans and followers had experience in such practices, whether by making incessant calls to antis, vandalizing their property, or in coordinating flash mob protests on a targeted anti's front lawn. These loyal pro-choicers were also experienced enough to know to cover their faces while they acted and thus shielded their own identities in case camera crews showed up.

These self-righteous secular and pagan jerks are just hiding themselves, she concluded now. *And they deserve to be exposed! Exposed and humbled!*

She noticed this single post mentioning the Avonport chapter had 152 Likes. There were also fourteen comments. But when she scrolled through the comments she only found one solitary negative response, and this was from someone Kiera didn't know. However, their comment, *"STUUUPID! Babies are destroying the planet!"* did make Kiera grin.

She was tempted to add a baneful comment of her own. To do this, though, might prompt one of the organization's moderators to look her up. Unlike the FB account used under her own identity (accessible only to approved family and friends), her Pro-Choice Krumme County ID was kept visible to the public, making it easy for her approved followers to message her.

Instead of lingering on the page any longer Kiera clicked on the button that took her straight to her Pro-Choice Krumme County account. Her settings disallowed anyone from posting or commenting unless she'd already approved the user. She scrolled down to the last post entry. It was a post written the Thursday of the week before.

Specifically, she'd made it to share information about an article from her favorite news source. The article in question addressed some proposed anti-choice Bill scheduled to be voted on by the state House in a matter of days. Kiera had added a good amount of fiery commentary along with the link to the full article, and urged everyone reading to contact their local representative and to demand the rejection of the Bill.

To her elation this post had already garnered 52 Likes. There were several comments, too. But she wasn't in the mood to read them. She clicked instead the option to begin a new post. There were a few things to report on regarding the escort work at the clinic: Wendell's praiseworthy repair of the utility shed roof. The decent weather the escorts had enjoyed for the last several days. What she mockingly referred to as the *Catholic antis' continued milksop protest* across the street from the clinic.

"*The papists are apparently terrified of our Tally,*" she typed, "*who patrols our side of the street with her unfaltering courage!*"

She also related the return presence of Reverend Pumpkin Head with his bunch of holy rollers.

"*Standing in the sun isn't kind to Pumpkin Head's ginger complexion. His face is starting to look like someone blew a wet fart on it!*"

She finished the post with a scathing mention of the Pagans And Secular People For Life bunch:

"*These local yahoos are a branch of a pseudo-intellectual organization that works under the illusion of enlightenment. While I don't expect them to be sitting down to dinner any time soon with the christofascists, this group is demonstratively as extremist in its efforts to crush women's autonomy.*"

She knew there was still a chance Tall Guy's filming friend would share her video somewhere online. This prospect was something Kiera wanted to discredit before it got much circulation.

"One man among the sidewalk trio," she continued to type, *"and whom I'll call Tall Guy was cursing at Tally earlier in the morning. Tall Guy had brought along a most offensive sign. Tally attempted to block it from street view but was unable because he held it raised over his head. The bully took much enjoyment laughing at Tally's small stature, proving himself to be just another typical male chauvinist jerk."*

After writing this Kiera provided her readers with a link to the *Pagans And Secular People For Life* Facebook page and another to their main website. With a finger punch to the *publish now* button, the post went up.

She still wished she knew Tall Guy's real name. The knowledge of his name would give her more power to invoke Cailleach's aid in exposing his personal details. There was, certainly, the chance one of her loyal followers would take it upon themselves to find that information. But she was anxious to get the ball rolling.

Kiera stepped away from the computer and slipped into the bedroom. She approached the cedar chest that stood at the footboard of the bed. This was where she stored all her tools for magical rites. Kneeling, she opened the lid and lifted out a brass candle holder along with a long unused red candle and a small electronic lighter. After closing the chest lid she gathered the items and stood up.

She returned to the den and taking a seat on the couch, placed the candle holder and lighter on the coffee table. The candle she clutched between her palms. She closed her eyes and began to pray to the dark hag.

Cailleach, hear my invocation. I praise your foreboding name in all gratitude for answering my fervent recent prayers. You have touched my son's heart and given him the initiative

*to contact me. For all these things am I ever grateful. Hail be
to you, most glorious and powerful One!*

As Kiera drew a long, deep breath, her hands squeezed
the hard cylindrical wax. Through her third eye she
summoned the vision of Tall Guy and his two companions
standing on the sidewalk. She focused on her repugnance
for them as she continued praying:

*O glorious Hag who works in the shadows—my family, my
colleagues and I have been confronted by new enemies. These
enemies have insulted us and mocked our sworn Cause. Like
our other enemies they seek to interfere with this Cause; unlike
the others they act on the behalf of pagan gods and goddesses
who seek to thwart your works. I plead Thee see these enemies
now, recognize them as I recognize them and cast your wrath
as a shadow over their work. I beg you, Cailleach, make
known their names to us your servants. Guide us to discover
where these enemies dwell. Grant us knowledge of the intimate
details of their lives. Give us your steadfast influence to deal
with them and to act without bringing retribution upon
ourselves. Allow us to take vengeance upon them in the name
of our sworn and sacred Cause. I beg this of thee, Cailleach!
So mote it be!*

The wax had grown warm between Kiera's hands. She
imparted a revered kiss to the candle and stood it upright in
the holder. Taking the lighter in hand, she pushed the
button to ignite a blue flame. She touched this to the tip of
the slender wick. A tiny spark of blue and yellow erupted
and the braided cotton was lit.

Kiera sat back to gaze at the burning light.

"There," she said with a satisfied smile, "I have done
my public service for the day."

Chapter 6

The next morning Kiera was out of bed before Wendell awoke. She came into the kitchen to find Tally sitting at the breakfast table. The girl was writing something on a large piece of pink poster board. Kiera wanted to ask Tally about the rather noisy return made during the wee hours since she and Wendell had both been awakened by Tally and Braeden laughing raucously from the kitchen. It was only after Braeden was heard leaving through the front that quiet finally settled over the house again.

Kiera decided that addressing this could wait until she was good and awake. Instead, she assumed a cheerful tone and asked Tally how she was and what she was making with the poster board.

"I've been busy," Tally answered. "I'm making my own poster to carry at the clinic."

Kiera was curious how long Tally had been working on this poster. "I hope you got at least a little sleep."

Tally shrugged. "I rested my eyes a while ago. But I want to finish this thing before we leave for the clinic."

That Tally hadn't slept all night was worrisome. Not that Kiera intended to ask about what she and Braeden had been doing during the course of the night. Tally too easily grew irritable when asked how she spent time with her friends.

Kiera looked down at the poster board. There was an opened box of broad line markers on the table, too. It was evident now Tally had just started on this project. As Kiera watched Tally chose a purple marker and wrote on the board:

HONK IF YOU SUPPORT
REPRODUCTIVE RIGHTS

It was a message Kiera liked, but the overall appearance was amateurish. Tally's letters were uneven, crammed together, with the ends of both lines markedly sloping rightward down the board.

Kiera and Wendell had taught their children to read and write but Tally had never developed much patience in her handwriting lessons. To be honest, Kiera knew that neither she nor Wendell had devoted a lot of effort teaching their children legible penmanship. At the time they had viewed such a skill as only something valued by the bourgeois.

It was only after the kids were adults that Kiera and Wendell noticed not only was Tally lacking in penmanship, but her general reading comprehension skills were deficient. Wendell had offered several times to help Tally hone her comprehension but Tally had predictably bucked. After his last offer, in fact, Tally practically accused Wendell of trying to turn her into a white colonialist. Wendell had thrown his hands up at the insinuation and never brought up the subject with her again.

Tally beamed proudly now. "What do you think, Mom?"

"I like the message," Kiera said cautiously. "But what's wrong with the posters Campaign Parenthood sends us? There are a bunch of those in the utility shed."

"I like mine better. Going to draw flowery vaginas in the corners."

"Ah."

Tally raised an eyebrow. "Don't you like it?"

"Sure I do." Kiera knew this wasn't exactly the truth, but she was also aware of the kind of reaction anyone could expect if they dared criticize one of Tally's artistic projects.

She decided to say nothing more about the poster, and hoped secretly someone else among the escorts could persuade Tally to use one of the professionally made posters.

"Have you fed the chickens, dear?"

Tally shook her head. "I taped a note on Dad's comb asking him to do it."

This was about the tenth time in less than a month Tally had neglected the one chore Kiera and Wendell expected of her. This wasn't fair to any of the rest of them and Kiera was tempted to say something about it to Tally. But she was reluctant to put her eldest daughter in a foul mood. They had the drive to make it to the clinic, and from experience, Kiera knew it would be an unpleasant drive if Tally fell into one of those moods.

So Kiera grabbed a doughnut for breakfast, got dressed and brushed her teeth. After this she went outside to go feed and water the horses.

As she walked the path to the barn, she saw Felicity standing in the pen. The sleek roan mare stood at the trough with its old-fashioned pump. Her head was lowered as she lapped water from the basin. Just as Kiera neared the fence, the dun, Little Crest, trotted out. He went to stand by his companion's side. Little Crest shook his head on noticing Kiera. It made his shiny dark mane and long whorl whip about his face.

"Good morning you two," Kiera called.

At that moment Felicity raised her head. Her ears pricked up as if listening to something and she made a little whinny.

"It's just me, silly," Kiera assured her. "Over here."

As she got to the gate and reached for the latch, a blood-chilling wail stopped her hand. It was a low, pitiful canine wail that seemed to emanate from the end of the walking path.

Kiera turned and looked that way. The shades stood still. Not even a breeze stirred the leaves.

The sad wail resounded a second time. It spoke of a wounded or frightened dog. But Kiera saw no sign of a canine or other beast moving among the trees. Nothing at all.

Felicity whinnied again. Kiera tried to soothe her, telling the mare it was just an echo from some dog down in the valley. But it must have spooked Little Crest. He pawed the ground his front hooves. And giving a loud snort, he head-butted Felicity in the side of the neck.

"Calm down, Little Crest," Kiera told him. "It's just some dog."

She watched as both horses suddenly turned away from the trough. With Little Crest leading, the two sprinted through the barn doors.

"You skittish cowards," Kiera grumbled. But she noticed the wail had raised the hair on the nape of her own neck.

Determined to ignore her unease, she lifted the gate latch and opened the gate. As she turned to close it behind her the canine knell sounded again.

This time Kiera was sure it came from the shades. It was possible this was just some stray, but there was also the possibility the dog belonged to some pesky neighbor. She didn't want the owner nosing around looking for it or calling authorities to say this was the umpteenth dog that had gone missing around the Scruggs property.

Kiera thought about venturing into the shades to search for the distressed dog. But what would she do if she did locate it? She couldn't very well take a wounded animal to the pound without questions being asked. Nor, was it likely she could do so without Wendell finding out. And he'd certainly know if she brought the dog home to provide medical aid.

Bringing a dog into their house would inevitably lead to an argument. Doubtlessly, her dominant personality would win out, and in time, Wendell would agree to let her handle the situation as she saw fit. But she worried that no promise she could extract would permanently protect the dog from Wendell's rifle. Besides, what aid she might offer a dog wouldn't be given for selfless reasons. Her only concern was the thought her family could end up blamed by some redneck neighbor for an injury to the dog. The last thing her family needed was for any of those people to start gossiping over the frequent disappearances of dogs. Gossip led to the authorities being called. There were few things Kiera despised more or trusted less than the police.

Even now she trembled with rage at the memory of men in tidy blue uniforms and shining badges pinned to their shirts. It was men like this who had led her Anthony to his death. The kind of men who held no respect for the love she bore him or cared that their actions had broken the dreams of her youth. She had never forgiven those men. She never would.

Her family's mountain home was her safe refuge from their kind. Wendell didn't understand how his reckless shooting of strays could inadvertently invite authorities straight onto their property. It was easy to forgive Wendell, though. When the two of them had met it had been Wendell who had consoled her mourning for Anthony, even while most of her family had acted hell-bent on faulting her. In some ways Wendell was like Anthony; he disavowed traditions and through his passion for reading, had pursued his own unique brand of higher education. And Wendell's dislike for convention had made him sympathetic to her need to have a home isolated enough that the narrow-minded couldn't constantly watch everything they did.

Kiera knew Wendell loved her without judgment. He supported her in every cause she was drawn to. She was grateful to him. And she realized that she owed him her courage not to live in constant fear of gossip.

This realization assuaged her nerves. She released a cleansing breath.

"The dog is wounded," she assured herself. "Death will end its suffering."

Feeling her anxiety wane, Kiera opened the gate and went about tending to the chores she'd come to do.

Later that morning Wendell drove them to the clinic. During the ride Kiera related that Rory had called and that he had promised to be home in two weeks or less.

"Good deal," Wendell said. "It's been long enough. I'll need him home to start the spring planting. With Elvira having died last fall, I'll have to harness the plow to Rory."

From the back seat Skylar made an exasperated sound.

"Dad, just buy a garden tractor!"

Wendell glanced at her reflection in the rearview mirror and grinned. "I'm kidding, Sky. But we do need a new mule."

Skylar smiled back. "You can still buy a tractor. Be easier for you than using a mule."

Kiera turned in the front passenger seat and looked at her. "No, Sky. Gas-powered engines are bad for the planet. And reliance on technology makes people dependent and stupid. You know better."

Tally, who sat in the back beside Skylar with her eyes focused on the phone game in her hands, piped up, "Mom's right, you igit."

Skylar threw her sister a hard sidelong look. "Sure, Tally. Technology makes people dependent and stupid."

Tally paid no heed to the comment. And Kiera, trying to ignore Skylar's point, turned back around in her seat and commented on the blooms burgeoning in the dogwoods that lined the highway. With this said the conversation about technology fell silent.

The morning was a peaceful one for the Pink Escorts. The patients came and went and no anti groups were seen near the clinic. In fact, the only group that did put in an appearance was the Catholic one with their Virgin Mary images. Again these people positioned themselves across the street with their signs, but they offered no catcalls to the patients.

Tally, with her freshly made sign, posted herself on the sidewalk. When Kerry arrived she wanted to join her, and asked Wendell to go to the storage shed to find her one of the Campaign Parenthood signs. The selection Wendell brought back had text which read: *Reproductive Rights Are Human Rights*. Kerry thanked him and hurried with it outside. From the sidewalk she and Tally faced the traffic, proudly brandishing their signs for the passersby.

Kiera was happy to see almost all the regular escorts were present. As the morning was so quiet most everyone talked among themselves. While Wendell stood around the tent with the other men, Kiera took a seat with Wanda, Kristen, Jayelle, Zoe and Leandra. It was only on noticing

Skylar sitting alone on the snacks table and talking on her phone did Kiera realize she hadn't seen Felix Henner since arriving.

"Did Felix not show up?" she asked the other women.

"He mentioned yesterday something about a job interview," Kristen said, pulling her fingers idly through her long purple-tipped gray hair. "That's probably where he is."

Kiera snickered. "Oh, I don't see Felicia Henner letting her son do that while he's still living free under her roof. She's such staunch supporter for the cause."

Leandra grinned suddenly and pointed at Kiera. "I read your post from last night, lady! Good digging. Somebody will find out the names and home addresses of those antis soon enough!"

"Which ones are these?" Jayelle asked.

Kristen clapped her hands and snorted back a laugh. "Pagans And Secular People For Life. Avonport chapter. Can you believe it?"

Wanda's mouth dropped. "Are you frickin' serious? Pagan anti-choicers?"

Kiera beamed. "Yeah, those dumbasses that were out front yesterday. With the ugly tall guy who harassed Tally."

"Oh yeah," Wanda said thoughtfully. "Hm. I figured all the anti-rights nuts were Christians."

The women congratulated Kiera for the information she'd been able to dig up on this latest enemy group. They also promised to do their best in helping to identify Tall Guy and his companions.

"They won't be anonymous long," Jayelle vowed. "And when we find out where they live we'll have a protest outside on their lawns."

"And maybe some good, old-fashioned house eggings, too!" Leandra suggested.

A feeling of pride washed over Kiera. It was times like this that she knew her leadership abilities did not go unappreciated.

Some moments later Skylar hopped off the snacks table and walked over.

"Mom, I know everything is pretty quiet, but somebody should be out there keeping an eye for patients who might want directions to the clinic door or help getting there from the parking lot."

Wanda laughed. "Shield the abortion patients with umbrellas if they ask, sure, but are we supposed to be bellhops, too? Geesh, girl."

Kiera noticed Skylar suck her bottom lip as if struggling against the urge to say something harsh. "Some of the women who come are cancer patients," she replied to Wanda. "It wouldn't hurt us to be polite and guide them to the entrance."

Wanda waved her hand dismissively. "I signed up to help keep abortion patients from the interference of uppity hecklers and protesters. Holding the hands of cancer patients is beyond my pay grade."

Skylar's eyes widened with disbelief. Kiera, hoping to diffuse the awkward moment, reached out and gave her hand an affectionate squeeze.

"That's thoughtful, Skylar. You go do that."

Skylar nodded. As she left the tent Kiera knew Wanda had truly shocked her daughter.

"I'm sorry, Kiera," Wanda offered. "Hope I didn't hurt Skylar's feelings. But well, you understand?"

Kiera did understand. If the escorts started acting like guides for sick patients it might undermine the principal reason for their presence.

"People die every day," she concurred. "It's sad, but we can't let it distract us from what's most important."

At around two o'clock that afternoon Jeremy Dinks returned to the tent from a smoke break. He came with the report that the sidewalk was getting congested with antis.

Kiera went out to investigate. She found Reverend Pumpkin Head and six members of his Creek View Baptist congregation positioned on the sidewalk west of the clinic entryway. They carried posters, and today every one of them had worn powder blue smocks with large white-framed navy crosses sewn over their hearts.

In turn, Tally and Kerry had apparently decided against meekly keeping to the eastern side of the entryway. The two of them were marching back and forth, proudly brandishing their own signs, right in front of the Baptist group. It was a tight spot for competing space, and at one point Kiera heard one of the Creek View Baptist women complain Kerry had stepped on her foot. The complainer was a heavy-set woman and Kerry pounced on this fact.

"It's a public sidewalk, you stupid cow!" Kerry screamed in her face. "You should have moo-ved!"

In fairness, Kiera thought, the aging Kerry was far from being able to boast a slim figure herself. But her remark made Kiera chuckle.

For a few minutes the Baptists endured Tally and Kerry's purposeful obstruction of their signs. But it wasn't long before they started to edge further down the sidewalk. Tally and Kerry kept up with them until the group reached the street corner. It was here that Jilly's –a small homestyle diner—was located. The owner had long before demonstrated she was no fan of either the escorts or the antis. She'd even gone so far as to place a large standing sign in the middle of her parking lot that read: DISPUTES SPILLING OVER FROM CLINIC WILL RESULT IN CALL TO POLICE.

The Baptists saw this warning sign and lowered their signs. They looked defeated. Tally cackled and she and

Kerry skipped back like happy school girls to reclaim their turf. Kiera, giddy with pride for Tally, returned to the tent to apprise the other escorts about the pair's victory.

For a little while it seemed the clinic property might be peaceable for the remainder of the business day. This was until a masculine voice, reciting a Biblical verse, pealed out from the direction of the sidewalk.

"For thou hast possessed my reins: thou hast covered me in my mother's womb. I will praise thee, for I am fearfully and wonderfully made. Marvelous are thy works and that my soul knoweth right well."

It was a voice the escorts all recognized. While the others groaned with disgust or covered their ears, Kiera got to her feet and headed out the door. Walking onto the grassy slope, she saw a familiar figure seated in a wheelchair on the sidewalk just beside the entryway.

The man's real name was Bill Hendrickson and he was a self-styled street preacher. His visits were irregular, yet when he did come he was fond of sermonizing. Today he had shown up wearing hunting fatigue trousers and a cap with the words *Proud U.S. Vet* printed across the front. Printed on his black tee shirt was an image of a cross with a dove flying overhead. From the hand grip of his wheelchair hung a duffle bag Kiera had seen before. He used this to carry the self-printed religious leaflets he tried to give away.

Hendrickson had lost both legs below the knee while on active duty in Afghanistan. He also had a glass eye. Through their digging on Hendrickson, the escorts had discovered he lived in an apartment at an independent living facility located at the edge of town. Because he was a disabled veteran the escorts were hesitant about confronting him. On the occasions he'd got too loud with a bullhorn they had simply called the police. But unlike with most other loudmouth protesters the cops refused to tell Hendrickson to move along.

Disappointment with the police had not stopped Kiera from bestowing on Hendrickson the epithet of *Squinty McGimpy*. The use of this name was the only time PCKC Facebook followers ever criticized Kiera (some deemed the epithet mean and disparaging to veterans). Kiera even lost a few followers completely over the name. However, as much as Kiera disliked losing followers, she felt that if followers could be so easily offended over a nickname, then it probably wounded the holier-than-thou Hendrickson right down to his abortion-hating core. And this prospect delighted her.

At the moment Hendrickson appeared to be focused on something in the parking lot. Kiera looked and saw Skylar walking beside a woman. Her daughter had thrown the protection of an umbrella over the woman's head and was leading her toward the clinic. Kiera surmised the woman must have come for an abortion as patients coming for other medical procedures typically didn't care if anyone could see their faces. As Kiera turned her head she spotted Tally and Kerry standing on the sidewalk. They were glaring at Hendrickson; their faces flushed and contorted with anger.

Hendrickson shouted out to the woman under the umbrella, "Please ma'am, if you are pregnant, don't go there! Give your unborn baby the same chance at life your mother gave you!"

Kiera was infuriated. She cupped her hands around the sides of her mouth and yelled at him, "Hey Squinty, go the hell away!"

Hendrickson shut his eyes. It appeared he was praying.

Tally and Kerry lowered their signs and walked over to his wheelchair. Kerry poked Hendrickson's shoulder. "Get out of here, Squinty McGimpy!"

Tally shouted something at him now, though Kiera couldn't understand what it was due to the sound of a large truck passing down the street.

Hendrickson opened his eyes and swiveled the wheels of his chair. It rolled along the eastern portion of the sidewalk. Here he stopped and turned it about so that he faced the clinic property.

He declared loudly, "And the Lord said, *Before I formed you in the womb I knew you, and before you were born I consecrated you!*"

Tally and Kerry followed the veteran. They both laughed at him, and Tally jeered, "Poor little Squinty McGimpy! What did your god consecrate for *you*? A disability check?"

Not to be outdone Kerry crowed, "Poor Squinty McGimpy, couldn't walk for his limpy!"

Hendrickson did his best to ignore them. "*Truly children are a gift from the Lord; the fruit of the womb is a reward!*"

Tally and Kerry suddenly threw their signs aside. To Kiera's surprise the two lifted their arms and clasped hands over his head. They began to dance in a circle around the wheelchair and recited Kerry's remark in a loud sing-songy taunt.

"Poor Squinty McGimpy! Couldn't walk for his limpy!

Poor Squinty McGimpy! Couldn't walk for his limpy!"

Kiera giggled. She thought Hendrickson looked pathetic as he tried to continue his preaching over their voices.

"Do you not know that you are God's temple and that God's Spirit dwells in you? If anyone destroys God's temple, God will destroy him. For God's temple is holy, and you are that temple."

From across the street the Catholics antis could now be heard booing and yelling "Shame on you!" Several cars slowed down in passing, with drivers and passengers gawking at the situation. Some of them were indignant and shouted at Tally and Kerry to leave the veteran alone.

Kiera was sure that soon enough Hendrickson would admit defeat and move along. As piteous as the image might be to others, Kiera was eager to share the moment with the loyal among her online followers. The last time she'd posted about Hendrickson someone among them must have tracked down where he lived, because two days later the veteran was in the local news after a burning sack of dog feces had been left on the porch of his home. The news article stated that the firefighters who had turned up reported the sack had been set too close to a large American flag posted at the top of the steps railing. Half the cottage had gone up in flames. The firefighters were able to rescue Hendrickson from his bed, though he had to be treated for smoke inhalation.

Kiera was sure none of her followers had planned for that prank to turn into a near-fatal event. Nor did she foresee such an unlikely event to happen again. So she took her phone out of her pocket and began to videotape. For almost seventy seconds Hendrickson endured the two dancing escorts. But at last he threw his hands down, and with a rough shove of the wheels turned his chair and reeled it ahead. Kerry had to lurch out of the way to keep from being hit.

"Watch it, turd!" she bellowed.

Hendrickson ignored her and continued rolling away. Kiera videotaped his progression until at last the wheelchair rounded the next street corner and moved out of sight.

The Catholics were still booing. Tally and Kerry, laughing with victory, responded by flipping them off. As the pair retrieved their signs Kiera clicked off her camera app.

At that moment she heard a voice close by, "So, this is what you escorts do?"

She saw her brother Daniel walking toward her from the parking lot. He was dressed in casual corporate – smokey black trousers and a pressed white dress shirt, as well as a pair of the fashionable Italian leather loafers he was fond of. His salon styled fair hair was, as always, perfect, without a strand out of place.

As he joined her Kiera realized this was the first time she'd known her brother to make his way out to where the escorts worked. Daniel was typically to be found either in his office or at a board meeting. His dealings with the escorts were phantomlike at best.

Kiera greeted him wryly, "What brings you outside, little brother? Finally decide to step your feet into the trenches alongside the callous-handed workers?"

Daniel lifted an eyebrow. "Seriously, Kiera. I saw that guy Tally and the other woman chased down the street. He's a veteran, right?"

She made a disdainful sound. "As far as I know, just a street preacher with a bad habit of coming here to taunt patients."

"But the man's clearly disabled, Kiera. And it is a public sidewalk, after all."

Kiera rolled her eyes. Daniel had always been bad about zeroing in on the most asinine points and missing what was significant. "What part of taunting patients don't you get, Danny?"

She noticed the ever so slight clench of Daniel's jaw. Ever since childhood this particular tic happened at times he felt annoyed or stressed.

"Taunting, hm?", Daniel quipped. "Yes, the man looks so very intimidating."

Kiera gave him an impatient look. "Whatever."

"Look sis, I didn't come out here to talk about this. But since I am here, let me mention that while passing by the Pink Escorts tent, I was surprised to count eleven people in there. All of them just sitting or standing around."

"Yeah, so?"

Daniel blinked as if surprised by her question. "Eleven people in there. You, Tally and that other woman out here. Skylar in the parking lot. That's what, fifteen people? The only one who appears to be doing anything resembling escort work is Skylar."

Kiera's skin prickled. "Daniel, you have no idea what it can be like down here! The shit we have to put up with from those anti-choicers! They are always hostile, and we never know when a group of them will suddenly get the notion to invade the property en masse. You should be grateful the clinic has this many people willing to give up their valuable time to help."

Kiera hoped to see her angry tone bring at least a glint of fear to his eyes. When they were young it had taken so little to intimidate her little brother. But now he only looked decidedly bored.

"Invade? That's one wheelchair-bound man, Kiera. There's no need for any of you to be out here behaving like what I just saw."

She felt like slapping him! Why was he being so obstinate?

"Jesus, Danny," she seethed. "How corporate and provincial you've become! Why I remember the times I bailed you out of jail. Many times, little brother. Don't forget."

He gave her a sharp look. The sharpest one she'd seen in ages. "I was a stupid teenager then, but no, I've never forgotten. And you may be interested in to know I actually came down here for a reason that has nothing to do with your flock of escorts."

She laughed cynically. "I knew you didn't care about rubbing shoulders with the proletariat."

"Can you dispense with the socialist jargon for just a minute? It's about our Mom."

The mention of their mother sidetracked Kiera. "What about Dorothy?"

"She's very sick, Kiera. Stomach cancer."

Kiera was incredulous. Their mother Dorothy had always been such an active, healthy woman. "Are you sure?"

Daniel told her that his wife Emma had been taking Dorothy to her medical appointments. Kiera didn't know Emma well. In fact, she'd consciously tried to avoid talking with her sister-in-law as Kiera had little doubt the woman was as artificial and snobby as Daniel.

"Mom wanted do-overs after the first results came back positive," Daniel said. "And we were both with her when her doctor gave her these latest results. It has progressed very swiftly, already stage four."

The world seemed suddenly to rush away and Kiera was enfolded in an embrace of conflicting emotions. For many years she had consciously worked to push Dorothy out of her life. She had exonerated her actions because she still blamed Dorothy for the divorce from her father. And when her dad had died Kiera had told herself she needed to shield her children from Dorothy's country bumpkin-bred influence. The truth was her rancor toward Dorothy had begun years before the divorce. She deeply resented Dorothy, for reasons she dared never speak of in front of the children. But learning now how sick Dorothy was, Kiera felt that comfortable resentment threatening to dissolve.

Kiera remembered Dorothy's easy smile. The woman's tinkling laughter resounded in her memory. She recalled the countless weekend shopping sprees the two of them had enjoyed in places like New York City and Atlanta. Their mother-and-daughter vacations in Savannah, their skiing trips to Luzern, Switzerland and the many holidays the two of them enjoyed at Redhead Bay. Even as Kiera remembered these places and the things they had done together, her senses were overwhelmed by the smell of blackberry pancakes. These had always been Kiera's favorite, and when she was a child Dorothy cooked up a batch every Saturday morning. A big batch, especially for Kiera.

Kiera felt an unexpected tear well at the corner of an eye. "Why didn't she tell me?"

"She did trying calling," Daniel explained. "But her calls apparently didn't get through. And I know it is the same number I have for you."

Kiera realized this was the truth. She had blocked Dorothy's number some years before. It had been right after a Thanksgiving dinner at Dorothy's house, when Kiera's kids were still quite young. Tally had been running around, chasing cousin Teresa's daughter and son around with a dead chipmunk she'd found near the driveway. It had just been a childish prank, of course, but when Dorothy saw what was going on she ordered Tally to take the chipmunk carcass outside. When Tally only laughed, Dorothy complained to Kiera and Wendell, *If you and Wendell aren't careful, your kids will turn out clingy, disrespectful little hooligans!* At that point Kiera's temper snapped. After a few choice words for Dorothy she and Wendell took their children and left. It was the last time Kiera had spoken to or seen her mother.

As clearly as Kiera knew she'd never been as close to Dorothy as she had Ira, or even his mother, Grandma Lucinda, the fond memories of her mother had not faded.

"I can call her tonight, Danny. Tonight or tomorrow."

Daniel rubbed the back of his neck. "Do more than that," he said warily. "She wants to see you, very much so."

"Of course." Kiera inhaled deeply. "She still at her house on Tarbert Avenue?"

"Yes."

Kiera promised to go see Dorothy just as soon as possible.

He nodded and looked down over again to where Tally and Kerry stood with the messages on their signs aimed at traffic. His next question sounded like a functional afterthought, "Make sure Tally and the others stay on clinic property from now on, okay?"

At any other time Kiera probably would have responded with a snide remark. But she was distracted over the news about Dorothy.

Chapter 7

Kiera and her family picked up pizza on the way home. After the box and plates were set on the dining room table and everyone was seated, Kiera told Wendell and the girls about Dorothy's cancer.

Skylar was immediately distraught. "Oh mom, I am so sorry. Poor grandma!"

"Can't say as I ever liked the woman," Wendell said, "but I am sorry she's this sick, sweetheart."

Tally swallowed the huge bite of pepperoni in her mouth and took a swig from her glass of lemonade. "That sucks, I guess."

"You guess?" Skylar snorted. "That's pretty cold, don't you think?"

Tally glared at her defensively. "Yeah, so it's cold? I really don't care."

Wendell, who was selecting a second slice of pizza from the box, threw Tally a dismayed look. "You might want to care just a bit. At least for your own mother's sake."

"Why?" Tally asked. "All I've ever heard is that my grandma abandoned mom when she needed her most."

Kiera was touched by Tally's loyalty. But for some reason, it was discomforting tonight to hear her daughter repeat what she'd asserted about Dorothy over the many years.

"Well," she said, hoping to get off the subject of the past, "I'm going to go see Dorothy tomorrow. Just take the jeep for a short trip out to her house. If you all don't mind working the clinic without me?"

"That will be fine," Wendell said. He reached over the table and patted her hand. "You're the better person, Kiera."

"I'll go with you if you want," Skylar offered.

Tally chuckled and imitated her sister in a childish voice, "*I'll go with you if you want.* What the hell, Skylar? You don't have to try to get in good with the old woman just because she's dying. Grandpa had all the money, and there's already a designated portion for you."

Skylar stared at her. "You are unbelievable, Tally."

Tally spat off some tart reply, but Kiera couldn't hear it over the sound of her own blood swooshing angrily in her ears.

"Enough!" she shrieked.

Her daughters at once fell silent— Tally with a snicker lingering on her face and Skylar staring off with an appalled expression.

"I just wanted to tell you all," Kiera said. "I think it's only right to visit the woman who gave birth to me. But I will go tomorrow, by myself. It may be uneasy as Dorothy and I haven't seen each other for so long. And then after that, Sky, maybe you can come with me on another day?"

"Sure, Mom."

Wendell had a faraway look on his face as he contemplated the slice on his plate. "I'm glad you picked the toppings, Tally. I never thought pork and pineapple would be so tasty for what is, basically, a dish for white colonialists."

Tally grinned. "I won't tell if you won't, Dad!"

They both laughed.

After dinner, Wendell went out to feed the goats, Skylar went to tend the horses, and Tally crashed on the sofa in the living room for a nap. Kiera busied herself in washing the plates and wiping down the table. The household was quiet by the time she was finished, and she took the opportunity to call Rory. It wasn't a long call, just long enough for her to make sure he was coming home. She was pleased to hear his confirmation that the plans were still on. The subject of Dorothy's cancer was not one she brought up with Rory, as she decided it could wait until he was back.

After Skylar and Wendell had returned to the house, they both announced they were going to bed. Kiera found herself thinking about Dorothy. Bittersweet thoughts these, and she detested the idea of dwelling on them. Besides, there was something she wanted to get done before retiring for the night.

In the den, she sat down at the computer and got online. She went straight to the Pro-Choice Krumme County's Facebook page. There just would be no sleep for her that night if she didn't make a move to further embarrass street preacher Hendrickson.

In a fresh post, she uploaded the video she'd recorded that day. In addition to providing the video, she wrote a lengthy, ridiculing description of how Squinty McGimpy had got himself into the predicament of, as Kiera described it, *"being danced into surrender by our pro-choice warriors Tally and Kerry."*

After publishing the post, she checked her notifications for any comments pending approval. There were three submitted for the post she'd made the night before. Two of these came from PCKC Escorts (Kerry and Leandra), and they were both congratulatory about Tally's diligent patrolling of the street. Kerry also included a scathing rant about the *Pagans And Secular People For Life.*

At one point, Kerry wrote that she hoped, *"someone will discover a name and details for this misogynist Tall Guy. HE NEEDS TO BE TAKEN DOWN!"*

The third comment came from a long-time online abortion supporter by the name of Ted Godsey. This Godsey lived in Knoxville and was very involved in Pro-Choice issues in all surrounding counties. He used his comment to throw shade at all three anti-groups Kiera had written about, and he didn't hold back the obscenities in doing so.

Kiera was pleased. She hit the Approve button for all the comments.

Shortly before midnight, Kiera took a shower. After this, she fluff-dried her hair and brushed her teeth. Lastly, she slipped on a knee-length night shirt and stepped out of the bathroom.

While passing the stairway she heard Skylar talking from upstairs. Kiera paused and realized the girl was on her phone.

"Sounds ideal for you," Skylar said to whoever it was. "And a ping pong table in the garage? That'll be cool. Hm? Yeah, but you'll have to teach me how to play!"

Kiera was curious about who it was that Skylar hoped to teach her ping pong. But she was too tired to eavesdrop any further. She stepped into the living room to turn off the overhead light and latch the French doors. This was when she discovered Tally was still lying on the sofa. The girl was on her back, snoring lightly, with an arm thrown across her brow. After latching the doors, Kiera approached the sofa. Her eldest daughter was bathed in sweat and Kiera detected a pungent, acrid smell to her perspiration.

"Tally," she said, bending over, "wake up. You'll be more comfortable in your own bed. And honestly, you need a shower, too."

When Tally didn't awaken Kiera nudged her shoulder.

"Hey, Tally?" There was no response, so Kiera nudged her a little harder. "Come on, wake up."

Tally rolled over onto her side. As she did so, her mouth dropped open and she sucked in a particularly sonorous snore.

Kiera felt a twinge of alarm, realizing the only time Tally ever smelled like this or slept this deeply was after she had spent time with Braeden Wilcox. She remembered, too, that she had found Tally awake all the night before and that Tally had spent some of that night with Braeden.

What if there was some legitimacy to Skylar's suspicions about Braeden? It was a horrible thought that Tally could be using hard drugs. Wendell and Kiera themselves occasionally indulged in marijuana, mushrooms and blue Lotus. But these things were all naturally grown pleasures. She and Wendell had assumed their example of staying away from lab-produced crap like meth, refined coke and heroin would be enough to keep their children from experimenting with them.

Kiera decided it was best to let Tally sleep it off. She departed quietly and walked to the master bedroom. Wendell was sitting up in bed, reading a book by the light of the lamp at his side of the bed. On noticing her, he flipped down the bed covers on her side.

She crawled in and lay on her side facing him. The worry she felt over Tally must have shown on her face for he closed the book.

"Is something wrong?"

A ball of raw anxiety formed in the pit of Kiera's stomach. "It's Tally."

"What?"

She told him about Tally's deep sleep on the sofa, of the awful smell of her perspiration. And of her fear, the girl had been using drugs with Braeden Wilcox.

"Ah," he said, stroking Kiera's temple. "You shouldn't worry about that. Tally wasn't raised in a trailer park. We've told her the hazards of using cheap man-made uppers and pharmaceutical-grade hallucinogens."

Wendell's cerebral-sounding denial did nothing to allay Kiera's fear. She understood he wished to believe they'd raised their kids to be percipient. In Wendell's eyes, their children could do no wrong. To admit that they were vulnerable to making mistakes was something difficult for either of them to accept. Doing something stupid was what the children of other people did. People not as intellectual as he and Kiera. People much less intelligent.

Kiera was beginning to understand her kids were far from being perfect. Rory, not content to stay home, was determined to enter the mainstream workforce. Skylar was getting more mouthy and independent by the day. Then there was Tally. Despite Wendell's refusal to believe otherwise (and just maybe in part due to that refusal), Kiera was finding it hard to dismiss the possibility their oldest daughter was a drug user.

"I'm afraid telling her hasn't been enough," she said. "The signs are all there, Wendell."

"You are mistaken," he scoffed. "We are with her every day. I would have noticed these so-called signs."

Kiera couldn't help but doubt this contention. Sure, when they'd first met in the office of their mutual parole officer years before Wendell had just got out of prison after serving two years for selling cocaine. He believed he knew all the signs of drug use. Yet he seemed blind to Tally's ever-increasing delight in aggressive confrontations and how her various interests so quickly turned into obsessions. But Kiera did see. And she was gripped by the sudden terror that whether by action or words, she was at least partly responsible.

Kiera shook her head. "I see the changes in her, Wendell. Today, she went over twenty-four hours without getting any sleep. This wasn't the first time. She gets obsessed with projects while ignoring the need to eat or bathe. She's quicker to anger, more aggressive. And her skin smells funny. I genuinely think Tally is tweaking."

He laughed softly. "Oh no, no. Tally simply takes after her mother. I don't mean the lack of bathing thing, of course, but when you get behind a worthy crusade you don't let trivial things distract you. This is all it is."

Kiera groaned softly. "Seriously? If she's like me, then perhaps I have blown it as a mother."

"Oh, c'mon Kiera. You have always been a conscientious mother, haven't you? You did everything right during your pregnancies. You gave up smoking. You gave birth at home instead of going to some hospital to be surrounded by stupid doctors and their textbook notions. You turned your back on so-called friends who said you were nursing our kids too long. You educated them in what needs to be learned. You taught them to be pro-active social warriors. I have always believed that a woman who cares enough to do all these things is the only kind of woman deserving of the title *mother*. So what if Tally wants to emulate you? It has to be a good thing."

Perhaps he was right, she thought, and she had just imagined the worst.

But something else crept into mind. Something she only occasionally thought about, for the few times it had previously slipped into her conscious mind she felt suffocated with guilt. Yet again it raised its ugly head out of the muck in which she'd tried to bury it.

"But Tally once came very close to dying because of me."

Wendell grimaced. "You're not going there again, are you? Not after all these years. It was an accident."

Kiera didn't want to think about the incident but she couldn't help it. Tally had only been thirteen when Kiera found her lying, convulsing and nearly unconscious, on the kitchen floor. The tiles underneath Tally had been pooled with her blood and her legs and summer shorts had been drenched as well. The poor girl's skin was bleached white, her lips a ghastly shade of purple. Kiera had called 9-1-1. With Wendell and their other two children piled in their vehicle, they followed the ambulance to the hospital. In the trauma unit the attending doctors discovered Tally had suffered a massive uterine hemorrhage. She was provided with blood transfusions. And later, when Tally was strong enough, she was given a gynecological examination and other physical evaluations. The results confirmed Tally's ovaries had been injured during the hemorrhage and would never be properly functional again.

The doctors had diagnosed Tally as having suffered acute uterine dysfunction. Only once Tally was home again did the entire truth come out. Tally admitted she'd eaten something from Kiera's pink cabinet in the food pantry, in fact, had consumed several ounces of crushed blue cohosh and sampled jars of toxic crèmes Kiera had made. At the time, Kiera kept this pantry stocked with abortifacients. These herbs were the ones Kiera grew and sold via the internet to women seeking natural methods of inducing abortions. Kiera had never imagined one of her children would try digesting these herbs, and so she'd never even bothered putting a lock on the pantry.

"I'm sorry, Mom," Tally had told her. *"I won't get into your herbs again."*

Kiera had been horrified by her own negligence. She spent that night with scrub gloves on her hands, washing every trace of deadly crèmes from the jars and flushing the collection of abortifacient herbs down the toilet.

"If I had been more careful," Kiera said now to Wendell, "Tally wouldn't have got into those herbs. And she would still be able to have children."

Wendell sighed. "You can't keep beating yourself up. Besides, you've never heard Tally blame you for what happened, have you?"

Kiera shook her head. "No."

"Well, there you go. What happened then has absolutely nothing to do with her state of mind now. She's an exuberant, determined young woman, nothing more. I see that. Our friends see that."

Kiera looked at him hopefully. "But why am I so worried about her now?"

Wendell kissed her brow. "It's your mother. Dorothy is dying and you feel helpless to make it not so. This causes you to feel guilty. And this guilt has, in turn, dredged up all the old contention between you and Dorothy. On a subconscious level, you want to hurt yourself for being unable to make Dorothy's cancer go away, so you are imagining things to feel guilty about, in particular things having to do with motherhood. This only makes sense, don't you see? It was your choices when it came to raising children that made for the rift between you two."

Kiera thought he was at least partially right. The rift between her and Dorothy had started long before any of the kids were born, still it hadn't helped that Dorothy had acted so judgmental about the way they raised her grandchildren. Kiera thought again about the chipmunk incident at Dorothy's house.

"If you and Wendell aren't careful, your kids will turn out clingy, disrespectful little hooligans!"

There had been other things, at least one major thing, which had come between Kiera and her mother many, many years before. It was something Kiera felt best left forgotten as much as Tally eating the blue cohosh.

Just perhaps, she considered, she feared seeing Dorothy would ignite the lingering resentment she held toward the woman. This guilt Wendell talked about, maybe it was, in its own way, an unconscious maneuver to keep from having to think about that resentment.

"You are probably right," she conceded. "Thank you."

Wendell nodded and shifted in the bed toward the lamp. He closed his book and placed it on the nightstand.

"I assure you I'm right, sweetheart." With a little chuckle, he added, "However, I do agree Tally could stand a shower. You ought to suggest it to her tomorrow."

He switched the lamp light off. The light from the kitchen seeped dimly down the hallway and through the bedroom door to grace the room with soft illumination. Kiera felt Wendell wriggle a bit as he got comfortable. When he turned over onto his side with his face toward her on the pillow she kissed his lips.

"Goodnight," she told him. "I love you."

He murmured back a, "Love you, too." The next moment, his breathing turned relaxed and heavy.

Chapter 8

Wendell's assurances eased Kiera's mind enough she drifted easily off to sleep. It was a restful sleep, one so deep in fact that when she was roused by a gunshot her perceptions unwillingly stirred and struggled to sink back into slumber's soothing darkness.

A dog's yelp pierced that lull. Kiera's mind snapped into full consciousness. She opened her eyes and saw only the ceiling above the bed and felt Wendell's chin weighted upon her shoulder. He was snoring lightly.

Kiera thought for a moment the snores had confused her tired mind and manifested the sound of it into the dream as well as the report. She turned over with her back to Wendell and closed her eyes.

Another yelp sounded clearly from just outside the bedroom window. Kiera groaned. The last thing she needed was for Wendell to be awakened by a dog. He would end up worried enough about the livestock to throw on his shoes, find his rifle and go out to shoot whatever mutt was out there.

The yelp came again and was followed seconds later by an anxious bark. As Kiera listened she was sure she heard movement outside the window.

"Good grief," she muttered. "Please don't wake up Wendell at this time of night!"

As quietly as possible, she peeled away the covers and got out of bed. She padded the floor around the foot of the bed and went to the window. There, she parted the heavy weave curtains and looked outside. The illumination from the waxing moon glazed the property. The herb garden, presently just a 10'x 12' patch of tilled earth, appeared as a large black rectangle on the lawn. Wendell's wooden tool shed stood silent. Just beyond the shed, dense grass which hadn't been touched by a mower since before the last autumn, could be seen under the faint starlight. The ground sloped deeply here, allowing her to glimpse the hilly property belonging to their nearest neighbors down that way.

Everything outside appeared to be sleeping and undisturbed beneath the night sky.

Kiera heard the bark again. She couldn't be sure, but it seemed to be coming from the tall grass.

"I hear you out there, you stupid thing," she growled lowly. "I don't need my husband running out to shoot you. Just please go away."

With anxious breath Kiera waited to catch sight of the dog. But it did not appear, nor did she see anything moving among the grass. After about ten minutes without hearing a yelp or bark, Kiera gave a sigh of relief.

"Good. Now stay away."

A sudden vein of purplish lightning appeared in the sky. A few moments later, Kiera heard a soft boom of distant thunder. Satisfied the sound of it had probably chased the dog home, she turned from the window and noiselessly slipped back into bed.

The coming morning arrived with heavy rain and sporadic high winds. It was Skylar's turn to drive the family to the clinic (something Kiera was silently grateful for as her youngest was a more observant driver than Tally and her vision was better in the rain than Wendell's). By the time Skylar reached the clinic drive, however, the rain had eased into a sprinkle. The parking lot was slightly flooded, although the standing water was beginning to wash down the driveway toward the street. As the Scruggs emerged from their jeep, Kiera noticed the rain clouds above were beginning to break up and move on. Only the gusts remained and they were already growing weaker.

The morning saw the arrival of a great many patients. To the escorts' surprise, the rain seemed to have kept the antis away. Even the diligent Catholics failed to show up at their regular turf across the street.

Kerry was in the tent, complaining this morning about the arthritis in her hip. She must have been hurting badly as she declined to join Tally in patrolling the sidewalk. So Tally struck out on her own, taking along her homemade sign to proudly flaunt at passing drivers.

The other Escorts seemed content to sit around the tent and talk. Skylar was the only exception. The young woman took an umbrella and set out for the parking lot. Once again, she was offering to walk patients to the clinic door, not just the young ones who might be there for an abortion, but the middle-aged and senior women who were surely there for other medical procedures. Kiera remembered Daniel's comment from the day before: *"The only one who appears to be doing anything resembling Escort work is Skylar."*

As unfair as Kiera knew it probably was, the idea that her youngest was trying to make the rest of them look bad did cross her mind.

The thought didn't nag her for long because Dorothy was foremost on her mind. By the time eleven-thirty rolled around there was a lull in the number of patients coming in. She decided this was a good time to head out to her mother's house.

Kiera found Wendell sitting with some of the other male escorts. She told him she was leaving, planted a kiss on his forehead and walked to the parking lot. She saw Skylar standing near the front door of the clinic. Her youngest was talking on her cell phone, but seeing her mother, Skylar smiled and threw a wave. Kiera waved back and got into the jeep.

Tarbert Avenue was on the opposite side of the city. It was part of the old working-class residential district where Dorothy and most of her family members had been born and raised. This section of Avonport was fondly referred to by locals as *Thunder Estates* because in the 1930s a couple of moonshine runners-turned-professional stock car drivers had grown up here. These drivers' names and stories were something that had never interested Kiera, since her father –who had grown up in the influential Monument district– had deemed the subject of stock car racing an entertainment for the ill-bred.

What Kiera most keenly recalled about the community was the number of old houses that lined the streets. They were generally roomy brick or wooden frame residences. Some of them had been built as far back as the late eighteen-hundreds. The last time Kiera had driven through she had seen that most of these homes had fallen into disrepair. The home Dorothy had grown up in had not fared any better until her divorce from Ira. By that time, Dorothy's parents were both long dead. But Dorothy had made many renovations, financed, Kiera assumed, from the alimony payments Ira had made following their divorce.

As Kiera drove through Thunder Estates she noticed some of the old houses had either been renovated or were undergoing restorations. A few others looked to have

recently been torn down or dismantled. Real estate signs stood in the emptied yards of these properties.

She turned from Holly Street onto Tarbert Avenue. Dorothy's home was the third on her right. Kiera pulled the jeep in behind her mother's old tan Cadillac parked in the driveway. She turned the engine off and drew the key out. This she placed in her leather pouch purse that lay in the passenger seat.

Kiera looked over the house and yard. She'd only been here once or twice since Dorothy had moved back in. The original white wood siding had been done away with and exchanged for cream vinyl. The modern windows boasted lovely shutters of dark green, while the worn white front door Kiera remembered from her childhood had been replaced with a nice modern oak one. There were evident updates to the yard, too. The old Mulberry tree had been cut down and in its place stood a ceramic bird bath with a fluted pedestal. Grandma Schwann's large peony bush still stood at one corner of the porch, but hydrangea shrubs had been added here and there along the front side of the house. Their blue blossoms were already beginning to open. Rose bushes now bordered the iron fencing that separated Dorothy's property from her next-door neighbors.

While Kiera admired the changes, she also felt an apprehensive twinge. It had been so long since she and Dorothy had spoken. Her mother would surely know why she had finally come for a visit and this would be awkward. For a moment Kiera felt the compulsion to just restart the jeep engine and drive away. But no, that would be wrong. Dorothy was her mother and she had most of the time, in her own flawed and conventional way, tried to be a loving one.

Kiera grabbed her purse and exited the jeep. The grass was damp under the soles of her cowboy boots. She walked up the steps and as she set foot on the porch, the front door suddenly opened. A head peeked out. It was Dorothy.

Her hazel eyes lit up with surprise. "Kiera? Oh my, I thought I heard a car door!"

They regarded one another for several quiet moments. At last Kiera managed a smile.

"Hello Mom."

Dorothy stepped forward to give her a hug. The fragrance of her mother's favorite perfume filled Kiera's senses. Dorothy's shoulder-length hair—once pure blonde but now white—tickled like strands of silk against Kiera's cheek.

As Dorothy released her, Kiera noticed dark hollows beneath the woman's eyes. Except for this, Kiera would have never guessed her mother had cancer. Dorothy had aged, of course, which was no surprise considering she was eighty-one years old. More lines now creased her brow and deeper wrinkles tugged the corners of her mouth. Age spots dotted the backs of her hands. But Dorothy's excellent posture had not been affected by the years. She was still tall, her poise as erect and eloquent as Kiera recalled. And her simple ankle-length beige cable knit dress complimented a slender figure which had escaped illness-related emaciation.

"I hope," Kiera said, "this isn't a bad time?"

"Bad time? Oh, pooh! You come inside."

Kiera followed her into the house.

The interior renovations Dorothy had made were more drastic than the changes to the yard. The foyer, once bare except for a few very old reproductions hanging from the old wood paneling, now boasted bright floral wallpaper and dark maple flooring. An exquisite crystal chandelier was mounted to the antique-like metal ceiling tiles. The original staircase had entirely been replaced. The new one was constructed of oak and outfitted with a plush carpeted runner of Oriental design. On a side table stood a large crystal vase. This was filled with long-stem pink satin roses.

Dorothy led Kiera into the parlor. It was a room once referred to by Kiera's maternal grandparents as the *guest sitting room*. This room had been given a more casual refurbishing than the foyer. The walls were papered with a subtle pastel pinstripe design, and several small cherub prints (Dorothy's favorite motif) hung here and there. The floor was covered by light blue wall-to-wall carpeting. The sofa and two armchairs were upholstered in royal blue velvet, the same shade as the heavy window curtains. The coffee table was a carven oak piece which looked to have been professionally refinished. The large coat rack that stood by one window was one that Dorothy's father had built before she had been born. The large fireplace was still open. The bricks had been whitewashed, though, which gave it a simple, eloquent appearance. And instead of real logs, Dorothy was using a faux log electric heater.

Kiera noticed that all along the mantle stood several framed photos of various family members. Included among these was one of Kiera and Wendell from their wedding. There was also one of their three children, taken when they had been much younger. The photo reminded Kiera how very long it had been since she'd given Dorothy any new photographs.

"Do sit down, Kiera."

Kiera saw an afghan had been thrown haphazardly across the back of the sofa. Assuming her mother had been using the afghan for warmth, she took a seat in one of the armchairs.

"I can get you some tea or lemonade if you'd like?" Dorothy offered. "Molly Ann is coming in a while with my lunch. Though I do have lemon cake in the kitchen if you're hungry."

Kiera shook her head. "No, thank you. Molly Ann? Isn't that your sister Vera's daughter?"

"Yes. She and her husband Matt live in the garage apartment behind Vera's house. Up on Winston Circle."

"Oh yes, I remember."

As Dorothy sat down on the sofa, Kiera noticed the little grimace that pinched her expression.

"Mom," she said delicately, "Daniel told me you have been sick."

Dorothy waved a dismissive hand. "It may not be so bad. I have an excellent specialist. I don't want you to worry."

"But it does worry me. Stomach cancer is serious."

Dorothy regarded Kiera in a way that couldn't be deciphered. With a weary ring she said, "Well dear, you know now."

"But Daniel also mentioned you asked to see me," Kiera said tentatively. Guilt inflamed her cheeks. "Oh Mom, it shouldn't be like this. We should have kept in touch."

Dorothy gave a sad shrug. "My darling, you're here now. That's what is important. How are my grandchildren?"

Kiera smiled. She assured Dorothy the kids were getting along well. Proudly, she related how Tally had opened a web shop from which she sold her handcrafted jewelry. That Skylar worked a part-time job online as a call distributor for a car insurance company. And about Rory turning out to be a natural-born farmer and that he was a great help to her and Wendell in all their planting and harvesting activities.

Dorothy listened attentively. When Kiera had finished, she asked, "So Rory still lives with you and Wendell?"

"Yes, Mom. They all do."

"Ah. I would have thought they would have left the nest by now."

Kiera felt a familiar prick of indignation. Ignoring it, she said, "There is no reason for them to leave. They are quite happy where they are."

A rueful purse wrinkled Dorothy's mouth. "But is it good for them to live on top of that little mountain, entirely away from the rest of the world?"

Kiera laughed. "Oh Mom, it isn't like we haven't taught them how to drive. And they have access to our vehicles. Why, Rory is in Kentucky at this very moment."

Kentucky. As soon as the word passed her lips, Kiera saw the astonished gleam that came to Dorothy's eyes.

Kiera immediately tried to clarify, "He drove there to look at a horse for me. He has a very good eye for horses."

It was all the details about Rory's trip Kiera was willing to give. But Dorothy's mind seemed at ease.

"Ah," Dorothy said with a light chuckle. "He must share his mother's affection for horses. Good, good."

Dorothy turned a little and pulled the afghan from the back. Very neatly, she covered her thighs and legs, and tucked the fabric around her waist. Kiera asked if she was cold.

"Not really. I get little chills every now and then."

"Let me turn the heater on?"

Dorothy shook her head and assured Kiera the chill would pass momentarily. But Kiera saw how sallow Dorothy's face suddenly looked! And how her lips had taken a bluish hue and how ever more pronounced were the hollows beneath her eyes. Kiera hurt for her.

But Dorothy's thoughts were not on her sickness. "Your brother was right. I do want to speak to you about something." She patted the cushion beside her. "Sit beside me, Kiera."

With a nod, Kiera rose and moved to the sofa. Dorothy turned to face her. Reaching her hand to Kiera's face, she smoothed a slender lock of hair at her cheek and tenderly folded this around Kiera's ear.

"I owe you a long overdue apology, sweetheart."

For a moment, Kiera thought Dorothy was referring to how she'd treated her grandchildren. But then Dorothy's eyes misted over. It was something more than the grandchildren. Kiera had an idea of what her mother was apologizing for, something she'd longed to hear for years— an apology for the way Dorothy had tried to get Ira to turn his back on Kiera when she stood at the mercy of a heartless criminal justice system.

Kiera sat up straight and offered a patient smile. "Go ahead, Mom."

Dorothy said in a quavering voice, "I wronged you, Kiera. I should have taken you and Daniel and divorced your father much sooner."

The unexpected statement dulled the victory Kiera had felt close at hand. It was confusing, too. For though Dorothy's filing for divorce had seemed to come out of the blue at the time Kiera had simply been too angry with her mother to care about the reasons behind her decision. Besides, the divorce had proven a significant embarrassment for Ira. And throughout the years, that embarrassment had provided Kiera extra ammunition in which to reproach Dorothy.

"What the hell, Mom?" she stuttered. "Isn't it enough you broke Daddy's heart when Danny and I were already grown?"

"It didn't break Ira's heart," Dorothy said. "Hurt his pride, yes. But you already know this, Kiera."

Kiera folded her arms over her chest and eyed Dorothy sharply. "My father gave you so much. Didn't you owe his pride at least a little something?"

"I was weak, Kiera," Dorothy answered in a penitent tone. "Once I truly was in love with Ira. After we were married, I also liked being part of the wealthiest family in town. And later, when Ira became mayor, I enjoyed that, too. But I should have cared more about the children I brought into this world. In this, however, I failed."

"Come on, mother," Kiera retorted, "are you trying to make me believe Ira Hambrick was an abusive or neglectful husband or father? Because that is something I will never believe."

"No, Kiera. Ira provided an enviable lifestyle, all the financial security one could ever hope for. Three beautiful homes. A river yacht. Social status."

"Then what are you driving at?"

As her mother reached for her hand, Kiera recoiled and snatched it away. "Tell me!"

Dorothy sighed. "Oh, Kiera...it took little time to discover Ira Hambrick wasn't in love with me. He didn't marry *me*, he married Miss Avonport 1960. He was proud to say he had the prettiest wife in town. Just as he was proud to have sired an intelligent, successful son to carry on his family name. There was something, however, that meant more to Ira than being elected mayor, more to him than even prestige and hobnobbing with the city elites. It was two things, in fact: his mother and you."

Kiera scoffed, "And here I thought you were going to apologize for trying to convince Daddy I was better off rotting in prison! But the truth is you have been jealous of me!"

Dorothy's expression took a sobered hardness. "That's not it at all, Kiera. Ira's love was not normal. The way he treated you and his mother was not normal."

"Not normal," Kiera said, mimicking her mother's voice. "Oh my god, Dorothy! I know you never showed anything but a veneer of politeness toward Grandma Lucinda. What the hell did that poor woman ever do to you?"

"Poor woman," Dorothy muttered. "She only snubbed me, Kiera. Snubbed, mocked and belittled me every chance she got."

Kiera responded coolly, "From everything I've ever heard or known about Grandma, she had a busy, full life all the way to the end of it. Had her gardening, had her community volunteer work, charity fundraisers and events. I highly doubt she had time to devote to mistreating you."

A flush swept over Dorothy's wan face. "As if you would have ever noticed. I wasn't of the acceptable mindset for Lucinda Townshend Hambrick. My kinfolk were what she ridiculed as *low-class white-bread*. Nobody in my family belonged to a union. None of them achieved political success. There was not one who was a famed anti-establishment activist like Lucinda. None of my women folk slept with Woody Guthrie or blew themselves up trying to set off a pipe bomb in the old county courthouse. And I, Lucinda's daughter-in-law, certainly had no interest in the radical ideas she deemed to be the socially superior way of thinking.

"She was fond of you, I think, in a reflection-in-the-mirror kind of way. In Ira's eyes Lucinda was the most flawlessly fascinating creature that ever lived. She could be demanding of him, even cruel at times. All the same, he lived for her approval. I felt sorry for your father, for it was, very honestly, as much idol worship on his part as it was love. When Lucinda died he was left with a daughter so much like her in looks, disposition, and temperament. Even the sound of her laughter echoed in your voice. The adoration Ira lavished on her, he also lavished on you. I saw this adoration, Kiera, yet I did very little to interfere. But I should have stopped it. I looked the other way instead. Why? Because I enjoyed the lifestyle Ira provided. I liked the social status. I knowingly failed to think about what was best for my daughter. Instead, I told myself that while I could never compete with Lucinda, then at least he does love our daughter."

Kiera felt disgusted by this outrageous tale.

"And what's your point in this histrionic story?"

Dorothy gave her a pitying look. "Oh honey. Don't you understand? My selfish choices led to Ira instilling in you the belief you knew more than everyone else around you. Of making you feel that you were entitled to hurt anyone who might stand in the way of obtaining what you wanted. It is my fault that you ended up in prison. Don't you see this?"

Icy rage formed in the pit of Kiera's stomach. She forgot the sympathy which had compelled her to visit Dorothy. She ignored the sorrowful tears shining in Dorothy's eyes. The only thing Kiera could focus on was that this woman was bound and determined to make her feel like Ira had spoiled and made her shallow.

"Apparently," she seethed, "your jealousy is what made you resent Daddy caring enough to do what he could to help me."

Dorothy's tears spilled down her cheeks. "I was never jealous, sweetheart, you must understand! But once you did that awful, awful thing, I saw how I had failed you as a mother. I couldn't bear to fail you again, or knowingly let your father fail you. So yes, I told him not to bribe that Kentucky parole board into granting you early parole. But only because I wanted you to have the chance to become a better person! The kind of person who knows right from wrong, who has learned from their mistakes." With the back of a hand, Dorothy wiped her cheeks dry. "But what I thought didn't matter to Ira. He and his high-priced lawyers got you out after only thirty-four months of serving a twelve-year sentence. And it was my fault you were there to begin with! I should never have allowed Ira to have corrupted you."

Kiera glared at Dorothy. She was unmoved by the tears, the passion in her words. Dorothy had turned her back on her own daughter, and now she was trying to blame a dead ex-husband for her indifference.

"You have no shame at all, do you? Here, blaming the only parent that cared about what I was going through!"

Dorothy shook her head. "I take the blame." She sniffed, and holding her hands in her lap, regarded Kiera sadly. "And over the last few years, my dear, you've shown me exactly why I deserve to carry that blame."

"What the hell do you mean, Dorothy?"

Her mother's jaw clenched. At length, she said, "I've seen you on the evening news. You, Wendell, my grandchildren. That bunch you call Pink Escorts parading around the clinic. I am also aware of the charges incurred because of the spectacles the bunch of you engage in outside the clinic. Public disorder. Assault. Stalking."

Kiera railed at her now, "All those charges were dropped, too! Those antis harass the women who come to the clinic! And don't forget my dear brother Daniel is the clinic's CEO. I don't hear you complaining about him! How anti-woman your delicate scruples are!"

"Daniel knows I don't approve," Dorothy replied. "It is wrong of him, but at least he isn't out working to stir up hostilities. This behavior, Kiera, this is why I know how deeply I failed you." Her voice faltered as if she were on the verge of crying again, "You didn't learn a thing from the short time you were in prison, did you? You have no regret. Now you and your family are out there assaulting and mocking people who simply want to save the lives of unborn babies."

The ice in Kiera's gut seemed to explode and she felt rime settle in her veins. She was so angry she thought of slapping Dorothy's pallid face.

"Such a close-minded piece of white trash you are," she shouted. "Daddy was better off without you!"

Dorothy's blue eyes widened and she began to tremble ever so slightly. The pitiful sight of her mother looking so frightened softened Kiera's anger. The idea occurred to her that her mother's conservative ideas would never change. She could not forget that Dorothy was trying to apologize, even if it certainly wasn't the thing for which Kiera wanted an apology. This blame, Kiera believed, was based entirely on a delusion. She almost felt guilty for yelling.

"I didn't mean that," Kiera offered. She placed a reassuring palm over Dorothy's hand. "You just don't understand how vital we Pink Escorts are."

Dorothy hugged her arms together until the trembling ceased. "I have failed," she said miserably. "I just wanted you to know how sorry I am. And to ask your forgiveness."

Kiera was determined to be the bigger woman. "Mother, I forgive you. As misguided as you are, it's evident you thought you were doing the proper thing by wanting to leave me in prison over some mere youthful indiscretion."

"Mere youthful indiscretion?" Dorothy repeated in a soft, disbelieving voice. "But Kiera-" Her words were cut off by the sound of the front door opening in the foyer.

From the foyer, a feminine voice hailed, "Dorothy, it's me! I brought you some lunch."

The door shut and approaching footfalls were heard. A moment later a woman carrying a covered dish stood at the parlor threshold. Although it had been years since they'd seen one another, Kiera recognized the graying, bespectacled woman as her cousin Molly Ann.

"Oh my gosh, Kiera! How are you?"

"Fine, Molly Ann. How are you getting along?"

"Couldn't be finer!" Molly Ann said cheerfully. She crossed the floor toward them. "What a wonderful surprise to find you here. Just yesterday Aunt Dorothy and I were reminiscing about all us cousins when we were kids!"

Molly Ann looked at Dorothy. A frown creased her pleasant brow as she noticed her aunt had been crying. "Aunt Dorothy? Are you okay?"

Kiera quickly interposed, "Mother, I will be going now. I'll give you a call soon. Take care."

She reached forward to kiss Dorothy's cheek. Her mother remained still as stone as she did so.

"Goodbye, Kiera. I love you."

Kiera stood up and gave Molly Ann a stiff goodbye.

"Alrighty, Kiera," Molly Ann said in a confused tone. "I come by practically every day. We'll have to sit down one day and have a nice chat and catch up."

Kiera moved past her. As she reached the foyer she heard her cousin question Dorothy, "What's wrong, honey? Did you two have a quarrel?"

Dorothy mumbled something Kiera couldn't understand. But it did not matter. Kiera was sure she'd call her mother soon, perhaps even stop by again in a week or so. But for now she only wanted to put space between Dorothy and herself.

Chapter 9

Upon the return to the clinic Kiera managed not to mention the visit to anyone. Typically she didn't mind venting her emotions to whoever would listen. But she couldn't get Dorothy's disease-wearied face out of her head. This image alone was something she didn't dare bring up. Hearing sympathetic remarks about her mother was just something she was not ready to deal with. Not when the woman was still determined against giving the apology Kiera expected. So she sat amid the other escorts and half-listened to their conversations until the clinic business hours were over.

While Skylar drove them home, Kiera rode beside Wendell in the backseat of the jeep. Off-and-on bouts of drizzle spat down against the vehicle during the drive. It felt like a mocking kind of rainfall to Kiera, the kind that only intensified the unresolved frustration left over from seeing Dorothy.

Wendell suddenly put his arm around her shoulders and asked how the visit with Dorothy had gone.

"It's my mother. No worse than I expected."

By the empathetic shake of their heads, the response must have suitably given Wendell and Tally the impression

Dorothy was as indifferent and uppity as always. Skylar, however, did ask if Kiera thought Dorothy was in much pain.

"She didn't seem to be, sweetheart," Kiera answered, swallowing the taste of her own doubt, "not at all."

Wendell made a shepherd's pie that night for dinner. After the family had eaten he went out to his garage to start work on a new chick pen he wanted. Braeden came by to pick Tally up for a date. Skylar went to care for the horses and later Kiera found her working on her computer in her room. She told Kiera that she wanted to put in some hours for her online collections job.

It was still sprinkling outside when Kiera had finished the dishes. She'd endured a dull throbbing headache since arriving home (a situation she blamed on all the rainfall). This, and the fact nothing eventful had happened at the clinic that day, convinced Kiera to stay off the computer. Instead, she took a couple of acetaminophen caplets and called it an early night.

For what seemed a long time she lay alone in bed with the lamp by Wendell's side dimmed to the lowest setting. Her mind was occupied by the discussion with Dorothy. Even after the headache let up, the conversation played out over and over in her mind. She couldn't seem to put away her mother's words: *It is my fault that you ended up in prison. Don't you see this?*

Kiera had never understood how a normal woman could happily leave their daughter in prison to suffer over one foolish, youthful choice. But Dorothy had. Kiera remembered being told by her father how Dorothy had argued against his decision to get their daughter out of prison at any cost. Daniel, as well, as young as he'd been at the time, had later affirmed their mother's opposition to helping Kiera. Yet even now with death's boot stepping upon the foot of her shadow Dorothy had no remorse over what Kiera had endured.

Most infuriating for Kiera was that the woman wallowed in regret for something that had never happened. Kiera refused to believe her father had pampered her or in any way given her a superior attitude! Yes, she could conceive that Ira had loved her more than Dorothy and saw it was possible Ira had felt closer to his mother than his own wife. But even if this were true, Kiera was sure it was a consequence of Dorothy's shortcomings and not a reflection on Ira or anyone else. For Dorothy to take it into her head that Ira had somehow emotionally or psychologically stunted their daughter...ah, this could be nothing but pure delusion!

Kiera rolled from her side onto her back. She blinked away the tears smarting her eyes.

"You're a pitiful woman, Mother!" she muttered softly. "You are delusional. So delusional!"

Even in bitterness, though, Kiera wasn't without sympathy for Dorothy. She thought if Dorothy had the capacity to love as much as Kiera loved her own daughters, then their own relationship might have been just as strong. As irritatingly conventional as Dorothy was Kiera did long for a deeper bond between them.

The bedroom door opened quietly and Wendell entered. He wore only a pair of flannel house trousers and his hair and beard were damp.

"You took a shower?" she asked.

With an affirmative murmur he padded around the bed. After he sat down Kiera watched as he pulled toward himself the soot-caked ashtray at his nightstand. Then he opened the drawer of the nightstand and removed a joint and lighter. After he'd lit up and drawn in a deep toke, Kiera asked how the chick pen was coming along.

He exhaled with a little cough. "It's coming along nicely. I should have it all finished by this weekend. Want some of this?"

Kiera sat up and accepted the joint. She took a deep toke, which she held in for several moments. Blowing out the smoke, she passed back the joint.

"You look like you've been crying," he observed. "What is it? Your mother?"

At her nod, his face tightened. "I'm sorry, babe. I should have gone with you. What happened? Is she a lot sicker than you made out in front of the girls?"

Kiera shrugged. "I really don't know. But it wasn't her illness."

Wendell drew another toke. This time, he was able to exhale it smoothly. "Let me guess. She's still harping about her grandchildren being raised out here on…what was she called it once? Our *commune paradise*?"

Kiera smiled weakly. "No, not this time. No, this time she felt she owed me an apology for not standing up to Daddy."

"Ah. I take it she's still not sorry for leaving you in the loving arms of the correctional industry?"

Kiera nodded. "She blames herself for me not being in there long enough."

"I'm sorry, honey," he said. "I truly am. But Dorothy will never change. Not at this point in her life."

Kiera accepted another hit off the joint. After the draw and exhale, she gave it to him and lay down again.

"I know. But it sure would be nice if she'd at least allow me to forget she was an attempted backstabber."

Wendell took a last draw before crushing the remaining roach in the ashtray. Turning the lamp off, he lay down beside Kiera and curled an arm snugly over her waist. She felt his face nuzzle against the nape of her neck.

"I know it hurts," he said tenderly. "But if she can't realize after all these years that you were a victim of circumstances, then she doesn't deserve your concern. Not a single iota of concern."

The weed had taken away the last of Kiera's headache. Her mind was pleasantly spinning now, her frustration turning into sands of angst that swiftly drifted away. As her eyes closed, the sands winked away into darkness.

Kiera slept deeply. When she awoke, she found Wendell had already left their bed. Sitting up, she glanced at the time on the alarm clock: 9:14. She had to blink and look again. She'd forgotten to set it! Now she was over two hours late in her weekday schedule.

Oh my god, we're going to be late!

She quickly arose, and yanking some clothes out of the closet, ran to the bathroom to get dressed. When she was finished with her early routine she went to the kitchen. To her surprise Tally and Skylar were seated at the table. They were having a meal of jellied toast and scrambled eggs.

"Why didn't anybody get me up?" she asked fussily.

"Dad said to let you sleep," Tally said. "He was up real early. Said he got woke up by some dog."

Kiera's eyes rolled in exasperation. "So he turned off the alarm? Of course."

"Mom, there's more eggs in the skillet," Skylar told her. "And I can make you some toast."

"Dammit, Skylar, we have to be at the clinic!"

"Good grief, Mom, it's not like they can't handle one morning without us."

Tally snorted and sucked down a forkful of eggs. "I don't know. Some of our people wouldn't take the initiative to deal with belligerent antis if we weren't there."

Kiera groaned at Skylar. "See, your sister understands! Why can't you?"

Skylar threw up her hands in resignation. "Sure. Fine."

The door opened and Wendell walked in. After he closed the door Kiera demanded to know if he'd used his rifle.

"Good morning, Kiera," he said in a sardonic tone. "I am well this fine morning, thanks for asking."

"And we are all late this fine morning, thanks to you!" She folded her arms across her chest and glared at him. "A dog, I suppose?"

He offered a faint smile. "Yes. It woke me up barking around six. As for the alarm, you looked so peaceful; I wanted to let you sleep in. After the hard time you had last night, you know?"

Kiera understood he had only been trying to be thoughtful. "That's sweet of you, Wendell. Thank you." She gave his whiskered cheek a kiss. With a little dread, she asked, "Did you already bury it?"

"No. Never caught up with the damned thing."

Kiera felt relief flow over her. From the table, Skylar speculated that the dog may have gone home.

Tally shook her head. "You should set out traps, Dad. Or if that fails, poison."

Skylar's face blanched. "Oh my god."

Her sister made a mocking face. "*Oh my god*," she crooned. "Really, Skylar. Why do you waste your pity on our redneck neighbors' dogs?"

Skylar protested that nobody knew where any of the dogs came from and that it didn't really matter where they came from. Tally mocked her voice again, which led to the beginning of an argument between the two.

"Enough!" Kiera shouted. "It's time to get to the clinic. And I don't want to hear any more arguing during the ride."

Tally got up with her plate and carried it to the sink. She let it fall noisily over the basin and then announced she was ready to leave.

Skylar rose from her seat. "Mom," she said, picking up her plate, "what about Little Crest and Felicity?"

"You didn't feed and water them when you knew I was still sleeping?"

An incredulous look came to Skylar's face. "No, Mom. I took care of your horses last night."

There was undeniable admonishment in her daughter's words. Kiera felt her hackles rise. If it was any other time, she would have taken Skylar to task over her arrogance. But their Escort work was waiting.

"Okay, okay, Skylar, I'll get to them this evening!"

Skylar looked agitated. "No, they need their food and water. I'll go now."

"The hell you will!"

Wendell addressed them both in a diplomatic tone, "It's all right, girls. The horses can eat late this one time."

Kiera and Skylar's eyes were locked on one another for several moments. At last, Skylar conceded.

"Fine, Dad. Fine."

Kiera smiled, feeling triumphant to have won this battle of wills. But the disappointed shake of Skylar's head made Kiera suddenly feel childish. She knew she had bullied Skylar, and simply over a mere suspicion her daughter felt she'd neglected the horses. It went against Kiera's constitution to offer a heartfelt apology, but she owed it to the girl. Before she could gather the words, however, Skylar turned on a heel and walked out.

It'll be okay, Kiera consoled herself. *Skylar will get over it. She understands that I must make the clinic my first priority.*

Chapter 10

While the rain had left the region sometime during the night, the sky was still slashed by lethargic dark clouds. Yet the weather wasn't bad enough to keep the sign-toting antis at bay. There were the Catholics, Pumpkin Head's Baptist group, and a large number of Pentecostals from a church that hadn't been around for some months. The congestion around the clinic was so thick Tally decided there was no room for her usual parole up and down the sidewalk. As an alternative, she brought her pink sign back to the tent and took up a megaphone instead. She carried this outside and took a seat on the grassy slope in front of the clinic. With the megaphone, she blasted the antis with catcalls. The words she chose were knowingly vulgar and designed. Words that, as Kiera had taught her, were used to abase. Tally didn't limit these insults to the various groups, but targeted many of their respective individuals.

Kiera proudly noticed some of the antis were so mortified by the catcalls they broke away from their groups to make their way toward the public parking lot. By one-thirty, enough of these people had slinked away that Tally returned to the tent. She looked out of breath as she exchanged the megaphone for her beloved homemade sign.

"There's finally enough room to walk out there!" she announced.

Kerry, who had been sitting and complaining about the heat (for which no one else noticed), looked up and asked Tally if anyone was giving her a problem. Kiera heard the waspish tone in Kerry's voice, and looking at the woman's face, saw a belligerent scowl over her brow.

"Just the usual anti crap," Tally told her. "You want to come with me, Kerry?"

Kiera heard the older woman give an uncomfortable grunt as she got up from her chair.

"Of course," Kerry said. "I'll show those pieces of shit."

Wanda, seated beside Kiera, must have also noticed Kerry's mood, for she sat up straight and suggested to Kerry that she remain in the tent.

"You promised to tell me about the kitten that showed up at your door, remember?" Wanda said.

Kerry's answer was a brusque harrumph. Wanda shot Kiera a worried glance. It was a glance Kiera understood.

"C'mon Kerry," Kiera coaxed the older woman, "stay here with us."

Kerry ignored her advice and stomped out of the tent.

"Keep an eye on her, Tally," Kiera warned. "She's having one of her *bad* days."

Tally gave half a shrug before leaving again.

"Oh lord," Wanda declared, "that poor ole gal! I hope she don't start screaming bloody murder at somebody again. Last time the people at the gas station down the street called the law, remember?"

Kiera indeed remembered. In an incident some weeks before Kerry had started saying rather lewd things to some teenage antis praying in a circle on the sidewalk. When her words failed to make them break hands or stop praying,

Kerry got all upset and screamed obscenities at the little group. Her ranting was so intense and shrill her voice carried all the way down to the gas station, where the attendant—having no idea what was going on—had reported it to the police. Wendell had quickly interceded on Kerry's behalf by telling the reporting officers one of the boys had said something inappropriate to Kerry. But Kerry had been so riled up she began cursing at the officers. In the end, Wendell managed to convince her to return with him to the tent. After some conversation with the teens the officers went on their way.

"Let's hope she's more in control today," Kiera said.

About twenty minutes after Tally and Kerry's departure, the megaphone-enhanced voice of Squinty McGimpy's blasted from outside: *"Your eyes have seen my unformed substance; and in Your book were all written the days that were ordained for me, when as yet there was not one of them!"*

Shaun Wilcox muttered from the back of the tent, "Jesus-frickin-Christ, that guy again?"

Kiera imagined Tally and Kerry would find a means to chase ole Squinty away. Maybe dance around him again. But while Squinty continued his acoustic sermonizing, Tally abruptly bound into the tent. For once, she looked genuinely alarmed.

"Someone come quick," she said, "Squinty's got Kerry in a bad state!"

Kiera immediately rose from her chair and Wendell ran up from the back. They hastened together outside. There, on the sidewalk right in front of the clinic property, Bill Hendrickson sat in his wheelchair. While he preached in the direction of the parking lot through his megaphone, Kerry stood directly in front of him. Her hands were balled into fists at her sides, her face was ruddy with rage. She was screaming at Hendrickson, though her words could barely be made out over his voice blaring through the megaphone.

Wendell suggested Kiera go try to calm her down. Upon reaching them, Kiera placed a comforting hand on Kerry's arm.

To her shock, Kerry growled and shoved her hand away.

"Stop it!" Kerry yelled. "The bastard's gotta go!"

"Kerry," Kiera told her, "you need to cool off a bit."

Hendrickson's voice thundered through the megaphone, *"Behold, children are a heritage from the LORD, the fruit of the womb a reward!"*

Kerry shook a fist at Hendrickson. "Get out of here, you misogynist freak!" she screamed.

Moments later, Wendell came down with a megaphone in hand. He aimed the speaker toward Hendrickson's head and raised the microphone to his lips. With a switch of the talk button, he began shouting one of the Bible verses he'd memorized just for such confrontations:

"As you do not know how the spirit comes to the bones in the womb of a woman with child, so you do not know the work of God who makes everything. Ecclesiastes 11:5!"

Hendrickson paused for perhaps half a moment, and clearing his throat started up again, *"Lo, children are a heritage of the Lord—and the fruit of the womb is his reward! Psalm 12 7:3!"*

Wendell was undeterred. *"May that man be like the towns the LORD overthrew without pity. May he hear wailing in the morning, a battle cry at noon. For he did not kill me in the womb, with my mother as my grave, her womb enlarged forever. Jeremiah 20:16-17!"*

The situation was now a competition of sermons. The two men continued thundering their selected Biblical verses back and forth, often interrupting one another so nobody hearing could possibly decipher what they were saying.

A handful of sidewalk passersby did, however, stop to gape at the scene. Among these was a young man who began videotaping with his phone. His female companion shook her head and placed her hands over her ears. Irked, Kiera yelled at the two to mind their own business. She couldn't be sure if they could hear her over the amplified argument. Her attention was distracted from the pair when Kerry suddenly gave Hendrickson's wheelchair several agitated kicks.

Kiera noticed the blood had drained from Kerry's face. Sweat poured down her brow and over her pale face. Once again, Kiera tried persuading the older woman to move back to the tent. Kerry angrily told her to *go to hell*.

Skylar appeared at Kiera's shoulder. "It's getting loud out here, Mom. A couple of patients complained while going into the building."

Kiera rolled her eyes, yet she was relieved Skylar had shown up. Together, they managed to drag Kerry away and lead her back into the tent. Once inside they released their grip on her arms. Kerry roared in fury, and spinning around, smacked at Skylar's head with a pudgy palm. Luckily, Skylar was able to dodge the blow.

"Calm down, Kerry!" Kiera shouted.

Kerry was in a tizzy. "Traitors! You all are nothing but traitors!"

Tally, sitting atop the snacks table, shook her head. "Calm your tits, Kerry, okay? You sound like a batshit crazy old woman."

This statement made Kerry's eyes glaze. She charged to the snacks table, where she brought her fists down over a bag of chips lying near Tally's butt. The bag burst open. Now Kerry honed in on an empty chair and kicked it over. She ran to the metal tub used for ice and sodas and kicked this, too. Kiera and the other Escorts urged her to calm down but Kerry only shrieked obscenities at them. This onslaught was so high-pitched it pealed over the amplified voices from outside.

In the midst of her tantrum Kerry started to sway on her feet.

Skylar was crying now. "Kerry, please sit down. You don't look well."

Kerry stopped shouting. Confusion shone in her eyes as she asked the girl breathlessly, "Julie? Julie, what are we doing here?"

Julie was one of Kerry's daughters-in-law, the daughter-in-law—if Kiera remembered correctly—that Kerry liked.

"Julie just wants you to sit down, Kerry," Kiera said calmly. "And you asked for something to drink, remember?"

Skylar pulled a chair toward Kerry. "Here. Take a seat, honey."

Once Kerry was seated, Kiera brought her a soda from the metal tub. Kerry's hands were quivering so hard she couldn't pop open the tab. Skylar pulled it off for her and lifted it to Kerry's blanched lips. After drinking several sips, the tension visibly relaxed in Kerry's muscles. The atmosphere in the tent also returned to normal.

"There you go, Kerry," Jeremy said gently. "Just relax, relax."

Kiera drew close to Tally and asked if she had a number on her phone for any of Kerry's relatives.

Tally pulled her phone from a pocket. "Think I got her husband's."

As Tally looked through the contacts list Kiera was aware of how quiet it had grown outside.

"Got it," Tally said.

Kiera instructed her to ask Kerry's husband to come pick up his wife. While Tally did this, Kiera was drawn to the tent door. She looked out and saw a police cruiser had shown up. It was parked on the street beside the sidewalk, its flashers silently turning.

Kiera exited the tent and walked to the crest of the little hilltop for a better view. From here, she saw two officers, a male and a female, had approached Wendell and Hendrickson. Both Wendell and Hendrickson were speaking to them, but Kiera could not make out any of what they were saying. It was apparent, though, that Wendell was angry, for he kept jabbing an accusing finger toward Hendrickson.

Kiera made her way down to them. Wendell was giving the officers his reasoning behind the megaphone contest while Hendrickson just sat shaking his head. She wondered who it was that had called in a complaint to the police department.

She read the officers' names from their badges. The female officer –Officer Tiffany Walters—looked at Kiera. Her eyes canvassed Kiera's pink outfit with an uncertain squint.

"Are you one of the people that work here, ma'am?"

Kiera cleared her throat. "I am."

Walters' attention returned to Wendell's version of what had happened. Once he was finished, the male – Officer Jodie Quill—asked Hendrickson to give his side of it. When Hendrickson was done with his version this Quill looked somewhat lost for words.

He remarked at last, "The complaint we're most concerned is about a woman kicking a man in a wheelchair. Would this be your wheelchair, Mr. Hendrickson?"

Kiera's chest clogged with panic. She had no doubt whichever anti had called the police had also injected exaggeration into their complaint.

Hendrickson made a dismissive wave. "She was elderly. Confused. And I'm not looking to press charges."

Kiera breathed a sigh of relief.

There was an annoyed note in Quill's next statement, "Sounds like the woman a couple of other officers were called about just this morning. Look gentlemen, we got three other complaints already today about all the noise out here. Mind you, this is a public sidewalk. It belongs to neither one of you. Just as importantly, we do have a noise ordinance. One can use a megaphone outside, but not if it disturbs the peace."

Wendell and Hendrickson both nodded. But Kiera resented the uppity tone she perceived in Quill's voice. She told herself her feelings had nothing to do with a deep-rooted hatred for cops, only that Quill was trying to show off his authority. She also suspected the officer opposed reproductive rights.

"Oh don't be a dick!" she told Quill. "That weirdo started all this! He showed up, as he's done before, with the sole intention of disrupting clinic business! His stupid wheelchair sure hasn't stopped him from harassing the patients!"

Officer Walters turned on her sharply, "Ma'am, unless you helped either of these men to bring these megaphones out here or encouraged them in some other way, you need to let us deal with this situation. So let me ask: did you help them or encourage them?"

"No," Kiera answered sarcastically, "I didn't help or encourage them."

"Then please step away, ma'am."

A stab of rage pricked Kiera's breastbone. But she caught the cautioning look Wendell threw her. She decided it best for the moment to let Walters have her way, so she walked to the end of the clinic drive. Here she turned about, hands on hips, and listened as Quill addressed the men.

"Having received complaints, we could reasonably cite both of you. But if you are both willing to stop with the megaphones and promise not to go looking for each other once we leave, I think-"–he cast a hopeful glance at Walters—"this will be sufficient."

Wendell agreed to comply.

"Mr. Hendrickson," Walters asked, "how about you?"

Hendrickson nodded.

The officers asked Hendrickson if he needed a ride anywhere. He told them his vehicle was in the public parking lot. They watched attentively as he set his megaphone in his lap, grabbed the wheelchair tires and began rolling the wheelchair down the sidewalk.

With him gone, Wendell gave the officers a peevish look. "You know, if the City would do something to keep those pests off these premises, you all wouldn't receive calls to come out here!"

Quill responded with a dry chortle. "And as we've told your people many times before, Mr. Scruggs, this clinic doesn't own the sidewalk. You and the other Pink Escorts should let that sink in. Now if Mr. Hendrickson comes back with his megaphone and causes a noise issue, do let us know. Otherwise, leave the man alone, alright?"

Wendell opened his mouth as if to argue with Quill, but before he could speak, Walters piped up, "And if we receive further complaints involving an alleged assault on a disabled person, we will hand it over to our detectives."

Kiera ached to slap this female officer! "You stupid cow!" she shouted.

Both officers looked over at her. Neither said anything, but instead wished Wendell a stiff *good afternoon* and then walked to their cruiser.

Kiera joined Wendell. Seeing the tight way he clutched the megaphone handle, she realized he was angrier than he'd let on to the officers. She gave his arm a caring squeeze.

"Ignore them, Wendell. They put in an appearance just to bolster their stupid pig egos."

"How much longer, Kiera?" he asked lowly. His brow furrowed deeply, his vision grew dark and abstracted. "How much longer before society is free of pigs and religious fanatics? They're all feral, uncontrolled *beasts!*"

Chapter 11

Daniel texted Kiera just as she and her family arrived home. It was a brief message thanking Kiera for visiting Dorothy the previous day. She replied as vaguely as possible:

Glad to have seen her. Will try to get back over there soon.

This must have satisfied Daniel for he responded with a simple: *Means a lot, sis. Have a good evening.*

Kiera was left pleasantly surprised. She'd expected Dorothy to go crying to Daniel to complain that his sister had upset her. But no. Apparently, Dorothy hadn't even mentioned their tense conversation to nosy cousin Molly Ann.

The weather was nicely temperate that evening. Tally secluded herself in her room, where she kept busy making some beaded necklaces for her online jewelry shop. Kiera took care of the horses herself so Skylar could put in some hours at her own online business. Kiera gave Felicity and Little Crest a good, needed grooming and checked their hooves. She saw that a rasping was unnecessary, though, as Skylar had been doing a diligent job.

Kiera stayed with the horses awhile, petting them and talking to them as she used to. It was getting close to dark by the time she walked back toward the house. She saw Wendell sitting in one of the two wooden chaise lounge chairs kept in the yard. He was smoking a joint and his face was one of tranquil peace while he watched the sun set over the western hills. As Kiera came up he offered a drowsy smile and a hit off the joint.

"Pull up a seat, my dear."

She exhaled smoke and returned the joint. Pulling the other lounge chair next to his, she reached over and patted his knee. "You look happy. Good to see."

"Tonight I am happy. The happiest man in creation."

"And what brought this on?"

"What's there not to be happy about? And you're going to make me even happier, I know."

Curiosity made her grin. "And how's that?"

"You're going to let me know tonight whether you think I should rotate last year's vegetable garden or till up a new location?"

"Ah." Kiera had not given the matter much thought. There had been a time, not so long ago, when she'd invested much energy into gardening and harvesting, of preserving and cooking the rewards she and her family reaped from their efforts. There had also been a time when she maintained a personal blog dedicated to the homesteading lifestyle. Her views on the subject, along with her anti-establishment perspectives, had won her a few dozen fans with similar mindsets. Her blogging time, however, ended when some of these fans got all butt hurt over certain posts she'd made concerning the inferiority of baby formula as compared to breastfeeding. They also weren't too happy about her opinion on the moral necessity of late-term abortions, especially such abortions for lower-class women. The hostile reactions from once devoted fans were something Kiera, at first, thoroughly enjoyed commenting about. But her comments didn't go far, as she found herself countered with insinuations. They claimed her unbending views on breastfeeding were unrealistic and intolerant. And when it came to the late-term abortion topic they accused her of being heartless. In the end, these whiners snatched away every bit of the joy she'd once taken from blogging. Thus, when Daniel had first mentioned the clinic was looking for Campaign Parenthood supporters interested in working as Pink Escorts, Kiera had immediately volunteered herself and her family. With a new cause to put her focus on, she had closed down the blog and never went back.

Since then the gardening, canning, cooking and such had become no more than functionary interests. While Kiera enjoyed that some of their friends still regarded her as an expert on self-sufficiency, the truth was she had lost all interest in talking online about things like turning bean curd into tofu and making facial cleanser out of oatmeal and beeswax.

Wendell still thrived in the belief he was a master homesteader, and boasted to friends that his son and daughters would be master homesteaders after he was long gone. Out of love for Wendell she was happy to let him think the subject mattered just as much to her.

"Rotate the garden," she answered him. "This summer you and Rory can decide on a new location for next year."

With a last draw off the joint, Wendell handed it over to her. He leaned his head back on the headrest of his chair and gazed up at the descending dusk.

"I miss our son, Kiera. I didn't want to say this before, but the boy has been gone long enough. He's had the experience of punching in the clock for capitalist pigs. Time for Rory to come home and put his head and heart back into working for sensible intelligentsia endeavors."

Kiera watched fondly as Wendell's eyelids fell shut.

"And help his old man get this year's crop up and going," he said sleepily. "I know the clinic is your passion. I don't begrudge it, I truly don't. Still, I miss the passion of working beside my son. Forgive me if that sounds patriarchal or hints of toxic masculinity. It's just that after you, Rory is my best friend..."

His words trailed off. Kiera found she could not resent his feelings nor could she feel jealous over his affection for Rory.

"We'll all be happier once Rory is home," she said softly. And reaching over, she kissed his cheek.

After full darkness had claimed the skies, Kiera helped Wendell into the house. Once she saw him in bed, she lay down herself. She crept under the covers and closed her tired eyes. She was happy to feel the cares of the day slip away.

She was nearly asleep when barking erupted outside. It was a frantic, high-pitched sound that rattled her repose.

You stupid dog, please don't wake my husband!

But Wendell was snoring softly beside her. As the seconds passed, the barking grew fainter. After several moments it ceased altogether. With a grunt of relief, Kiera turned onto her side and waited for tranquility to return.

It was Friday, the last working day of the week for the Pink Escorts. Kerry was not there when the Scruggs family arrived. This was not out of the ordinary for Kerry, of course, but Kiera couldn't help but wonder if the old gal would show up at all.

Kiera hadn't eaten much that morning and was still hungry as the family entered the tent. She went to the snacks table and selected a package of doughnuts. Tally walked up just as she finished off the doughnuts.

She told Kiera she had just received a phone call from Kerry's husband, Frank. He had wanted to let the escorts know Kerry wouldn't be in that day as there had been little improvement in her state of mind. In fact, Frank had made Kerry an appointment with a geriatrics specialist. Tally also said Frank had asked if Kerry's car could be left in the clinic parking lot over the weekend.

"I told him I guess it's okay," Tally said. "I know Frank is getting up there in years and rarely drives himself. And I don't think they have good enough a relationship with their neighbors to ask for their assistance."

Kiera knew the clinic frowned on anyone aside from physicians and maintenance people leaving their vehicles in the lot through the weekend. Yet, she supposed it couldn't be helped this time.

"A shame Kerry got so upset yesterday," she remarked. "This is Squinty McGimpy's fault, you know? Upsetting a vulnerable senior with his sermonizing."

"Oh, that reminds me!" Tally announced, pulling her phone from her back pocket. Kiera watched as she brought up her internet browser. With the pad of a forefinger, Tally swiped the front screen over to icons of saved material. She tapped one of these.

"Found this last night."

"What is it?"

"Something the Catholic antis posted last night on their website."

"I thought you were working last night?"

Tally shrugged. "I got bored. Besides, I know you keep up with all the antis on Facebook, but the freaks from St. Gerard's don't do much there. So I visit their website regularly, just in case they're bitching about us."

She handed Kiera the phone. The page that appeared was from the St. Gerard Majella Church website. Kiera scrolled down past the church logo and found an uploaded video. The text appearing just below it gave a brief description:

Kiera snorted. "Jesus, what drama queens!"

She tapped her finger over the start button. The video had definitely been shot from the Catholics' verge across the street, and began playing just as Kerry approached Hendrickson the day before. Hendrickson was sermonizing through his megaphone and Tally stood a few paces away. The filmmaker hadn't muted the audio, so Hendrickson's preaching was recorded. It also captured Kerry's voice. To Kiera's dismay, Kerry's screaming carried just as distinctly, and nearly as ear-splitting as Hendrickson's amplified preaching.

At one point in the video Kiera heard the filmmaker observe, "This is ridiculous."

Kiera watched Kerry make her first kick to one of the tires on Hendrickson's wheelchair. Tally was seen running up and saying something to her elderly friend. Ignoring Tally, Kerry kicked the tire again. At this point Tally shrugged and trotted off toward the tent.

There was no option to leave a comment for the video. Kiera irritably tapped the screen again to stop the play.

"Damned busybodies! Tell me they didn't film your dad coming out?"

Tally nodded. "They did. Got you in there, too. They filmed until the cops drove off."

Kiera assured herself the video was insignificant for the escorts. Squinty McGimpy and Wendell had both complied with the two cops.

"Oh well," she said, handing the phone back to Tally. "We know the St. Gerard people aren't in the custom of posting videos to social media. And so what if they do? All it shows is the daily abuse we go through defending reproduction rights. Their only success is showing the world what loonies they are by having this at their website."

Tally stuffed the phone into her pocket. "If they show up on our side of the street they'll get a fitting welcome. They are no different from the other hate-mongers that trespass here."

Kiera was unhappy though. She was used to, and took delight in, trolling the videos made by antis and spread across social media. She was able to leave scathing comments for most of these. But there was no way to leave even an anonymous comment at this particular Catholic website. The best she could hope to achieve in inviting public derision was to provide a link for this site from the PCKC Facebook page. Her fans and followers definitely could mock it from there. Yet she was disappointed fans and followers wouldn't be unable to say something snarky regarding the video directly at the St. Gerard Facebook. That group's moderator was quite diligent in blocking criticism.

Tally patted her shoulder. "Don't get down, Mom. We can't get back at them on social media right now, but I'm sure an opportunity will open somewhere soon enough."

Kiera couldn't help but smile. Her eldest daughter understood her concerns so well.

Tally's prediction came true quicker than Kiera would have expected. While carrying her homemade sign out on her sidewalk Tally found several St. Gerard people already lined up on the verge of the clinic's side of the street. Tally excitedly returned to the tent to tell her mother.

Kiera knew what they must do. She found the biggest Campaign Parenthood sign they had in the tent and together the two of them marched down to the sidewalk on the eastern flank of the clinic driveway. There were five antis standing on the verge, and every one of them was displaying awful pro-life signs for passersby to gawk at. Kiera walked onto the verge and squeezed herself between it and the curb. It made for a tight squeeze as she walked along and she was glad to see the surprised looks on the antis' faces. Carefully she sidled down the line of them, checking each of their signs. Among the five were two women with particularly large and visibly heavy signs that forced the women to hold over the ground. Kiera positioned herself directly in front of one of their signs: an offensive image of a newborn swaddled in a pink receiving blanket. The message *Protect the Unborn* was printed across the top.

Kiera planted her own sign on the ground right in front of it, effectively blocking the anti's sign from view. The two signs were so close they touched.

The anti spoke up, "You're right in my face, ma'am."

Kiera stuck her tongue out at the woman. With a whistle and a gesture of her hand, she directed Tally to do likewise to help block the other lowered sign. This one touted the image of a mother cradling a baby, along with the message: *This Is What Co-Existence Looks Like*.

Tally wormed herself between this anti and the curb and dropped her sign in front of the cloying message. The woman she blocked was rather weighty and dressed in sweats, with only bedroom slippers on her feet. Someone that Kiera instantly decided she would nickname *Ms. Fat and Frumpy*. And it was obvious Ms. Fat and Frumpy was annoyed by Tally's maneuver.

Kiera noticed the woman take a step back, pick up her sign and walk to one end of this line of antis. There she posted herself and displayed her sign again.

Tally dashed toward the woman, managing to clomp over the foot of the male who stood just beside the woman Kiera blocked.

"Hey!" the man exclaimed.

Ignoring him, Tally shoved her sign down to obscure the mother and child image. The woman moved again, this time to the opposite end of the line. Again Tally scrambled to get in front of her. This time Tally managed to run over the man's other foot.

"Stop doing that!" he hollered.

Tally deposited her sign with a thud to the ground in front of the chased woman.

"You're deliberately pressing against my sign," Ms. Fat and Frumpy grumbled.

Tally sneered, "I guess you'll have to back up then."

"I don't have to back up. But you need to stop shoving your sign into me."

Kiera glanced over and saw that Tally indeed was pushing her weight behind her sign so that it pressed against the woman.

Tally gave a mocking pout. "Poor baby! Prove I'm shoving it into you!"

The man whose feet had been stepped on spoke up, "I've brought my phone. Should I videotape what you're doing, young lady?"

The condescending remark triggered Kiera. She lifted her sign quickly, turned to the man and tamped it forcefully down over both of his feet.

The man yelled in pain. The woman Kiera had been blocking complained there was no call for what she'd just done.

"Shut up, papist bitch!" Kiera hoisted her sign again and planted it once more in front of the Madonna sign.

The woman closed her eyes, and to Kiera's amusement began to softly pray. Kiera knew this was an excellent opportunity to make some silly fake prayer to Satan. It would unnerve the whole lot of them! But just as Kiera opened her mouth to spout off some evil-sounding babble her train of thought was interrupted by a male voice from the sidewalk.

"What an exemplary way to show support for women's rights!"

Kiera's attention snapped toward the speaker. She was irked to see it was the Tall Guy from the damnable *Pagans And Secular People For Life* group. Accompanying him were the same woman and other male who had shown up earlier in the week. Both men had signs tucked under their arms (though Kiera couldn't make out the messages), while the woman carried her phone in hand.

"Mind your own damned business!" she shouted.

Tall Guy's male companion laughed. The female friend lifted her phone and began videotaping.

"How about you, Ms. Women's Rights?" Tall Guy called out. "You have plenty of space out here, yet you choose to be right up in that woman's face." His eyes turned to where Tally stood pressed up against the other Catholic woman. "And you...we saw you run over that man's feet. Now you're purposely pushing into that lady."

Tally glowered at the Tall Guy, angry crimson dots washing over her cheeks. "What's it to so-called seculars or pagans? These Catholics hate you anyway!"

Ms. Fat and Frumpy spoke up, "We don't hate anybody, miss."

"Was I talking to *you?*" Tally screeched. She was so irked now she bared her teeth and thrust her face less than an inch from the woman's nose. Tally began to hyperventilate as she continued, "Stupid christofascist! Ignorant white trash!"

She cut loose with several explicit comments. With each angrily enunciated word she pelted saliva into Ms. Fat and Frumpy's face. Tall Guy, his male companion, and the other Catholics scolded Tally for being disgusting. Even Kiera suspected if Tally didn't reign in her temper she might lose control of her composure altogether.

"Tally," she cautioned lowly, "don't let them get to you."

Tally threw her a dark look. "I'm not *letting* them do anything! They need to hear the truth since they're obviously too stupid to take a good look in the mirror!"

Kiera watched warily as Tally tore again into Ms. Fat and Frumpy, "And especially you! You hang out with these other losers because there's no man in his right mind who wants to fuck you! No man who could get it up long enough to knock your stupid ass up anyway, you pathetic, ugly cow!"

Tally punched her sign against the woman with such force Ms. Fat and Frumpy was knocked back on her feet. She stumbled, looking like she might fall, when Tall Guy caught her by the arm and righted her footing. It was now the other Catholics warned Tally that if she didn't leave them alone immediately, they would call the police.

Tally dropped her homemade sign and spread her arms out beckoningly. "Go ahead, call the pigs! Nothing will happen, it never does!"

She began to laugh and to inch back on her feet. Kiera saw the heels of her shoes slip precariously over the curb.

Kiera spun toward her. "Watch out, Tally!"

Whether Tally heard her or not, Kiera would never know. The next instant Tally stumbled over the curb and fell into the street. The back of her head struck the pavement with a *clunk!* Kiera froze as she saw a truck advancing down the street.

In this moment Kiera's sign fell from her hands. Just as she started toward the street one of the Catholic men leapt past her. In a flash, he crouched down, seized Tally's wrist, pulled her up and shoved her back onto the verge and into Kiera's arms. The wheels of the truck screamed to a halt inches in front of Tally's rescuer. He rushed back onto the verge and gave a little wave to the truck's driver –a woman whose face was ashen with horror. With a shudder, she continued driving.

Kiera was aware her daughter was safe in her arms. Tally was gasping and her eyes were wide with terror but she was alive. The other Catholics encircled them both. They asked Tally if she were alright. Even the Tall Guy and his male companion looked relieved.

"Is your head hurt?" Tall Guy asked her.

"You should take her to the hospital, let them check her out," suggested the woman Tally had been cursing only moments before.

Kiera felt Tally's every limb tremble.

"Excuse us!" she raged at the antis.

They moved aside and let Kiera lead Tally away to the tent.

The fall on the street had left a large bump on the back of Tally's skull. Worried, Kiera asked Skylar to drive them both to the emergency room. As Kiera put Tally in the back seat, Wendell promised Tally he'd annoy the antis while they were gone. Tally –left dazed and uncharacteristically quiet by the incident—could only give her father a nod.

The city hospital's extended Covid policies allowed for only one companion per patient. So while Kiera signed Tally in at the emergency room, Skylar stayed in the jeep. It took almost twenty minutes before Tally was taken into an examination room. There she and Kiera waited for at least another fifteen minutes before a doctor came in. After questioning Tally about what had happened and a brief examination of her head, he ordered some X-rays. Kiera stayed while they waited for an attendant to take Tally to the radiology department.

By this time Tally's stupor had worn off a bit. She began to curse about how the antis had made her lose her balance. She also hated the antiseptic smells all around them and fussed about how hungry she was. Kiera took the complaints as positive signs. In a few minutes the attendant arrived with a wheelchair. Kiera, who was shivering from the chill in the emergency room, watched as Tally was rolled out of the examination room.

Kiera then made her way out of the hospital to warm up.

As she approached the jeep she saw Skylar seated inside and using her cell phone. It appeared that Skylar was texting with someone. Kiera opened the front passenger door and slid into the seat.

Skylar looked up questioningly. "Is she going to be alright?"

Kiera explained Tally was having X-rays. "Guess we'll know after that. She was talking more, though, like her old self. It's so cold in that place. Thought I'd warm up out here a few minutes."

Skylar nodded. Her attention returned to the phone in her hand. Kiera watched as she thumbed the keyboard.

"Messaging your father?"

"No. It's Felix."

"Felix Henner?" Kiera's nose wrinkled in distaste. "What does he want?"

Skylar didn't answer right away. Instead, she finished typing and sent her text. Then, clicking the text app off, she slipped the phone into the pocket of her light jacket.

"He asked me to go out tonight."

"Oh geesh. Please don't tell me you haven't already told that boy to blow off!"

Skylar flashed a mirthless smile. "I have to disappoint you there."

Kiera's eyes rolled. "You know he only worked as an escort to make his mom happy. He doesn't care about reproductive or women's rights at all!"

"According to you."

"According to me *nothing*. He quit!"

Skylar looked exasperated. "Felix has a full-time job now, Mom. He's also moved out of his mother's house and into an apartment over his Uncle Mike's garage. That doesn't make for much time to work at the clinic, now does it?"

"You've been talking with him ever since he left, haven't you?"

At Skylar's nod, Kiera felt the hackles rise on her arms.

"Felix Henner's mother is wealthy enough, Skylar! He doesn't *need* a job. That's just an excuse for flipping off Felicia and the ethics she has tried to instill in him!"

Skylar drew a deep breath. As she exhaled, she said patiently, "As shocking as this may be for you, Mom, some people want to make their own choices in life. To pursue dreams and ambitions that aren't solely determined by what will or will not satisfy their parents' expectations."

It occurred to Kiera that now she could probably explain the recent change in her youngest daughter's personality. Felix Henner had brainwashed her!

"You have to stay away from him, young lady! He's a horrible influence."

Skylar rubbed her brow as if it hurt. "Look, you can like Felix or not like Felix, but I am twenty-five years old. I won't let you speak to me like I'm a kid. And I refuse to let my choices be swayed by your hyperbole and melodrama."

The words were hurtful to Kiera. That Skylar would accuse her of such things just to excuse her interest in some stupid boy was unbelievable!

The fingernails of Kiera's right hand dug mercilessly into the pleather door panel. If it weren't for the fact they were at the emergency room, waiting to see if Tally was alright, she would have screamed at Skylar.

The response she delivered instead was given with poise and dispassion, "Skylar, allow me to say this as plainly and free of hyperbole as possible: you don't have a job that will support you financially. You don't have a vehicle of your own. You cannot access funds to what your grandfather left you without my signature. If I told you to get out of the home that *my inheritance* paid for, you'd have no choice but to walk off the mountain and live without a roof over your head. So go out on your little date with Felix. Spread your legs if this is what it takes to get that little shit out of your system. But if you want to keep enjoying my generosity, then you'll get Felix Henner out of your system quickly. And you will get in line with the program."

"Program," Skylar muttered thickly. "Yes, mother. Let me get in line with the program. Because I owe you this, huh?"

"You owe me everything. A fact you have overlooked lately."

Skylar turned her face to stare outside the driver-side window. In the reflection Kiera saw tears rolling down her daughter's cheeks.

A stab of remorse tempted Kiera to soften. She couldn't honestly see herself ever throwing one of her children out of their home. It was only she could not stand idly by and let Skylar discard the ideals in which she'd been raised. And especially not for the sake of a man as happily conventional as Felix Henner. Kiera decided the best way to compel Skylar into making smarter decisions was to act unaffected by the girl's emotions.

Kiera opened the passenger door. "I'm going to check on your sister."

Chapter 12

Almost two hours later Kiera and her daughters left the hospital and returned to the clinic. Kiera was relieved she could tell Wendell that Tally's x-rays revealed no damage to her skull. The doctor had diagnosed her with only a slight concussion.

"But she's tired, Wendell," Kiera explained. "And we have to make sure she stays awake for the next six hours."

Wendell agreed they should go home. As Kiera drove the four of them home, he sat in the back seat with Tally, and regaled her with the report all the antis had gone away after she fell in the street.

"I think your fall worried them," he laughed. "You should have seen them flee like rats from a sinking ship."

The story delighted Tally. Kiera, however, knew her husband had somewhat exaggerated. When Skylar drove her and Tally to the hospital she had noticed the antis were still gathered at the verge. Their signs had all been lowered as they talked together, probably discussing what had happened. It was very possible they'd concluded the incident had been enough excitement for them and called it a day. But she knew they had hardly fled like rats. Of course, any other tale would have disappointed Tally.

Wendell was simply doing his best to cheer up their wounded daughter.

Once home Kiera made Tally sit on the living room sofa. Her daughter was cranky and still complaining about the antis.

"I think we should contact your lawyer, Mom," Tally said. "It's their fault I fell! I could have been killed, you know?"

"I know," Kiera smiled. "We can talk about a lawyer later. Just take it easy for the rest of the day, alright?"

Kiera turned on the television and found Tally's favorite true crime network. Once it was evident her interest was piqued by the show, Kiera went to the kitchen to make dinner.

Kiera served their dinner in the living room. She had made tacos since they were Tally's favorite. After eating, Wendell found a pack of cards and brought out a bottle of wine. While they played several hands of Crazy 8's, Kiera noticed Tally forgot her anger with the antis. Her competitiveness returned, but it was more light-hearted than usual.

Skylar excused herself at dusk to go feed the horses and Wendell went out to take care of the other animals. As Kiera washed dishes, she peeked into the living room every few minutes to make sure Tally was alert. Thankfully, the girl was sitting up and completely absorbed now by some anime series.

Around eight o'clock, Kiera was searching the cabinets for microwavable popcorn when she heard a car pull up outside. Moments later Skylar, who had evidently seen the car from her upstairs window, entered the kitchen to announce Felix had arrived.

Kiera offered a stiff chortle. "Well, do have fun."

While Skylar went to fetch her phone and purse, Kiera peered out the kitchen door window. Felix's older model red SUV was parked there and she saw him standing outside of it and smoking a cigarette. He was actually nicely dressed this evening in crisp blue jeans, a short-sleeved button-up shirt and no hoodie. He'd even taken time to comb his longish golden hair. Kiera imagined Felix thought this look would impress Skylar.

She noticed how his eyes darted skittishly toward the house.

Good. He must know I don't approve of his sorry ass.

When Skylar reentered the kitchen she told Kiera she would likely be home before midnight.

"I see your true love out there likes cigarettes," Kiera said.

"Yes, so? You smoke weed."

"Big difference between nicotine and weed. I gave up tobacco a long time ago, you know."

"Yeah okay," Skylar said. She threw open the door. Giving Kiera a curt goodnight she went outside and shut the door behind her.

Kiera held the door open and watched as Skylar ran out to Felix. They exchanged a few words, then to Kiera's alarm, Skylar let Felix open the car door for her!

"Oh, my god...just look what that toxic male is turning my daughter into!"

With the car engine started, Felix turned it around and began the long drive down the narrow gravel drive. Kiera growled under her breath.

"You bastard!" she groaned. In her outrage, she burrowed her fingernails into the outer door edge. The ivory paint peeled away as she slowly raked the wood.

Kiera spent some time watching television with Tally. When she was sure the six hours had passed and it was safe to let Tally fall asleep, Kiera dimmed the living room lights and covered her daughter with a throw blanket.

It was a relief Tally was going to be okay. But Kiera was still upset with Skylar. Kiera's temples throbbed with anger as well as the gnawing desire to vent to somebody.

She went to the bathroom to find aspirin. As she washed the pills down with a glass of water she contemplated getting on her Facebook page. In case any of the antis started online gossip over Tally's fall, she felt there needed to be some post addressing what had happened. She remembered the secular and pagan group woman who had been filming. Kiera had no doubt the cunt had uploaded the video somewhere. The thought that anybody seeing it might criticize Tally was unacceptable to Kiera.

But between the headache and the anger with her youngest daughter, Kiera doubted she could write anything without emotions bleeding into the words. The post could be put off until the morning. The only thing she felt like doing right now was to relax.

She kicked off her shoes and socks and left them in the bathroom. In the kitchen, she opened the refrigerator and looked through for liquor. There were a few cans of peach vodka left on the second shelf. She took one and carried it outside. The stars and moon shone softly over the yard as she walked over to the chaise lounge chairs.

Even as the weather wasn't quite warm enough for flitting insects, the temperature was comfortable. The birds were silent in their early year nests and the only sound Kiera heard in the night air came from the direction of Wendell's workshop. It was the familiar erratic *whrr* of his band saw. Friday nights were the usual time of week he spent time in his workshop. There he would repair structures used around the farm or work on new projects. Kiera rather hoped he'd take his sweet time about it this night. Wendell always had a strong opinion when it came to their children and right now, she didn't want to risk stupidly blurting out any hint that she was upset with Skylar. If she did Wendell would offer an opinion on how to referee the situation, and inevitably that opinion would be saturated with all his fatherly blindness. The last thing Kiera was interested in hearing was some excuse for Skylar's behavior.

The dew was chilly under Kiera's bare feet. As she stood gazing numbly at the landscape, she understood that Skylar's rebellious behavior and the infatuation with Felix Henner was something she herself would have to handle. She also wasn't sure how to go about doing this. She would give the girl this one last chance. Let her have her insufferable little romantic date. She'd let Skylar get her thrills in the back seat of Felix's car or wherever else they decided to do. But Skylar had flaunted everything she'd been taught, and from here out, Skylar would have to be managed much differently at home. Kiera would make Skylar keenly aware of how very much she disappointed her mother.

Kiera would give the outward appearance of wounded resignation. Pretend she was accepting of Skylar's choices. She was certain that if the ruse was executed properly Skylar would come to feel guilty, and without feeling righteous in insinuating Kiera was being melodramatic or using hyperbole. The act would require some days to play out convincingly, but in the end, Skylar would feel she had betrayed her mother to the very foundation.

The process was not one which came naturally to Kiera's volatile nature. It would involve sheer willpower and pure focus of intent to carry through. Yet Kiera remembered that when she'd committed herself to this tactic in the past, she had reaped very pleasing results. Such had been the results when Kiera was a child and forced to deal with a stubborn mother. It had also succeeded those occasional times when, as a teenager, Kiera found her father obstinate, too. It had worked often during married life, most notably when both daughters were toddlers sharing her milk and Wendell complained Rory was too old at eight years of age to continue nursing as well. The guilt tactic had worked well enough then that Wendell never brought up the subject of prolonged nursing again. Kiera realized she'd never had reason to use the tactic on her Rory. She also knew now that she was fortunate it was Skylar and not Tally she had to deal with. Tally, so uncannily like Kiera in mindset, would see right through the act. Skylar was an entirely different psyche: artless, sentimental, and innately tender. In other words, easily controlled.

Kiera took a seat in one of the lounge chairs. With a firm plan and the determination to commit to it, she felt the anger beginning to subside. As she pulled the tab back on the vodka can a welcome sense of satisfaction washed over her. She stretched her legs over the footstool of the chair and smiled up at the ebony sky with all its disinterested, nonjudgmental stars gazing down. The sound from Wendell's band saw was almost lulling.

She had no idea she wasn't alone until she felt the quick warm lap at her toes.

With a gasp she jerked her legs back. Now she could see the figure of a small dog standing in front of the footstool edge. The starlight allowed her to tell it was a fully grown dog with smooth hair and features reminiscent of a fox hound. But Kiera's father had raised fox hounds, so she knew by this animal's dark coat and ropey tail it was no fox hound, at least not a purebred.

As she regarded the dog, its head cocked to one side.

Kiera waved her palms at the dog. "Go, dog, go home!"

The long, ropey tail began to wag. Kiera couldn't help but smile. It was a winsome dog that certainly didn't act vicious. And though Kiera couldn't remember seeing a mutt like this before, she thought there was something very familiar about it.

She thought about the reaction Wendell would have if he knew it was here. The dog had to leave. Sitting straight up, she leaned forward and gave its chest a light prod with her hands.

"Go! Go home now before Wendell sees you!"

The dog whimpered but did not budge. It stared at her with its large, sweet brown eyes in a way that almost made Kiera want to pet it.

"You don't listen well, do you?"

She started to prod it again when she noticed the collar at its neck. It was a cute red and black plaid thing, with a brass snap buckle and D ring.

Just as with the dog, there was something familiar about this collar.

"I think I've seen your collar," she mused.

She tried to remember if she'd noticed any dog with such a collar hanging around one of the neighbors' yards. None came to mind.

The temptation to stroke the animal was great. But it was cruel to give the wrong message. The animal might take such a gesture as an invitation to stay. Besides, a dog as pretty as this and with such a nice collar surely had an owner.

The dog gave a frisky bark and wagged its tail harder. As much as Kiera hated doing it she knew the dog had to be chased away for its own sake.

"Shoo now!" she ordered. When it did not offer to move, she stretched her legs over the footstool and thrashed her legs up and down. The balls of her ankles made a clatter over the wood.

The dog backed up a little but failed to show any interest in taking off. Kiera rose from the chaise lounger. She stomped a foot on the ground in front of the dog and clapped her hands.

"Go, go home!"

The dog finally turned. It trotted toward the higher grass. To her dismay, it stopped and looked back at her. Its tail was no longer wagging and its perky demeanor seemed to have been replaced with mere curiosity.

Kiera clapped again. "Shoo! Go!"

The dog gave a little yelp. The next moment it ran on, disappearing at last into the dark grass.

"Sorry little dog," she whispered ruefully. "But if my husband caught sight of you that'd be all she wrote."

Kiera sat down again. She stared at the high grass for some time. The image of the little dog in its plaid collar scratched at her brain.

If only I could remember where I've seen that dog before, she thought. *I could at least tell its negligent owner to come get it and keep it off our property!*

After drinking two more cans of peach vodka, Kiera went to bed. Her sleep was so deep she wasn't even aware if Wendell came to bed and she did not awaken until she was roused by Tally shaking her arm.

"Mom. Mom, you need to wake up."

Kiera opened an eye. Her head pounded again and this pain was exacerbated by sunshine that poured in through a slit between the window curtains. As she sat up she realized her mouth was dry and slight dehydration had glued her tongue to the roof of her mouth. Tally stood by the bedside. Kiera forced her tongue to move. With a little inaudible pop it detached from the roof.

"What time is it, Tally?"

"Almost one. I would have let you sleep longer, but Skylar is leaving."

The words confused Kiera. She rubbed her throbbing temples and shifted in the bed with her back to the window.

"What do you mean? She went out on a date last night with that idiot Felix, right?"

"She got back from that," Tally explained, "I'm guessing sometime after you went to bed. But Felix showed up again about thirty minutes ago. Right now Skylar is packing. She told Dad and me she's leaving with him."

A splinter of panic struck Kiera's breast. As she rose from the bed the hangover squeezed her brain. For a moment, her legs felt like noodles. She caught Tally's hand to keep from losing balance and inhaled deeply.

"You okay, Mom?"

"I'm fine. What do you mean she's *leaving* with him?

Chapter 13

Kiera ran upstairs to Skylar's bedroom. Tally followed and together they stood at the threshold of the open door. Inside, two of Skylar's canvas duffle bags were laid out on the bed. Her closet door stood wide open and her clothing had been pulled off the hangers and heaped on the mattress alongside the duffle bags. Skylar was busy emptying more clothing from her dresser drawers.

As Kiera stared in disbelief she remembered her vow about outward resignation made the night before. It galled her now to have to play the ruse out when her head hurt so badly. But it was evident Skylar would give her no other choice.

"I hear you are leaving."

Skylar pitched an armload of underwear onto the bed. "I tried waking you up earlier, before Felix got here."

Kiera glanced at Tally and gestured for her to go downstairs. After she'd left Kiera stepped into the room. "Perhaps you think I don't deserve a real goodbye before you set off?"

Skylar opened the last drawer. She crouched down and began scooping the clothes into an arm. "I would have waited till you got up. Just thought I'd pack in the meantime."

"I see." Kiera's apprehension was managing to stifle the ache in her head. As she watched Skylar carry the last of her clothing to the bed she sought for the right wounded tone to use. "So you're going off with Felix?"

Skylar sat down on the bedside and began rolling her clothing. Without looking at Kiera she said, "Yes. He asked me and we talked it over. And he says he has plenty of room at his place."

"The rooms over his uncle's garage, right?"

Kiera sighed at Skylar's nod. "Well, I suppose you know what you're doing. A garage apartment in the city, is it?"

"It's the city, yes."

"A big change for you. No more horses to feed. No more bossy big sister to contend with. No more responsibilities."

Skylar rolled her eyes. "Felix wants to help get me enrolled in the community college."

"Ah," Kiera replied with a consciously pained note. "Isn't that what your father and I offered to help you do?"

"You and Dad wanted me to take courses online. I'm interested in becoming a dental hygienist. This would involve training that cannot realistically be pursued online. And from what I've discovered, looks like I will have to take some remedial courses before I can even enter the school's hygienist program."

Kiera grunted. "I supposed we failed with your homeschooling, too?"

"I never said you failed, Mom. I'm just tired of you living my life for me. Felix understands. It was the same with his mother."

Bile rose to the back of Kiera's throat. She had to fight to keep her voice even, "I understand. You think you need Felix to help live your life."

"I do need Felix," Skylar answered, "but not the way you make it out. I love him, Mom. If you want to make a crack about how this makes me a weak, dependent woman, go ahead. I don't care."

Kiera's arms crossed. She felt her fingernails dig into the tender flesh on the underside of her arms.

"If running off from your home," she said, "and the people who only seek to provide you a sense of being a strong woman makes you unhappy, who am I to judge?"

Skylar finally met her eyes. "Just stop, Mom. Let me get packed."

Reaching for Skylar's hair, Kiera stroked the little curl at her daughter's cheek. She resisted the urge to yank it. "Of course. If this is what it takes to make my daughter happy."

Kiera stood just outside the house as she lit up a joint. Wendell and Felix were both out here, standing casually by Felix's SUV. The two of them were talking about, of all things, car stereos. Kiera thought a stranger passing by would have taken the two for old friends. She was staggered by Wendell's nonchalance. It was as if he didn't care this conventional lowbrow boy was waiting to drive off with their youngest child!

Felix fished out a cigarette from the pack in his shirt pocket. He stuck the cigarette to his lips and raised the lighter to the tip when he noticed Kiera standing there. It was apparent he was suddenly uncomfortable, even as he offered a, "Good morning".

Kiera knew that until Felix actually left with her daughter, there was a chance she could get Skylar to change her mind. So she gave Felix a stiff *hello* and perfunctory *how are you?*

"I'm good, thank you."

She watched as he lit the cigarette. His hand was noticeably shaky as Wendell said something about USB extension cables. As Felix returned to their conversation, Kiera imagined the skies suddenly growing dark and a lightning bolt striking the boy dead where he stood.

The scenario did not manifest. Instead, there he stood, chuckling over some humorous comment Wendell had made. Kiera's hatred for Felix suffused through her pores like flaming daggers. She could not recall the last time she felt such vehemence toward another person.

God, I hate your laugh as much as your smarmy face, she thought.

The door of the house opened. Skylar emerged with the stuffed duffle bags in tow and her sister following behind. Felix noticed and walked toward them.

"I'll put these in the cargo space," he said, taking the bags from Skylar. "The back seats are kind of hard to move."

As he went off with the bags, Kiera dropped the remainder of her joint and stamped it on the ground.

"How gentlemanly," she said. "He must think you're too delicate to lug them any further."

If the implication registered with Skylar, she didn't show it. She instead embraced Tally. The two said their goodbyes, and exchanged promises to text or call one another by the next day.

Skylar turned to Kiera. "I won't be that far away, Mom. I will call. I will visit."

Kiera's toes dug into the soles of her slippers.

"If he decides to bring you over, huh?" Kiera asked. But she deposited a kiss to Skylar's brow, invoking a silent prayer to Cailleach as she did so.

Dark, formidable Mother, keep her here where she belongs!

Skylar's face tightened. "Bye Mom. I love you."

Kiera watched as she walked over to Wendell and told him goodbye. Then Felix opened the passenger side door to let her in. Emotion ballooned in Kiera's chest. As Felix got into the SUV and started the engine, black dots swarmed in front of her vision.

Cailleach, no! Don't allow this!

But moments later the SUV turned and began its journey down the windy hill drive. Kiera struggled for air. When at last her lungs filled, she charged at Wendell. She raised her arm and with a palm struck him with a loud slap across the face. She heard Tally gasp behind her.

"How could you just stand there chatting with that awful, stupid boy?" Kiera screeched. "Anyone can see he wants to control our daughter's life!"

Wendell rubbed his stinging cheek. The look of pained disquiet on his face only further irritated Kiera.

At last he said, "We both know *who* wants to control her."

"And what the hell is that supposed to mean?"

Wendell didn't answer. Instead, he walked around her and stomped toward the house. Kiera heard Tally ask if he was alright.

Kiera stood alone outside. She glared at the drive, her mind blind with rage. Her baby was gone, gone off with her vapid small-town hero. Gone off to be exposed to ideas contrary to everything Kiera and Wendell had taught her!

Her head fell back and a scream tore through her throat.

"Dark Mother Cailleach, *why? WHY??*"

She crumpled to her knees and slammed her fists over and over into the ground. Obscenities flew from her mouth with each impact. Like arrows these words sailed, hurled at Felix Henner and at her goddess who had chosen not to intervene. She even cursed her foolish Skylar who had repaid her parents' lessons with nothing less than treason.

Her hands were aching and her knuckles were bleeding when Tally returned. Tally crouched beside Kiera and gently stroked her back.

"Mom, it's going to be alright."

Kiera let herself be cradled. In the comfort of Tally's arms she was aware of the river of tears that spilled over her face and down the front of her blouse. She blubbered as she continued to weep. *Skylar* and *traitor* were the only intelligible words she could utter.

"It will be alright," she heard Tally say. "And I will never leave you, Mom. I will never betray you. This, I promise."

Chapter 14

Kiera devoted the rest of the day to writing the post she'd put off for the PCKC Facebook page. It was imperative for her to discredit anything the anti-groups might post online about the events of the day before. So she posted her own interpretation of what had transpired, carefully crafting her words so that anyone reading them would believe the antis had caused Tally's tumble in the street.

Once finished writing her account, Kiera summarized:

All escorts have encountered pushy antis. But I have never personally witnessed such aggressiveness as demonstrated by the woman holding the inflammatory sign Tally tried to block. This burly woman forced her weight into my daughter and caused her to fall onto the pavement. The male anti who ran forward and pulled Tally out of the street was obviously not concerned about being a Good Samaritan. Like the rest of these bullies, he was terrified at the thought of legal repercussions.

Kiera spell-checked the post. Next, she found on her computer a photo she'd taken of Tally some weeks before. In this photo Tally was standing next to the family jeep out in the front yard. She was dressed in shorts and a halter shirt which emphasized her thin physique. Anyone seeing the photo would naturally assume Tally could be easily pushed around by a larger person. Satisfied, Kiera uploaded the photo along with her post and hit the publish button.

Curious if the woman who had filmed the incident had uploaded her video, Kiera went to the *Pagans And Secular People For Life* Facebook page. She skimmed through the few new posts here but none of these related to or even mentioned an incident in Avonport. Eventually she came to older posts she'd already read.

She laughed cynically. "I guess these assholes are smart enough not to try embarrassing abortion defenders online!"

Satisfied, Kiera switched off the browser.

In the evening Kiera made sloppy joes. Wendell had shut himself up in his workshop and refused to come to the house to eat. So Tally took him his dinner.

Kiera resented the blithe way Wendell had handled Skylar's leaving. Yet it pained her that he was still angry. She took comfort in reminding herself he was just a male and that even the best of males were prone to do stupid things.

She resolved to apologize to him for the slap. It was nearly two in the morning when she was awakened by the sound of the front door being opened and shut. A few minutes later, she heard him enter their dark bedroom. He crawled into bed, and without a word lay down with his back toward her.

"I'm sorry," she said. When he did not respond, she turned to him and gingerly laid a hand on his shoulder. "Forgive me please? I should not have hit you."

He didn't answer. Within minutes, he was snoring lightly. The scene with Skylar played out again and again in Kiera's mind. She'd been betrayed by someone she loved dearly, and now the person she counted on most for consolation was ignoring her. Wendell's attitude, she knew, could be blamed on Skylar, too.

All the same Kiera felt her anger with her youngest crumbling beneath general worry for the girl. She did not know the location of Felix's home or if her Skylar was safe. She also couldn't rid her mind of the nagging fear Skylar might never deign to see her again. She could not understand why Cailleach had allowed all of this to happen. Kiera had dedicated her adult life to patterning her behavior in a manner befitting a follower of the powerful, volatile One!

Every winter of her adult life, as a show of continued fidelity, Kiera had sacrificed a living creature to Cailleach. There had been so many stray cats, chickens, lambs and even mice captured in the horse barn! She had renounced every fair and tender-hearted goddess that was antagonistic to her power. Male gods were Kiera's sworn enemies. Every mortal adversary Kiera had ever avowed vengeance on, she had done so in Cailleach's name.

This veneration had begun when Kiera was just a child, under the instruction of Grandma Lucinda. Kiera had been only eleven years old at the time. She was enraged at her parents for bringing a third baby into the world. It had been a girl child that her parents had named Monica, an infant with a pink rosebud mouth and wisps of blonde curls upon a shapely head. The baby's nose, ears, and bright blue eyes so resembled Dorothy she could have been a miniature replica. There was no resemblance to the meaty members of Ira's Hambrick side of the family, nor had the babe inherited –as Kiera had—the milky pale complexion and dark hair from Grandma Hambrick, who had been born a Roydon. From the moment Kiera first laid eyes on Monica she knew the child would not only be a rival for her father's affections but also a constant visual reminder of Dorothy as well. And Dorothy, Kiera had learned early in life, was not a parent so easily managed as was Ira.

It was hard enough for Kiera to bear the annoying Daniel. At least she knew her brother stood no chance of replacing her in Ira's heart. But enduring the tiny, beautiful Monica was something Kiera found insufferable.

Some days after the baby's birth, Grandma Lucinda took Kiera to the woods that grew behind the luxurious house that had been Kiera's childhood home. There Grandma explained to Kiera about the powerful Cailleach and how the Goddess had no use for women like gentle Dorothy. Grandma told Kiera how Cailleach rewarded followers for sacrifices and courage made in her foreboding name. Kiera had been eager to become like Grandma and to enjoy the gifts Cailleach promised those who were bold enough to follow her ways.

So had Kiera happily knelt before Grandma and she accepted the scratch of the woman's long fingernail across her chest and over her heart. It had hurt and bled as Grandma dug the ancient symbol into her skin. Kiera kept her eyes open, though, and watched in pain as Grandma Spat into the fresh wound.

"To receive Cailleach's blessings," Grandma had said, "one's desire must be as eager as the hungry spider's. Their resolve has to be as unbending as a steel web. To hesitate or cringe from eliminating our obstacles is a weakness. The power Cailleach rewards only the fierce."

Later that day, as Grandma instructed, Kiera went to her room and chose from among her favorite toys the plush owl Ira had given her on her fourth birthday. She carried the owl, along with some kerosene and a lighter, down to the playroom of the house. She laid the owl into the cold, unused fireplace. She poured the kerosene upon the plush and threw a lit match into the soggy mess. She watched the flames kindle. She witnessed the small inferno as the toy burned away. She watched as the flames crackled and glowed and eventually died down until there was nothing left of the stuffed owl but ashes.

The reward Kiera hoped for by the sacrifice was determination. She received this the very next day. While her parents and young Daniel slept, Kiera made her way to the nursery. Kiera snatched away the quilt that had lain across Monica's little body. The movement made the baby stir and open its big blue eyes. Kiera endured its wondering gaze and the stupid infant's gurgle only long enough to fold the quilt. Then she placed it over Monica's face. She bore her weight upon the folded cloth. The baby wriggled in silence, more wildly than Kiera would have imagined. When at last the limbs fell still and Kiera took away the quilt, Monica appeared merely to be asleep. She did not breathe, however, nor did her tiny arms and legs twitch or stir.

To Kiera's profound joy her wretched sister never moved again. When Kiera returned to her bed that long ago morning, she quietly praised Cailleach for giving her the courage to do away with the child.

During the days following Monica's death, while her mother and father mourned and even Daniel was given to tears, Kiera giddily awaited the scratches Grandma had given to heal and scar over. This scar, Grandma had promised, would be the proof Cailleach had accepted Kiera as one of Her select disciples.

Yet after all Kiera's years of loyal veneration, despite living her life as she knew Cailleach demanded of her female devotees, the goddess had now turned a blind eye to her supplications.

"You let my daughter leave, Dark Lady," she whispered vehemently. "And no matter her failings, I raised her in accordance with your will. Why have you seen fit to punish me by allowing her to leave?"

Kiera's sense of abandonment made for much tossing and turning before she finally fell into a dreamless sleep.

When she awoke, it was to find Wendell already up and gone from bed. She went to the kitchen to find the room fragrant with the smell of fresh coffee. Tally sat at the breakfast table with a cup in front of her.

"Did your dad put on the coffee?"

Tally nodded and rubbed her still-sleepy eyes.

As Kiera poured herself a cup she asked if Tally had seen her dad.

"He went into town to buy nails and tin sheathing. Oh, and chicken feed."

"Ah. Okay."

Kiera brought her cup to the table and took a seat. Tally gave her a pursed-lipped look.

"You ought to know, I heard Dad yesterday. Before I woke you up. He tried to convince Skylar not to leave."

Kiera was mildly surprised. "Really?"

Tally nodded. "He sure did. I would have told you yesterday, but I figured you weren't in the mood to hear it."

An uneasy knot formed in Kiera's stomach. "Was I that pissed?"

"You were." Tally shrugged. "I can't blame you for being angry at Skylar. But I think you hurt Dad's feelings."

Kiera thanked her for the information. She felt terrible, though, knowing if this were true, then her reaction toward Wendell had been completely unwarranted.

"And oh," Tally mentioned, "Skylar texted me last night."

As much as Kiera wished she didn't care to hear about her youngest, it was impossible.

"That's nice. Was she alright?"

"She sounded happy. She told me all about Felix's place. Said she got to meet his Uncle Mike and Aunt Lara, who she says are real nice. She was all excited Felix was making her a special dinner. Chicken Fricassee."

"Skylar's favorite," Kiera sneered. "That calculating bastard."

Kiera was walking to the house from having groomed the horses when she saw the jeep pull up the drive. Wendell got out with three shopping bags.

She watched him carry the bags inside. When she entered some moments later he was in the kitchen, just placing the bags on the breakfast table. She asked if he needed some help.

Wendell pulled a carton of truss head screws from one of the bags. "Nope."

Kiera sighed. "Did you hear my apology last night? If not, I give it again. I am sorry."

"Yeah, I heard it." His lips pressed tightly but he finally gave her a look. "I just thought you'd stopped giving in to those kinds of reactions years ago."

"Forgive me please?"

"Of course," he said with a resigned sigh. Hurt still shone in his eyes. Kiera stepped to him and gave his lips a tender kiss. She was relieved when his arms encircled her waist.

"Tally told me earlier how wrong I was," she said. "That you did speak to Skylar. I was so very wrong."

Wendell sat at the table while Kiera got them both a soda from the refrigerator. As she placed these on the table and took a seat, he gave a sigh.

"I talked to Skylar before Tally went to wake you up yesterday," he told her. "When Felix showed up, she was all sunshine and smiles. She announced she was leaving. I think she believed I'd be fine with the news. But it was my duty to remind her that our family has made it our duty to serve and guide the less fortunate and the unenlightened.

And I told her I was afraid that if she hooked up with somebody like Felix, she would forget her moral obligations."

"I see," Kiera said. "What did Skylar say to that?"

Wendell popped open the soda and took a long sip. "She said she loves us all, but that she wants to live her own life and make her own decisions. I asked her why couldn't Felix just give up working for the man and come live here? She looked aghast at the suggestion. Told me that neither she nor Felix want to live like *cult members*."

Kiera shook her head in disbelief. "Like cult members? What the hell?"

"That's what I was wondering. Anyway, at that point I was riled myself. Told Skylar that she was talking like an ignorant plebeian. That's when she said she'd heard that kind of *ideological prattle* all her life and was fed up with it. It made me mad, I don't deny it. I cussed a little, told her she was being unappreciative. But finally I literally just threw my hands up. I went outside where Felix was. I thought if I'm going to lose my daughter to this jerk, I should at least talk to him a little. Start to get to know him."

Kiera laid a comforting hand on his arm. "There was nothing more or better you could have said. And you handled it much better than I did."

After Wendell swallowed down the rest of his soda, he gave her an affectionate smile. Kiera could tell everything was copacetic between them. Still, she was disappointed Cailleach had failed to prevent Skylar from leaving. She mentioned this to Wendell.

Wendell said pensively, "It is very possible the goddess has done you a favor by not intervening. Despite the example I've tried to set, and that which Tally has always willingly accepted, Skylar cannot see you as the sacred embodiment of the dark lady. She doesn't venerate you as the embodiment of the female divine incarnate. When she looks at you, my dearest, she only sees the woman who gave birth to her, who raised her. Her obstinacy is a weakness that contributes nothing to the important missions for which you have been called."

Kiera thought upon this. It made so much more sense than the idea that Cailleach had abandoned a daring and resolute adherent as herself.

"I think you are right," she replied. "Skylar is my daughter, whom I will always love. But she has chosen false romantic notions and social narratives over feminist ideals and activist pluck. I could see her misguided views were becoming more and more of an impediment for our work at the clinic. Cailleach apparently saw this, too, and she provided Skylar the means to pursue her silly dreams. The means by which has got her out of our way."

Wendell squeezed her hand gently. "Yes. Hail Cailleach. And hail you, my dearest, before whose fierce bearing I gaze upon Her countenance."

Chapter 15

They made love later that day. Wendell was not the energetic lover he'd been in their younger days. But his touch remained as deferential as any man who dared seek the pleasure with an earthly representative of Cailleach.

As they lay together in the bed afterward, Kiera felt against her ear the uneven beat of Wendell's heart in his chest. It worried her. She looked at his face and noticed how pale his sweat-filmed skin was.

"Do you feel alright?"

Wendell beamed drowsily. "I am fine for you are my goddess," he whispered. "And I am forever your awed and devoted consort."

After he fell asleep a few minutes later Kiera noticed his heart was beginning to beat normally again. She kissed his cheek and got out of bed. And getting her clothes on, she left him to nap.

A half hour later Kiera and Tally were riding the horses bareback around the property. It was a long, relaxing ride. When they were finished and the horses returned to their pen, Tally helped her brush them down, then feed and water them. The sun was hanging low in the western sky as the two of them returned home.

Tally helped her make dinner. They chatted while they worked, and Tally told some jokes that made Kiera laugh until tears streamed down her face. Wendell came in, and bemused by their laughing, asked what he'd missed?

The mood was cheerful during dinner. Wendell opened a bottle of wine, and the lasagna Kiera and Tally had made was delicious. After the meal, Rory called Kiera's phone. He gave her the happy news he was starting for home in just a few days. Kiera was elated.

Happiness followed her to bed. She lay for a time alone in the darkness. There, she prayed in gratitude, thanking Cailleach for taking the ungrateful Skylar away. She would have preferred having her youngest back home, of course, but she also knew Skylar had to learn for herself that Felix was a provincial jerk and that she would never find true happiness outside the haven of her parents' home and their carefully selected group of friends. These things Skylar would never see until she experienced firsthand the ugliness of the outside world. Once Skylar saw this, Kiera was sure, she'd be compelled to return home. All Kiera had to do was wait.

Monday welcomed the escorts with a warmly pleasant spring day. The only protesters around this morning were the Catholics at their usual spot across the street. Tally was in good spirits and ready to be back strolling the sidewalk with her homemade sign. When the others asked where Skylar was, Kiera let them know that their youngest had gone MIA after deciding to go play house with Felix Henner.

Not very long after the Scruggs' arrival, two women were heard arguing outside. Kiera, along with Wanda and Jayelle, stuck their heads out of the tent. The commotion was coming from the eastern side of the clinic drive entrance. Tally stood there, her face flushed with emotion, as she confronted two females. One of these was a middle-aged black woman. She wore a black tee shirt with white lettering that read: *Black Pre-Born Lives Matter*, the signature slogan of the *Pro-Black Pro-Life* sidewalk counselors group. The other woman was white and quite young, surely no more than seventeen years of age, with long honey-brown hair. Only a few yards away stood a tall elderly black woman and a young black boy around fourteen years of age. Both of them sported the *Black Pre-Born Lives Matter* tee shirts. The elderly woman hugged against her chest what looked to be a stack of leaflets.

Tally appeared to be enraged at the white girl. She barked at her, "I don't know what this woman told you, but just because you scheduled an appointment only this morning doesn't give you the right to skip it! That is so inconsiderate to the doctors and staffs, not to mention the person who could have had the time slot!"

The middle-aged woman poised herself between Tally and the girl.

"You heard her say she wants to talk to me," she told Tally. "So you need to rein in that attitude, young lady, and back off."

Tally ignored this and addressed only the girl, "Are you going to let some anti-reproduction rights vulture guilt you into breaking an appointment? C'mon, don't be a pussy!"

The girl replied in a small voice, "I think I've changed my mind. I want to talk to this lady about adoption and pregnancy resources."

"So you're going to break an appointment," Tally scoffed, "and throw away your future just to bring another hungry mouth into an already overly populated world? How selfish!"

The middle-aged woman thrust a hand on a hip and threw Tally a hard look. "You need to mind your mouth right now, missy."

Kiera resented this woman speaking to Tally as if she were scolding a child. Irked, Kiera hurried over to stand beside her daughter.

She pointed at the white girl and demanded of the older woman, "Why the hell are you even here? Are you blind? Can't you see that she's white?"

The woman eyed her squarely as she answered, "I don't care if this girl is pink and purple plaid. If she wants to know her options before going into that place, I will talk to her! And don't you dare try to interfere!"

Kiera gave a belittling laugh. "And if you or any of your brainwashing crew set foot on this property I will call the police!"

A humorless smile crossed the woman's face. "I saw you, both of you, in those awful videos. Harassing that poor veteran. Jumping into those people's faces. Making fools out of yourselves. I would say you should be old enough to feel ashamed of yourself, but considering what you do here, I doubt you know the meaning of shame! You and your friends like to call yourselves Pink Escorts. The truth is you are *deathcorts*. And make no mistake, if any of you people ever touch one of us or assault somebody we are speaking with, we will be the ones who call the police."

Kiera's first reaction was to hurl some kind of dare or comeuppance. But she couldn't get the woman mentioning *those awful videos* out of her head.

Tally had either missed it or didn't care. Kiera heard her daughter shout at the woman, "Go on, you stupid black crow! Help that idiot make the worst mistake of her life!"

Kiera was stunned by her daughter's racist choice of words. It contradicted all the diversity acceptance ideals she'd been taught. If the woman was offended, though, she didn't show it. She instead placed an arm around the white girl's shoulders and guided her over to where the old woman and young boy waited.

Tally folded her arms angrily across her chest and said with a huff, "What a selfish jerk to waste a good appointment slot, huh?"

Kiera gave a distracted nod. She knew she should admonish Tally for the insensitive thing she had said. But Kiera was preoccupied with the woman's comment about videos. She watched silently as the white girl headed eastward with her three new companions. They walked until they slipped completely from view. Kiera was left to stare at the sidewalk, while apprehension gnawed at her stomach and Tally continued to grumble about the white girl.

There were no further confrontations that morning. The parking lot remained peaceful, with patients coming back and forth to their vehicles. No more antis, neither in the form of protesters nor counselors, showed up. In fact, everything was so quiet Tally grew bored with her one-woman patrol and returned to the tent. She put her sign away, took a chair and got on her phone. The blips and tinny sounds coming from the game she played were audible enough to be heard over the conversations inside the tent. Kiera, sitting in a chair trying to show interest as Jayelle told her about a sale on flip-flops and loafers at the dollar store, was almost relieved by the phone sounds. They kept her from falling asleep right where she sat.

It was nearly three o'clock when Kiera's phone buzzed. Taking it from her pocket, she saw she had received a text from Daniel. While Jayelle continued talking to Wanda and Kristen about the sale Kiera read the short message.

Sis, please come to my office. Need to talk.

Kiera expected her brother had some bad news about Dorothy. Not wanting to put it off, she excused herself from the other women and found Wendell, who was standing in the back talking with Jeremy. On seeing her, the two men fell silent, but the half-grin on Jeremy's face told Kiera their conversation probably involved the sharing of some stupid or insensitive joke that men liked to tell. She'd caught Wendell engaged in this type of juvenile behavior before, a few times actually, even as he knew how very much she disliked it.

But right now Kiera didn't care about their jokes. She informed Wendell about Daniel's message.

"I think he may want to tell me Dorothy is worse."

Wendell laid a hand on her shoulder. "Want me to come, too?"

She told him it wasn't necessary. Giving him a quick kiss on the cheek, she exited the tent.

Daniel's office was located on the top floor of the clinic building. Although there was an elevator Kiera preferred using the stairwell as she considered riding elevators a choice made by the obese or lazy. The office was one among a nest of large offices shared by the Board members, the doctors, the resources director and pertinent operational personnel. Kiera came up here once a month to meet with the resources director, Raven Goldbaum, to discuss the latest Campaign Parenthood initiatives and to sign for the monthly sustentation checks the organization sent for the escorts.

Kiera hadn't entered Daniel's office in quite some time. As he offered her a seat across his desk now, she remembered why she didn't like coming here. The dark oak paneled walls and expensive Persian rug seemed to Kiera to reek of corporate entitlement. Even the fancy mahogany filing cabinets smelled of affluence. Adding to these displeasing odors was the lingering fragrance of cotton candy-flavored vape mist.

She mused quietly that had this been their father's office, the wealth would have been similarly flaunted. But at least Ira Hambrick had smoked cigars instead of inhaling flavored water like her prosaic brother!

The temperature in the office was somewhat on the humid side. Kiera was still garbed in her bulky escort jacket and the warmth made the fabric irritate her neck. She was aware, too, her jacket was grubby and smelled of old sweat and the women's work boots on her feet needed a good cleaning. Other women, she thought, might feel slouchy walking into a nice office in such garb. But Kiera hoped her attire would remind Daniel that despite his refined lifestyle and high position at the clinic, it was his sister who put in the grunt work every day to defend abortion.

If he was affected by the sight of her outfit, though, his manner gave no indication.

"Can I get you a water, sis, or maybe some coffee?" he asked.

She watched as Daniel reached for the glassed bottled water at his desk and began to peel at the edges of the label with his thumbnails. It was a nervous habit he'd developed when they were children.

"No, thanks. What's up? Is Dorothy worse?"

Daniel assured her their mother's condition had not changed.

"I'm sorry, sis, no improvement there. But on the positive side, her condition is no worse either."

Kiera felt reluctance in his demeanor. And that he'd called her *sis* twice in the span of minutes told her something was indeed on his mind.

"Okay, there's some other reason you asked me up here. What is it?"

Daniel pushed the bottle of water away. Shifting slightly in his chair, he pulled on his professional face.

"Some videos have come to our attention, Kiera. From an anonymous tipster. Videos taken outside, involving escorts, specifically you, Tally, Wendell and Kerry Halker. The videos show the four of you engaged in some rather disturbing behavior."

Kiera felt apprehension quaver in her stomach again.

"Yeah, so?" she snapped. "Don't forget all the disturbing behavior we have videotaped involving those infernal antis. Shouting at patients, showing off their graphic signs, using their bullhorns. You know how they are."

"I'm not disputing they can be annoying, even intrusive at times." Daniel sighed heavily. "But punching a man's sign out of his hands? Tally getting so hysterical she falls into the street? And Jesus Christ, Kiera, you all badgering a disabled veteran? The optics these videos convey is one of deliberate harassment. Some may say even outright cruelty."

Kiera snorted at his austere tone. "Don't believe everything you see on a video, Daniel. People are known to manipulate those things."

"Our legal department has already had the videos looked at by a professional analyst. Her verdict is they were not manipulated."

"Your analyst is in error," Kiera retorted. "I'm sure whoever wanted you to see the videos have at least edited them to give the optics they want!"

"It's possible they may have been somewhat edited," Daniel conceded, "to cut out any preincidental antagonism on their part. But I assure you there was no image fakery involved."

Kiera shrugged. "So what are you trying to tell me? That some anonymous tipster is trying to threaten the clinic with a lawsuit?"

Daniel answered patiently, "The videos are posted at some conservative patriot website called The National Constitutionalist. They have already been linked to by numerous like-minded forums and media outlets. We've had no word about a lawsuit yet. However, bear in mind Avonport isn't a large city, nor is this a blue state. Our state legislators are already close to passing stricter abortion laws. Even now it would only take one local lawyer or legal firm to see those videos and then go look for the people in them. They could find out their names, they could track down that disabled veteran. And if that happens, Kiera, we will have a lawsuit to fear."

Kiera waved the air dismissively. "That's a major leap of assumption if you ask me."

"No one is asking you," Daniel said rigidly. "Time and again the Board has gone to bat for the escorts. And yes, the court cases have always been determined in our favor. But you know as well as anybody abortion is not popular in this region. That veterans are held in high regard here. And on top of this, Judge Slaughter, who we've always counted on hearing our cases, retires this year. As it stands right now even if we get to pick another judge to hear potential future cases there is no guarantee the replacement would be as sympathetic as Slaughter. For this reason the Board feels the reactions these videos may provoke are problematic. The decision has been made to take proactive measures."

Kiera felt her nose wrinkle. "What's that supposed to mean?"

Daniel looked down at the desk, his face twitching slightly as if he was taking great care in choosing his next words. His tone was benign as he finally said, "We need you, Wendell, Tally and the Halker woman to take a hiatus from the escorts."

"Hiatus?" Kiera sputtered. "What the hell, Daniel?"

"At least until the uproar over these videos is over with, Kiera. Until we figure out a way to make the damned things disappear from the internet. Our legal department is of the opinion we can probably allege the website owners are promoting fake news or something to that effect. This tactic has worked with Campaign Parenthood's partners involved in similar situations."

Kiera still couldn't believe he expected her to turn her back on her Pink defenders! "But you can't forbid me from being here. Our father built this clinic. Not to mention I am still a shareholder!"

"Your inherited shares do not entitle you to break corporate policies regarding clinic procedures and the day-to-day running of the physical domain. These policies were updated after the last time Tally faced a lawsuit. Don't you recall? After she poured hot tea on a woman?"

Kiera shook her head angrily. "I wasn't told a damned thing about policy changes!"

"The changes were outlined in the quarterly memorandum," he said, "which was mailed to every shareholder. I guess you didn't open the registered letter?"

Kiera remembered she hadn't bothered to read the last quarterly memorandum. She'd had no reason to think any policies had been changed, and especially not for those which affected escort activities.

She saw a slightly sympathetic expression come to Daniel's face, one she found incensing.

"You never wanted me involved, did you?" she roared. "You've never wanted to share Dad's legacy! And now you've come up with a strategy of cutting me out altogether!"

"First off, Kiera, that's simply not true. I love you, I always will. I stood with you and the escorts every time you went to court. And secondly, I didn't come up with this strategy as you call it. Look, I was against the policy changes. And if this matter was entirely up to me we would just take our chances in court as before."

"You're the CEO, Daniel. You should have more say than anybody on the board!"

"It doesn't work that way here," he replied. "We receive federal grants for what we do here. I can't just act like a dictator or else it could lead to an internal inquiry." He gave a hopeful smile. "Look, it won't be forever, Kiera. I assure you."

"Well, you will be losing me as liaison between Campaign Parenthood and the clinic! Have you even considered that?"

"Kiera, yours was an informal agreement with that organization. As of today Michael Burgie is taking over those responsibilities on behalf of the clinic."

She laughed bitterly. "Didn't waste much time, did you? And here I am, a card-carrying member of NOW and a committed activist for Campaign Parenthood, but all this time my own brother has seen fit to bar me from a position in this clinic because I am a woman!"

Daniel groaned. "Don't try that bullshit with me. You know there are more women sitting on the Board than men. You also know exactly why it was Dad made the decision to keep you off of corporate operations."

"Yeah," she sneered, "because I don't have a scrotum!"

Impatience pinched Daniel's face. "Because of what happened in Kentucky, Kiera. You know this perfectly well."

This mention of the past raised the hair on Kiera's arms. The shafts felt like red-hot needles just beneath her skin. They not only scorched, but aggravated the resentment she had long felt not just for Daniel but also for the father who had, intentionally or not, let her down.

She trembled with fury. "I was practically a child then, Daniel! That you would throw it against me now only shows what a pathetic excuse for a human being you are."

"A child..." Daniel murmured. He clasped his hands together as if he were praying and touched the fingertips under his chin as in thought. "That excuse aside, Kiera, there is nothing more I can do about the current situation. I truly am sorry for this. The four of you have no choice but to vacate the premises and stay away until it is decided your coming back is in the best interest of the clinic. I will be in contact with you as soon as the Board is satisfied that time has come."

Kiera's hands moved under the back of her legs. Her fingers clawed into her thighs and the nails pressed so tightly through her pants they dug through and into her flesh. She wanted to shout at Daniel, to curse him out, to grab something, anything heavy in the room, and throw it into his damned face. But this wasn't something she was willing to grant. For she had no doubt such a fitting display of her pain would only give her brother a measure of satisfaction.

Instead, she stood up and gave him a grim smile. "How generous of you. Goodbye Daniel."

As she started to turn he said, "Kiera, please remember this only applies to the four of you. Rory is welcome to continue volunteering here. Skylar, too. And I sincerely hope she will."

Daniel, she was sure, knew nothing of Skylar's running off with Felix. But this offer, spoken with what she deemed his artfully designed attempt at consolation, only scraped at the other wounds he'd made over the years.

She thundered at him, "You just would, wouldn't you?"

Daniel flinched. "I'm sorry, Kiera, I thought it'd mean something to you to know two of your children are at least here-"

"Amazing, Daniel! Even when you aren't trying to be a little shit, you still manage to be a little shit."

Kiera moved to the door and let herself out. As she marched down the corridor she heard Daniel call her name from behind the office door. Once, only once.

Chapter 16

Kiera arrived back at the tent and told Wendell he was to drive them home. When he asked what was going on, she offered no explanation. Tally was obviously not happy about leaving—Pumpkin Head's group had just shown up and she was anxious to confront them in some way. But to Kiera's relief her eldest daughter offered no complaint. Wanda seemed to recognize something was amiss and asked Kiera to text her later. Kiera responded only with a stiff-mouthed nod and the three of them piled into the jeep.

During the drive home Kiera told Wendell and Tally about the Board's decision.

Tally did not react with the angry hysterics Kiera had expected. She merely groaned, cursed a little and observed that she couldn't believe the Board was so stupid.

Wendell reached over from the steering wheel to give Kiera's hand a little squeeze. "I'm sorry, honey. This is totally unfair. The board doesn't realize how much the clinic depends on their escorts. They're lucky to have every one of those willing to come out five days a week to protect their patients."

Tally asked Kiera how long she thought they were supposed to stay off of the clinic grounds. Kiera shrugged and said she just hoped it wouldn't be long. She glanced in the rearview mirror and saw Tally drop her head back on the seat and glare at the ceiling of the jeep. But Tally said nothing more during the drive. Once they reached home and Wendell had parked the jeep Tally jumped out and slammed the passenger door shut. As Wendell and Kiera got out they watched as she ran to the house and unlocked the door with her key. She entered, leaving the door open for them, but they could hear her cursing as she stomped upstairs toward her room.

Wendell paused on the threshold. He looked livid. "This isn't right, Kiera. You've worked so hard for that clinic."

Kiera felt tears brimming in her eyes. She was aware of how icy the tears felt, how they poked her lids like tiny shards of broken glass.

"So help me, Wendell, one way or another I will see to it Daniel comes to regret this. Everyone on that Board will come to regret it. And those video-sharing antis will regret it most of all!"

The first task Kiera set herself to was to get on her computer and find The National Constitutionalist website. It was easily enough found. Once at the site, Kiera was not surprised to find it was not abortion-friendly. The front page was laden with articles bearing headlines that would appeal to Right-wingers, patriots and Constitution-adoring Libertarians. The videos Daniel had told her about, however, were not located on the front page. She had to search through the menu to find the Pro Life News section. Upon clicking this link, she was taken to another page. And here the very first article gave the sensationalist headline: DISTURBING VIDEOS OF AGGRESSIVE PRO-CHOICE BEHAVIOR AT ABORTION MILL.

Kiera had no desire to read the article and she had to scroll past a few paragraphs before finally getting to the videos. There were three of these. Kiera pushed the Play button for the first video. It started out with a black background, with only a date in the text and details that read: *"Anti-Lifers at Avonport abortion mill get aggressive with Pro-Life advocate."*

After the black background faded, the video showed the footage of the confrontation Tally and Kerry had had with the tall guy from the Pagans and Secular People For Life group.

There was no narration or other text to give a clue as to the identity of the person who had filmed it (though doubtlessly, it had been the woman Kiera had observed videotaping at the clinic). The credit captions below the video simply read: *"Provided by Pagans and Secular People For Life."*

The article writer had bestowed the title for the next video: TANTRUM THROWING PRO-CHOICER FALLS IN STREET. Kiera recognized it as having been filmed by the same woman, and it revealed what had happened the day Tally tumbled in the street. This one was more difficult to watch as it detailed not only the activity leading up to Tally's fall, but also the Catholic man who had pulled Tally out of the street to save her from the approaching truck. Kiera cringed to know some people watching the video might deem the guy's actions had been heroic.

The credit captions below this video were the same as the first.

The third video was placed under the headline: PRO-CHOICERS ASSAULT DISABLED VETERAN WITH MEGAPHONES.

This video contained no text, though a continuous timestamp of taping ran across the bottom of the image screen. The video had been shot just days before, in fact, the last time Squinty McGimpy had shown up. The imagery started out with the scene of a furious Kerry screaming right in the veteran's face. Whoever had taken it had taken their time, for it included Wendell's coming to intervene, the megaphone fight between him and Squinty, and even the appearance of the cops. The audio of the video was unfortunately quite sophisticated, for nearly every word exchanged in the spectacle was recorded. Dismayed (and quite disapproving) observations from an unidentified female were occasionally heard in the background. It was only after the police were seen leaving and Wendell walked back to the tent did the male video maker give a comment.

"Screaming at a handicapped veteran, getting in a battle of megaphones with the poor man," he observed. "Just the everyday brouhaha dished out by our friendly neighborhood abortion clinic defenders."

Underneath the video placement was the credit: *Provided by Anonymous in Avonport.*

Kiera felt none of these videos posed any more of a threat to the clinic than did the one which had been brought to court by the woman Tally had doused with tea. Sure, the writer's sensationalist headlines and the comment at the end of this last video had the power to inflame anti-choice sentiments. But such commentary, she believed, had been added specifically for prejudice's sake. Surely these comments would prove no more useful in court than those in the tea lady's videos.

"And Daniel and his stupid Board are scared by this propaganda!" she grumbled.

It was infuriating for Kiera; the videos gave the impression Tally and Wendell were antagonists. And she was left disappointed she still had no names to identify the person or persons who had done the filming.

She resisted the urge to read the article. The day had so far been too upsetting to put herself through any senseless aggravation. Besides, she had work to do at the Pro-Choice Krumme County Facebook page.

After logging onto that page she sought out the options and settings. She had always said the PCKC page was created for the benefit of the entire clinic's Pink Defenders. But she knew secretly, truly, it was her page. It had always had been hers. She had created it, she had moderated it, she had been the one who had devoted hours to writing posts. She'd provided the links to posts of pertinent abortion news. She had shared dozens of pro-choice memes with her followers. It was her commentaries that had been written to encourage the pro-choice supporters. She had been the one who had videotaped coverage of the silly behavior from antis that went on outside of the clinic. She and she alone had bestowed upon individual antis the mocking epitaphs her followers found so hilarious.

Nobody was going to take this away from her. She wouldn't allow her work to be used to the advancement of anti-choice haters who had made cowards of Daniel and his precious Board. She was also not willing to turn over ownership or moderation privileges to anyone else. Without her the page would just hang there in cyberspace; everything she'd ever posted, a potential treasure trove waiting to be gathered and weaponized in reverse by the antis.

So she took the steps that deleted the page altogether.

Kiera turned off the computer and went to Tally's room. She found her daughter sitting on her bed and playing a game on her phone. Tally's mouth was clenched as her thumbs tumbled over the tiny keyboard and Kiera noticed that her knuckles were white.

"Will you contact Kerry," Kiera asked, "and tell her the situation with the Board?"

Tally nodded at Kiera. "Yeah, I'll do that."

"And don't go into great detail about this with your sister? Last thing I care to deal with is Skylar gloating or saying I told you so."

"I sent her a brief message about it, but she hasn't contacted back yet," Tally said with a dubious expression. "You really think she'd gloat about it? I always thought she supported us."

The innocence of this admission made Kiera smile. "I'd like to think your sister does. But she's changed so much being around that Felix. Once she understands what he really is she will surely come back down to earth. I hope so anyway. I miss her. But until that time comes we shouldn't take the chance of either of them blabbing about our personal affairs."

"Okay, I'll leave it to you to give her the full details." Tally sucked her lips together tightly and Kiera saw a little shudder pass over her limbs. "Mom, this is all so unfair! And by the way Uncle Daniel reacted, I am scared these awful antis will retaliate. What if they do take us to court, and worse, find a judge that won't just dismiss their case outright? Their stupid lawyers will be digging into our personal lives! And nothing about our lives is anybody else's business!"

Kiera kissed the top of her head. "I will not let that happen, Tally," she promised. "I simply won't."

During the afternoon of the following day Wendell was lying in bed in their room and smoking a reefer while reading a book when Kiera brought him a glass of wine. She knew the aggravation over the clinic situation still bothered him, but his first question was to ask how she was doing. Kiera told him she was fine, and reminded him to let her be the one to inform Skylar what had happened.

"However you want to handle it," he said.

She forced a breeziness into her tone. "I've decided to play it out with Daniel and his precious Board. If they decide they don't want us back, there are other ways to help the cause of reproduction rights."

Wendell smoked the last of the reefer and accepted the glass of wine.

"You're taking this better than I expected," he remarked sleepily. "But yeah, why not? There's that clinic that recently opened in Crowsdale. It may be over in the next state, but I guess it's worth the drive."

"I'm thinking of becoming a contributing writer for Campaign Parenthood," Kiera told him, watching as he took a sip of the wine. It was the elderberry she'd made three years before, his favorite fruit variety. "They're advertising for writers at their national blog."

"Sounds like a plan there," he said. "You have experience with writing for the Party newsletter and they love having us involved in the local campaigns. And the primaries are coming up soon enough. We can find a way to stay busy. A place for you to direct your energy. That's what really matters to me."

Kiera told him how sweet he was to always think of her needs.

"Of course," he answered. "You are what keeps this family driven. Without you I would likely have just hermitized up here on the mountain top. And imagine how boringly conventional our kids might have turned out."

She smiled brightly, patient as he took three large gulps of the wine.

"Mm, Kiera, this is good. Some of yours?"

"Uh huh. Made three years back."

"Aren't you having some?"

"The bottle is in the kitchen. I'll get some later."

After he drained the glass Kiera saw his eyes were growing glassy. He yawned.

Kiera took the glass. "Why don't you take a nap? There's nothing you need to attend to right now."

Wendell nodded and lay down. "Think I will. Love you."

His eyes closed and he folded a forearm over his eyes. Moments later he was snoring. Satisfied, Kiera carried the empty glass from the room.

Kiera found a length of corded rope in a junk drawer in the kitchen. This she stuffed into the back pocket of her pants and then made her way outside, where she walked to the far southern side of the property.

It was here the family kept the chicken coop and just a few yards away stood the goat pen. The chicken coop was a three-leveled structure with a posted barbed wire enclosure, while the pen was simply a shed with a surrounding wooden fence. While the coop provided the chickens ample space to stretch their legs, the enclosure gate was always kept locked. However, the gate for the enclosure around the goats' pen was left open during the daytime hours. This allowed the animals to come back and forth to eat grass or visit the little stream which ran through the woods on this side of the property. Currently the family owned six goats: Bobbin, an aged white and gray billy, along with three nannies and two kids.

As Kiera approached the pen she noticed two of the nannies with their babies wandering in the field by the edge of the woods. She scanned the area for a sign of Bobbin. Her attention was drawn to the cleared path Wendell had cut some years before so he could drive the truck in to collect firewood. The path only extended into the woods for about five yards. The goats often meandered on this path as they were fond of the thick moss and dandelions that grew abundantly there.

Kiera caught sight of a rough patch of white moving in the nearby trees and hedging the path. As she waited silently, she saw this was indeed Bobbin. He was sniffing tree roots and sampling the leaves of various small bushes, occupied with his munching and quite unconcerned with the other goats or Kiera.

This was as Kiera had hoped. Old Bobbin was rather protective of the others. Even stiff with arthritis in his legs, he could move quickly when he was agitated.

Kiera opened the pen gate and stepped into the enclosure. Entering the shed, she found Lily standing on the planks between the little stalls. Lily was the youngest nanny and arguably the prettiest, with a coat the color of chestnuts and a white star at the crown of her head. She was also pregnant.

Kiera stroked the nanny's chin. Lily's eyes closed, indicating she enjoyed the attention. "You're a sweet girl, aren't you, Lily?"

From her pants pocket, Kiera removed a length of cord. She made a simple loop knot at one end and slipped this over Lily's head. She adjusted it down over the nanny's neck and pulled it just tight enough to lead the animal.

"We're going for a walk now."

Grasping the end of the cord securely, Kiera led the trusting nanny out into the sunshine.

***

Behind the horse barn was a slant of thick shrubbery. The slant ended at the very border of their property. A high old rusty wire fence separated their place from the owners of the adjacent land. The owners of that property – a family who owned umpteen beagle hounds—kept their farmland well-maintained. Kiera thought their last name was Redmond, though she really wasn't sure. But she knew the family kept busy most of the year with their crops of corn, pumpkins and tobacco allotments. If one stood at the fence and looked out, there was more to view than just the little farm. From that point the entire next valley spread out before the eyes, giving a panoramic view of numerous houses and trailers, the trout pond beside the old Murray place, the First Baptist Church, and even the road that wound past The Woodsman and into Avonport.

On the Scruggs side of the fence was a small area between the horse pen and the initial shrubbery of the slant. The ground was quite fertile due to the rain that tended to wash down. Some years back, Wendell and Kiera had tried their hand at growing ginseng here. The soil had unfortunately proven to be too peaty for ginseng. But, as Kiera remembered, the earth had been soft and easily turned. Wild spring violets flourished here every year and the mugwort grew in abundance throughout summer and fall.

Lily was exhausted by the time they reached the foot of the slant. She was content to nibble at the last sprigs of violets as Kiera left her to go into the barn. The horses were both here, nuzzling each other's noses as Kiera entered. She gave them a good-natured hello but did not linger to stroke them. Instead, she walked past their stalls to the tool rack that hung on the wall beside the shelved gear board. From this she removed one of the round-point shovels. And from the top drawer of the board she took a long-bladed utility knife.

Kiera had honed the instrument just a couple of weeks before. Though she'd not had cause to use it since she was sure the blade was still sharp.

As she turned she saw the horses regarding her. They had ceased their nuzzling and as Kiera walked past them again, she heard Little Crest give a snort. It was a rough snort, an angry sound she wasn't accustomed to hearing from the gelding. For a moment she thought to stop and reassure him.

Ignore him, it's nothing, she told herself. *But it is time to show resolve as unbending as a steel web.*

On returning outside, Kiera found Lily chewing a plantain leaf. Lily paid no attention as Kiera laid the shovel to the side, nor did the little goat offer resistance when Kiera straddled her legs across her back. Lily was so oblivious to anything but eating she did not even flinch when Kiera's legs clenched about her swollen body.

But Kiera braced for a reaction as, with a left hand, she clutched the hair on the back of the goat's head and forced it back upon the neck. Only now did Lily offer a meek bleat. But to Kiera's amazement, the little animal remained standing peaceably between her legs.

Sweat broke over Kiera's brow as she placed the knife tip against Lily's throat. Kiera sucked in a breath and plunged the blade into the nanny's flesh. Lily bucked at once. As she struggled to wrestle free, Kiera yanked the blade across the width of her throat. The nanny gave a shudder as the blood gushed, and a shriek —wet and thick, airy and terrified at once—caught in her throat.. Kiera held fast as Lily crumpled between her legs.

Kiera watched as the blood poured over the ground. It even splattered over the toes of her old loafers.

She held firmly to the goat until she was sure the life had at last seeped from the body. Only then did she spread her legs and let the nanny's body sink to the ground. Kiera backed away a few paces. As the blood pooled around Lily's head Kiera's attention was drawn to the round, full belly. This twitched several times, indicating that the unborn kid was still alive.

A moment's regret gripped Kiera. But stronger than this sensation was the burning hatred for her enemies. If it were not for their interference in her and her family's affairs, she would have never thought to make this sacrifice.

It took several minutes before the unborn goat stopped moving. When Lily's womb was still at last, Kiera tossed the knife away. She knelt on the ground and dipped the fingers of both her hands into the blood-saturated grass. This blood she smeared across her brow.

Kiera closed her eyes. She focused on the dark and cherished face of her Cailleach.

"Dark mother, I make this sacrifice unto Thee," she prayed. "Please accept it along with the adoration of you I hold. In turn, most formidable One, I ask that you shield me from my enemies. Shield me from retribution, shield me from any and all lawsuits. Keep them from giving public exposure to my life and whereabouts. Dear Cailleach, grant me thy protection as I request. I petition thee in great need and make this sacrifice willingly, without remorse now or ever. So mote it be!"

Kiera got to her feet and took up the shovel. It took less than an hour of digging to make a suitable grave. The spot she'd selected was not a place her family members often had reason to visit. But she wanted to be sure it was deep enough so no wild animals would be tempted to molest the goat's remains and bring the carcass out into the open where somebody might possibly see it.

By the time the pit was ready, perspiration had pelted Kiera's body. She was also tired. But there was little time to waste, for although Wendell rarely even visited the horse pen, there was always the chance he might wake from his nap and come searching for her.

It took more backpower than she'd expected to pull the dead pregnant goat to the pit edge. Once achieved, however, all Kiera had to do was get the carcass deposited in the cool earth. She sat down on the other side of the corpse and, using both feet, gave it a hardy kick. This was enough to make the body teeter forward and fall over the edge. With a heavy thump the dead nanny fell into the freshly exposed soil.

Kiera shoveled loose earth over the body. When at last finished, she lay the shovel down and sat down beside the grave to catch her breath. Her mouth felt as parched as soda bread and she rued the fact she'd forgotten to bring something to drink.

But the rite was finished and done with. For this, she could congratulate herself. She also harbored no doubts Cailleach had accepted the sacrifice. Lifted now was the sense of dread Daniel's news had brought her. Whatever the antis planned to do with their videos, it would be left for the clinic board to contend with. Cailleach would be generous now that Kiera had again demonstrated her strength and resolution.

She got to her feet and brushed away the soil that clung to her forearms and the clunks that dirtied the knees of her trousers. Just as she reached for the shovel something fluttered in the peripheral vision of her right eye. Turning her head, she saw a dog standing in front of the shrubbery leading up the slant.

It was the same small dog with the plaid collar she'd seen some nights before. This time, she could determine it was indeed a mutt, with a mesh of dark tan and white hair. Its ropey tail was solid tan with a tuft of long, darker hairs at the very tip.

Kiera straightened and eyed the canine wearily. "What are you doing back? Don't you know it's dangerous for dogs to be up here?"

She expected it to start wagging its tail again. Instead, the dog bared its teeth and growled. Kiera had no idea how long the animal may have wandered around loose, but with her stress just newly relieved she did not care to waste any concern over a stupid dog. Especially not for one that growled.

She leaned down quickly and grabbed the shovel handle. Turning to the dog, she struck the ground in front of it with the blade tip.

"Get out of here, doggie!"

The dog responded by barking. Kiera shook the shovel blade at it.

"Go!" she shouted. "Get the hell out of here!"

The dog continued to bark. Kiera anxiously pounded the shovel blade over the earth again and again. At last the animal stopped barking and began to slowly move back. Kiera glared at it and waited. Finally, the dog shrank completely into the shrubbery branches. It was only a shade now, its little feet planted firmly in the dirt, its big dark eyes glinting at her from the shadows.

"Dumb thing," she snarled. "Keep hanging around here and my husband will shoot you for sure."

The dog seemed to melt into the very shadows where it stood. Kiera blinked, but she could not see it. There was no movement among the shrubbery to indicate the animal had moved further back. It was just gone as quickly as it had appeared.

"Sneaky little shit, aren't you?"

She was glad to be rid of it. Now she could return home, and there savor the knowledge her sacrifice had been perfectly executed.

Chapter 17

Wendell walked into the kitchen while Kiera washed the dinner dishes. He'd just returned from feeding the chickens and goats and making sure all the animals were penned up for the night. He was perturbed to report Lily was missing and admitted his first thought was that a pack of dogs had got to the nanny. But, he reported, there was no blood or anything else to indicate such a possibility.

He took a seat at the table. "I searched the wood where the goats all like to hang out. No luck. So I went down to where the scrubby southern slope starts down. I called but Lily didn't come. I am worried. That slope is so steep and pitted with those potholes. All those high scrub bushes, too, made it difficult to get a good look even with my flashlight. Tomorrow I'll have to go back. It was just too dark tonight."

Kiera dried her hands and walked over to him. "Tomorrow will be much safer for you."

Fret crumpled Wendell's brow. "I just wish she weren't so close to giving birth. Those potholes aren't deep, but in her condition, if she has tripped over one, she might have broken a leg, maybe even her neck. But as I said, with all the bushes out there, I can't tell."

Kiera massaged his shoulder. "What will be will be," she said coolly. "You can't feel responsible if a goat makes an unwise choice."

He smiled tiredly and conceded she was right.

Kiera awoke before Tally or Wendell the following morning. She felt charged with confidence and looked forward to finding a new outlet in which to focus her passion for activism.

As driven as she'd been in the work as clinic escort, she had guided the others long enough to feel secure they could get along without her. She was also confident that she didn't have to wear the pink uniform of a defender to be an activist for reproductive rights. Campaign Parenthood had always appreciated not only her work with the escorts, but also her generous donations and her participation in online forums. She was eager now to contribute her time to the organization in another capacity. And if that capacity excluded her pig brother's corporate interests, then all the better.

After drinking a cup of coffee Kiera got on her computer and visited the Campaign Parenthood website. She clicked the link that took her to the Professional Jobs page. Here there were listings for local strategists, media consultants, content designers and even nurses for local facilities the organization supported. At the very end was the header for the job listing for which Kiera felt she was qualified.

NOW TAKING SUBMISSIONS FOR CONTRIBUTING WRITERS! IF YOU LIKE TO WRITE AND ARE PASSIONATE ABOUT PROTECTING WOMEN'S REPRODUCTION RIGHTS, WE WANT TO POST YOUR STORIES AND ESSAYS!

She'd never read the complete listing before. As her eyes now pored over the entire thing, she learned that the pay was rather low, only five cents for each article per viewer hit. Kiera wasn't overly disappointed by this as financial compensation was her last consideration. She knew she could write a grammatically correct sentence and she certainly doubted the organization could find anyone more passionate than she when it came to the subject matter!

Kiera clicked on the provided link that read, CONTACT NOW TO SUBMIT AN ARTICLE PROPOSAL. This whisked her to a new page. Here, she found a single email address in black lettering. But right above this, in bright pink letters, was a short message: DUE TO A FULL SCHEDULE OF FORTHCOMING PUBLICATIONS, ARTICLE SUBMISSION PROPOSALS ARE CLOSED UNTIL OCTOBER 15TH OF THIS YEAR. UNSOLICITED PROPOSALS AND DOCUMENTS WILL BE AUTOMATICALLY DELETED FROM OUR SYSTEM.

"Well damn," Kiera grumbled.

This was definitely disappointing. There were, however, still plenty of other pro-choice websites around. She couldn't imagine they were all closed to writing submissions. Even if she were mistaken, there was nothing to stop her from creating her own blogging site dedicated to abortion. Although she wasn't a technical expert she did have the resources to hire someone to open and maintain blog pages for her. She also had the money to promote such a blog page.

She remembered, too, that both her daughters had some experience with video markets like YouTube. One of Tally's friends had a channel where he uploaded videos devoted to hallucinogenics throughout known history. Kiera imagined that she and Tally could learn all the technical know-how needed to create their very own videos. They'd buy the appliances needed and open their own liberal pundit channel! It would be pro-choice activism at its most state-of-the-art, where their voices would be available to a great many people.

We'll be social influencers, she thought, *and the hell with Daniel and his Board!*

Kiera heard Tally's and Wendell's voices from the kitchen. She turned off the computer and joined them. Wendell was in a hurry to go and continue his search for Lily, but he stayed long enough to let Kiera make them omelets.

As she set the plates on the table, Kiera told Tally she had something she wanted to discuss with her. Tally gave an agreeing murmur before taking her fork and devouring the egg. Kiera laughed, asking if Tally was starving.

Tally swallowed the bite in her mouth and wiped a morsel of egg off her lips with the back of a hand.

"Sorry. It's just that Braeden is coming to pick me up. We're going to the lake for the day."

Kiera was reminded of Skylar's insinuations about Braeden and of her own concerns that Tally might be doing drugs. This sudden announcement from Tally made Kiera wince. Quickly, she searched for something that might compel the girl to change her mind.

"You know," she suggested, "with your time freed up now, you might consider getting back to making jewelry for your online shop."

The truth was Kiera hadn't thought twice about Tally's little jewelry business. But she hoped mentioning it would inspire the girl.

Tally shrugged. "That can wait."

Kiera glanced desperately at Wendell. But she knew already he would never believe Tally used hard drugs. And by the worried, faraway look on his face, it was evident he was thinking about Lily anyway.

"I do hope you'll be back by evening, Tally," Kiera said. "There's something I want to talk over with you. Something potentially exciting."

"Potentially exciting?" Tally asked. "What about?"

"Just some ideas about how you and I can stay in the forefront of the cause. How we can become social influencers, stuff like that."

Tally grinned. "Sounds good. Tell me your ideas when I get home?"

Kiera's compulsive nature resented that the talk would have to wait. Even more galling was this postponement issued from Tally wanting to spend the day with a young man Kiera didn't exactly trust. At least Tally sounded interested in hearing her ideas. So Kiera patted her hand and told her to enjoy the visit to the lake.

After Braeden picked up Tally, Kiera found herself obligated to go help Wendell search the southern slope. The effort of looking for Lily was an exercise in futility, of course, and certainly not something she was willing to confess to her husband. They made a thorough walk down the slope, with Wendell checking behind every shrub and peering down every pothole. They shouted Lily's name until their throats hurt. Once Wendell was convinced the nanny was not here, he wanted to check the woods all over again. And when it was clear Lily wasn't in the woods he became bent on searching the rest of the property.

As exerting as the useless effort was, Kiera accompanied him. It was the only way she could ensure she was the one who inspected the ground behind the horse stable. After a couple of hours, they had covered the entire property. Wendell, his face red with angst, conceded that the search was a lost cause.

Kiera persuaded him to come inside. As she poured glasses of iced tea for the two of them Wendell sat down at the table. He slammed the tabletop with both fists and cursed loudly. He was convinced now some dog or pack of dogs must have dragged away or chased off Lily.

"I'm going back out to check all the fences," he fumed. "Replace any that are damaged or anything that appears even close to being damaged. And though I know how you feel, Kiera, I'm going to have to shoot every single damned dog I come across. They are killing our livestock, and that I will not tolerate!"

She set his glass on the table and gave his shoulder a pat.

"I understand, of course," she said empathetically.

With the house to herself in the early evening, Kiera used the time to mop the kitchen floor. She had just finished up when she heard the tone of her cell phone ringing from the bedroom. She walked in and picked it up from the dresser. Skylar's number is identified across the display.

Kiera tapped the answer button and bade Skylar a tepid hello. Skylar asked how she was. Kiera answered that she was well.

Skylar mentioned Tally had left her a brief text message about them being let go at the clinic.

"Did something happen, Mom?"

"Just politics," Kiera told her. "My brother and the Board have apparently decided they would rather cower from outsider intimidation than stand up for those who defend the rights of women."

After a few moment's silence, Skylar said, "This must have come as quite the blow. I know how important serving as a Pink Escort is to you."

Kiera found it difficult to believe Skylar gave a damn how she felt. "Yeah, well, their loss will be somebody else's gain. I don't plan to hide in the shadows or act mute when the reproductive rights cause still needs people with more balls than my brother. I will find another avenue to pursue."

"I don't doubt that," Skylar replied pleasantly. There was another second of silence and then Skylar asked how her sister and father were doing.

The rest of the conversation was stiff but cordial. Skylar told Kiera that she and Felix had got a kitten. She had also signed up for remedial classes at the Avonport Adult Education facility and these classes were to start the following month and last for five weeks. And that in the meantime, she was enjoying learning to cook Greek dishes. Kiera responded to all these things with dull murmurs.

When it seemed Skylar had run out of things to say, Kiera remarked, "Well Sky, it certainly sounds like you are well and couldn't be happier. I have some cleaning to get to, but it was nice talking with you."

There was a strained note now in Skylar's voice, "Okay Mom. Please give my love to Dad and Tally."

"Uh huh, will do. Bye." With a thumb, Kiera tapped the button to end the call. The conversation had left her once again irritated with her youngest. The girl had to be lying, there was just no way she could be as happy as she was making it out! How could any intelligent woman be happy living in the backward little town of Avonport? Or in living with Felix? Or in holding onto the delusion that she could find fulfillment without the guidance of a strong feminist role model?

Kiera threw the phone on the bed. It struck the mattress edge and bounced before ricocheting and falling to the floor. Her hands clamped into fists. In her momentary hatred for the phone, she was tempted to kick it straight across the room.

She decided instead it was more important to find something to eat. Anything that might calm the feeling of churning acid in her gut. So she left the phone where it lay and made her way to the kitchen.

Chapter 18

The phone conversation played out again and again in Kiera's head for the rest of the day. As she prepared dinner that evening she was so distracted that she didn't realize she'd made far too much soup until after she put the corn muffins in the oven. Only then did she really look at the concoction boiling on the stovetop—winter squash with chickpeas and bits of tofu. She had measured and sliced everything without really paying attention to what she had been doing. The vegetables and little blocks of frozen homemade tofu appeared to be fine (though in truth, she couldn't recall if she'd even rinsed the vegetables). She had added an excessive amount of water. And as she saw the bubbles slowly form, she remembered she'd forgotten to add corn starch to provide a brothy texture.

She sighed and hoped at least the corn muffins would turn out alright.

Wendell walked in just as she placed the finished pan of muffins atop a trivet on the counter. The vexed expression on his face warned he was in a sour mood and the sweat pouring down his brow and his ruddy complexion was worrisome. She took a can of cold soda out of the fridge and handed it to him.

"You've been working on the fences?"

The answer he gave was a mere muffled growl. He apologized almost immediately. "I'm sorry, don't mean to grumble at you. But yeah. Got as many repaired as possible while I still had light."

Kiera didn't realize herself that it had grown dark. Now as she glanced out the window she remembered Tally and wondered where she was.

She mentioned this to him. He was swigging down the soda and offered only a shrug.

"She and Braeden only went to the lake," he assured her, "not halfway across the globe. They'll be back soon."

Kiera asked if he was ready to eat. He shook his head and tossed the emptied can into the trash bin.

"What I want is a shower. And probably a nap. Save me some leftovers?"

Kiera was not a fan of eating meals by herself. Wendell knew this about her, too. But she saw how exhausted he looked.

"Yeah, sure."

"I hope you leave the dishes for Tally," he said. "You've worked enough today."

He kissed her cheek and went to the bathroom. Kiera stared glumly at her huge pot of soup. It would be simple enough to resent Wendell for leaving her alone since his exhaustion came from spending the entire blasted day worked up over the goats. But no, this wasn't his fault. He feared the other goats were under threat from dogs because he couldn't find Lily. Lily was gone because Kiera had a need for her to be gone. And who had created that necessity?

My enemies, she thought, *the antis. And the clinic Board. My weakling brother. Even Felix who stole my Skylar away!*

She reminded herself all this would be rectified very soon.

The ritual went perfectly and Cailleach rewards the strong. She knows my desire is as eager as the hungry spider's, my resolve as unbending as a steel web.

She felt a little better. With a smile, she ladled a serving of soup into a bowl and buttered herself a muffin.

After Wendell took a shower he fell asleep in bed. As the orange of the evening sky was replaced by darkness, Kiera grew more anxious that Tally wasn't home. When she tried calling Tally did not answer her cell phone. Disappointed, Kiera shot her off a brief text: *When are you coming home?*

At eight-thirty, Kiera went out to take care of the horses for the night. It was well after nine o'clock by the time she returned to the house. Wendell had wanted Tally to do the dishes, but there was no guarantee she would be back any time soon. So Kiera washed them, if just to keep her mind occupied and distracted from the worry for her oldest daughter.

After finishing the dishes, she stood in front of the kitchen sink and gazed out the window. As she waited for any sign of Braeden's vehicle coming up the driveway she noticed that her feet, especially her heels, began to ache inside her sandals. She was also aware that her arms, folded over the edge of the recently used sink, were wet. So was the front of her shirt.

Kiera realized she'd been staring out the window for some time. She cursed under her breath and knew she'd be more comfortable if she changed into a dry shirt. Maybe even change into some night clothes? She could watch the living room television until Tally got home. It was a good idea; she could open a bottle of wine and watch one of her favorite TV shows. Relax a bit while she waited.

Just as she started to turn from the window, a flash from outside caught her attention. She saw lights flickering through tree limbs and foliage surrounding the long, high driveway. A car was ascending. Kiera grunted and walked out to the lawn to wait. She had many choice words in mind for Braeden Wilcox. And probably some for Tally, too, once she was inside the house. Experience had taught Kiera it was better not to encourage the girl's volatile anger by scolding her in front of others.

The vehicle topped the driveway and veered slowly to a spot close to the family jeep. The headlights glared in Kiera's vision, making it impossible for her to make out much in detail about the vehicle. A few seconds later, the headlights turned off. Kiera took a few tentative steps forward. She blinked hard and was able to determine that this was definitely not the older Toyota Corona Braeden drove. No, this was a flatbed truck, and hitched to the mount was a horse trailer.

The driver opened his door and the interior dome light switched on. With a heartened little shock, Kiera saw it was Rory! He stepped out of the truck, his face bright with his familiar, beautiful smile.

"Hey Mom!"

"Oh thank Cailleach!" she cried. She ran forward and threw her arms around his neck. In that moment, every disappointment and aggravation she'd felt over the last several weeks vanished.

She heard a muffled laugh in her ear. "You're cutting off my air supply, Mom."

Kiera let go and wiped an unexpected tear off her cheek. He was home; her sweet, perfect boy was home!

Rory sat at the kitchen table while Kiera heated him some dinner. He said he wasn't very hungry, that he'd stopped on the road for lunch that afternoon. But he didn't turn down the leftover soup and corn muffins. Kiera thought he looked well. He didn't appear to have lost weight and he already had the golden tan he usually developed after working outdoors all summer. His full dark beard had been trimmed and styled into a Van Dyke. It was shorter than Kiera preferred, yet it was too becoming to fuss about. And his hair! His lovely reddish-brown hair, which she adored, was still longish, even though it was obvious it had been professionally cut and styled. He had never had his hair cut by anyone besides Kiera and she deemed it too short for her tastes. But she also couldn't deny the look was attractive.

After Rory finished the meal and said he was full, Kiera suddenly realized she had nothing for dessert. She offered to make something, perhaps pudding or his favorite cake.

"No, Mom, stop trying to feed me," he laughed. "Just sit down. Catch me up, tell me how everyone is?"

Kiera smiled and took a seat beside him. She told them they were all well, his dad, sisters and she. Next she gave an abridged version of the things he had missed while away: that his dad was planning the vegetable garden as he did every spring; Skylar had moved in with Felix; and that she, Wendell, Tally and Kerry had been barred, at least temporarily, from their work at the clinic. This last, she explained, was due to some stupid videos posted by certain antis. She also emphasized that the ultimate blame lay with her cowardly brother.

What she didn't divulge to Rory was anything about the video which showed the treatment dished out to Squinty McGimpy. Nor did she tell him about Tally injuring her head when she stumbled in an outrage and onto the street.

Rory shook his head when she was finished. "Wow. I missed quite a bit, didn't I? And I'm sorry about the clinic work. I know how much it means to you, Mom."

"It means a lot to all of us," she said. "You, too, of course?"

Rory gave a little shrug. "Mom, you've always felt a need to get involved in the things you believe in. And I've always been impressed by your passion."

Kiera felt such pride in him, unlike Skylar, who seemed bent now on contradicting everything dear to her.

She stroked his arm lovingly, and told him not to worry about her as she had other opportunities – probably even more dynamic ones—that would allow her to contribute to the issue of reproductive rights.

"Never forget though," he reminded her good-humoredly, "You and Dad vowed to one day write a book on the homesteading life. You two certainly have the experience in gardening, canning and self-sustenance."

Kiera did remember. "Some day we will. Maybe when your dad slows down a bit and I am satisfied I've made my contributions elsewhere."

A faint note of unease sounded in Rory's voice, "Dad's still a workaholic, isn't he? He really needs to slow down." He sighed and then mused, "And Skylar is living with Felix? Well, I knew they liked one another, though I didn't realize it was so serious. It's hard to imagine her living somewhere else. You were okay with this?"

Kiera waved a hand dismissively. "Your little sister is going through a certain stage, shall we call it? All uppity. She thinks she knows more about this world than her parents. It will do her well to find out the truth. And when she's done playing house with Felix, she will be back. Of this I have no doubt."

Rory looked thoughtful and said he hoped Skylar would be happy with whatever choices she made.

Kiera asked him to tell her about his adventures while in Kentucky, reminding him in a jovial way that, as his poor, concerned mother, she had the right to know about everything that had kept her child away for so long.

"Okay," he grinned. He sat back in the chair and folded his arms behind his neck. "The details will probably bore you though. And I guess you'll hear it all again when I get to see Dad."

"Go ahead," she urged, "tell me."

He started out his story by assuring her the Dutch Warmblood he had gone to check out had proved to be nothing like it had been described in the classified ad.

"The couple selling him didn't seem to know much about horses," Rory said. "I didn't find them dishonest, just ignorant. They didn't even have the correct form of breeder's certificate; just a handwritten note from the man who owned the mother."

Kiera knew it was just like Rory to be so generous about somebody's motives. If she had been the one to drive all the way to Kentucky in hopes of buying this horse, she would have sued the would-be sellers for false advertising.

"I was all set to just drive home then," he went on, "but the girl who runs the motel I stayed at told me about a Mr. Geelen, who is a breeder right outside of Raywick. She said Mr. Geelen raises a variety of breeds. So I took a chance and went out to his farm and ranch. He didn't have any Warmbloods, but he was a very friendly elderly man. Very talkative, rather lonesome, too, since his wife passed away. Mr. Geelen owns mainly Tennessee Walkers, Quarters and Paints. A couple of Icelandic ponies, too. Anyway, while we were chatting I mentioned I had come to look at that Warmblood and that my mother was a well-trained horsewoman. Told him how I have been riding your horses since I was a little kid, that you taught me quite a bit about them. After a while, Mr. Geelen said it was a shame I was coming back home as he was looking to temporarily hire someone to help around the stables. His granddaughter – or actually, his dead wife's granddaughter—helped him sometimes with the stables. He also had a hired man.

However the granddaughter had another job that required her to go out of town for a while. Just days after the granddaughter left the wife of his hired man was diagnosed with cancer and quit in order to take care of her. I felt sorry for Mr. Geelen. And I have to admit, I loved being around so many very nice horses. So I offered to stay and help him at least until his granddaughter came back."

"Always my charitable boy," Kiera beamed. "I do hope this Mr. Geelen at least paid you?"

Rory assured her that not only had he been paid nearly three hundred dollars a week, but Mr. Geelen had also given him a nice room and fed him very well.

"I think you'd like Mr. Geelen, Mom," Rory said. "One of the most decent people you would ever want to meet."

"I suppose the step-granddaughter showed back up?" Kiera asked.

Rory nodded. There was a subtle change in his expression that sent a suspicious chill across Kiera's flesh.

"Don't tell me this is the friend you mentioned was going to follow you here?"

He blushed. "In fact, she is. But please, before you get upset, Mom-"

"Upset?" Kiera echoed, self-conscious of the resentment already welling up inside. "Why would I be upset? You have a right to date whoever you wish, right?"

Uncertainty shone in Rory's face. "I trust you mean that. I know you had a rough going with the other girlfriends I've had."

Disdain lifted the corners of Kiera's mouth. "Of course, they were airheads."

Rory appeared as if he were digging for just the right way to address her comment. If this embarrassed him, Kiera didn't care. She knew it was her prerogative as his mother and the leading guiding force in his life to have high expectations about the kind of woman he dated.

"They are all in the past," he replied patiently. "But I like Jacey very much. She has a few years more maturity than other women I've dated. A few on me, too."

The words *older woman* screamed inside Kiera's head. She imagined some lecherous cougar after her baby. With much effort, she managed to keep her worry from being expressed.

"We get along so well, Mom. I care for her very much, and I hope you will give her a chance."

Kiera was torn now between what to be more angry about – that Rory had invited some aging floozy to follow him here all the way from Kentucky or that the floozy considered herself too good to make ride in the truck Rory had driven?

"I am always happy when you are happy, Rory, you should know this by now. But I thought the plan was that this Jacey would stay here. Why did she change her mind? Is it our home isn't good enough for the granddaughter of a horse breeder?"

"No, no," he said, "nothing like that. It's my fault. I assumed Jacey would stay here. But she explained she wants to meet my family before taking a bed with me under your roof. So I'm going to stay here tonight, while she has taken a room at a motel in Avonport. At least until you all get to know each other. Jacey is a very bright woman, Mom. We have a lot of fun together, too, share similar interests. It's only that she is a little on the shy side."

Not too shy to wrap my son around her little finger, Kiera thought. She could see, though, that Rory was very taken with this Jacey. If Kiera made a stink over her just yet then Rory could be tempted to drive off and join her in the motel in Avonport. No, what Kiera saw she needed to do was to meet Jacey. She needed time to gauge the young woman's personality and determine her weaknesses and flaws. In knowing these things (however small and perhaps otherwise insignificant they were) lay Kiera's hope to hone and wheedle them until they stood out like polished thorns on a dove's face. Twisted, sharp, ugly things that Kiera could make seem repulsive to her son.

Kiera forced a buoyant trill into her voice, "Perfectly understood. Not all women are going to be as outgoing or proactive as your mother, are they? But it will be nice to meet her. Especially since she seems so important to my son."

The tension vanished from Rory's face. "She is important, Mom. And I am so relieved you feel this way. Jacey is planning to drive up tomorrow from the motel. I really do look forward to her meeting you and Dad. Tally and Sky."

Rory took Kiera's hand and kissed it and told her how much he had missed her. She believed this was the truth. He was still her beautiful boy, her loyal son. This conniving Jacey obviously wanted to come between them and take her boy from her. But this, Kiera vowed silently to herself and to Cailleach, would never, ever be allowed.

Chapter 19

Rory was tired from the day's long drive and did not wait long to go to bed. After he'd said goodnight, Kiera took a shower and then tried again to reach Tally. But the girl did not respond to either text or phone call.

Kiera crawled into bed beside her still-sleeping husband. In her prayers she thanked Cailleach for returning Rory again, safe and well. She did not forget to ask the Dark One to watch over Tally and to bring her home soon.

"Keep Tally safe, bring her home," Kiera uttered softly in the dark. "Help her understand the importance of letting us know where she is, how she is." Kiera suddenly was overcome by the suspicion she hated most. This suspicion could not be avoided, no matter how Kiera wished it was just her mind acting out of some irrational fear, no matter how Wendell denied its justification.

She finished the prayer with an impassioned appeal, "And please, Cailleach, keep Tally, who walks so proudly in Your shadow, safe from herself. Keep her away from those that would supply her with harmful drugs. I beseech thee to protect my daughter in these ways. Please, dark Mother. So mote it be."

The prayer considerably eased Kiera's mind. Soon her conscious drifted into sleep's void. For a length of time she rested there, safe and devoid of worry. This was until she was roused by the whistling wind.

Kiera found herself in a room inside a spacious chalet. She admired the beautiful things that surrounded her: the great stone fireplace, the open wooden beams, the floors of solid marble. It was the type of eloquently rustic place she'd truly longed for, the very kind of house she believed Wendell could have built if he'd only had the patient temperament to hire skilled workers instead of insisting on doing everything himself.

She was seated at a hickory log sofa with leather-bound cushions. It was a grand and costly piece of furniture, even if the cushions were hard and uncomfortable. She perceived a current of air penetrating the walls. These were unusual walls, fashioned of latticed wrought iron and she knew somehow that the exterior of the house itself was constructed of wrought iron fitted with barbs sharp as syringe needles. She was also aware that the chalet had been designed in such a way that prevented the sun from fully infiltrating the interior rooms. Anyone who dared get close enough to the barbed lattice could see nothing inside but shadows. Thus, she was always safe here from the sun's glare and heat, and more importantly, the eyes of the curious.

The wind began to blow through the spaces among the lattice. It tossed itself about the room, chilling Kiera's skin here and there with its erratic, indifferent gusts.

She walked around a bit in an effort to cast away the chill and came to pause at the fireplace. On the mantle stood four photo frames. She knew they were supposed to hold pictures of her family: one for Wendell, the other three for their children. As she inspected them, however, she saw the photographs were nearly indiscernible as each image metamorphosed into a mirror.

Kiera's attention was suddenly distracted by an uncertain sound from outside. Looking to the near wall, Kiera saw through the iron-wrought lattice a figure ambling in the soft green grass outside. She squinted for a better look and realized it was a woman passing by. The woman was barefoot and wore a long, flowing dress. Her lengthy, flaxen hair, shining like gold from the sun, tumbled over her shoulders and down her back. She appeared to be cradling something in her arms.

The woman stopped in her stride. She turned and cast her clement countenance upon the chalet. Kiera knew this was no mortal woman. It was the goddess Frig, looking exactly as she had in the painting Kiera had seen in the room Micky had performed the fortune-telling. Yet this being was more than Frig, she was the embodiment of every softly feminine attribute that was obscene and contrary to Cailleach.

Even as Kiera was sure no human could possibly detect her behind the lattice, she felt this fair and graceful being clearly regard her. A breeze ruffled the cloth of Frig's gown and gently moved the golden tresses to expose what was cradled in her arms. It was a newborn goat, still wet with afterbirth.

With a little shock Kiera saw Lily step out from behind the length of Frig's gown.

The nanny bleated anxiously and the goddess spoke some comforting words to her. Lily hid herself again behind the gown and Frig once more regarded Kiera. It was a bold, unflinching look that made Kiera want to shrink away.

"Enjoy the sheltering protection Cailleach gives you," Frig told her. *"I would have instead offered redemption and strength beyond petty retaliation. But you choose to cling to*

*chaos which rewards hate with hate and revels in the despair it
brings."*

Kiera gasped. She could not bear these judgmental
words, especially from a goddess she loathed so dearly.
Turning from the lattice, she saw now she wasn't alone in
the chalet. Standing close by and looking as handsome as
he had the last time he'd held Kiera in his embrace, was
Anthony. Her Anthony – whom she had loved with an
abandon she'd never been able to feel for Wendell. This
passion had remained with her even after she and Anthony
had been torn apart by the act which sent them to prison.
While forgiveness had been an emotion Kiera generally
credited as weakness, the love she felt for Anthony had led
her to forgive him for the relationship he'd developed later
with a Lonely Hearts inmate pen pal. The corrections
department had allowed Anthony to marry that woman
while he was incarcerated. They had even let him
consummate the arrangement before he was executed. Yet,
Kiera's passion had never wavered.

She simply had found it impossible to blame Anthony
for that marriage. It was not his fault he had been isolated
from the rest of the world, that he'd had a need for the
touch of another human being. She understood loneliness
after she had been sent to the women's correctional facility.
For three years she'd been imprisoned. Then, after her
father convinced the State to give her early release, she
took up heroin and pills in order to deal with the separation
from her beloved. During this same time she threw her
energy into pleading with the State of Kentucky to
commute Anthony's sentence. Her efforts had proven futile
and they also had made for contention between her and
her father. But regret over these efforts she had never
known.

Now she saw a wistful smile come to Anthony's lips. He
raised an arm and Kiera saw he held a wicker basket. It was

a fancifully weaved thing, covered over with a spotless handkerchief.

In that voice she had missed so dearly, he said, *"The broker sent me with your receipt, babe."*

The statement confused Kiera. She asked him what he meant. The moment the words left her mouth she noticed a droplet of liquid seep out of the bottom of the basket. She knew this was dark blood and it clung for a moment to the wicker weave before falling to the floor. Another droplet oozed out and spilled down. A third, a fourth, more and more droplets poured out. In seconds blood was streaming from the base of the basket.

She didn't want to know whatever butchered and bleeding thing lay inside the basket. It was something she dared not lay eyes upon, something so terrible that her limbs quaked in dread.

"Please Anthony," she begged, *"please do not make me look at it!*

Kiera awoke. The bedroom was cozy and dark and her heart pounded wildly from the nightmare. Wendell snored peacefully with his back toward her. As distasteful as fear was to her, she scooted close against him. His warm, familiar form gave comfort. After a long time the things she'd seen in the dream faded enough that she was able to go back to sleep.

Kiera awoke in the morning to the smell of pancakes and the sound of laughter. The laughter seemed to come from the kitchen and the pancake smell had a fruity redolence to it. She assumed it was Skylar cooking in the kitchen as her youngest had frequently made pancakes for the whole family, always adding blackberries or blueberries or other fruit. Only as she sat up on the edge of the bed did Kiera's memory serve her better.

Skylar moved out.

But she had the happy knowledge Rory had returned home. She arose from bed and walked to the kitchen. The family was gathered here: Wendell at the stove, flipping pancakes on a skillet, while Rory pulled clean plates out of the cabinet. Tally sat at the table and both men listened as she talked.

"So after their dog got done sniffing Braeden's car," she was saying, "he told them, 'unless you know for a fact we threw weed to that duck, you'll have to take it to a veterinarian and have the poor thing dissected, won't you?' The dumb cops just shook their heads and went about their merry way."

Wendell chuckled at the story. Rory noticed Kiera standing there.

"Good morning, Mom."

"Mom!" Tally exclaimed, "You should have sent me a text or called to tell me Rory got in last night!"

Kiera noticed dark circles under Tally's eyes and her overall unhealthy blotchy complexion. Trying not to stare at the girl, she explained to Tally that she'd tried reaching her the night before.

Tally grinned. "I know. Just teasing you, Mom. Oh gosh, isn't this a wonderful morning? Rory's back, Rory's back! And Dad's over there making blackberry pancakes!"

Kiera nodded even as she knew Tally's exuberance level was off the charts. "You look like you could use some sleep, babe."

Rory began arranging the plates on the table. Tally skipped over to the utensil drawer, pulled it out and began removing forks and knives.

"I'm good," she assured Kiera, "good as gold! Gosh, what a beautiful morning!"

Wendell looked over at Kiera, contentment beaming in his face. "It was a very nice surprise to walk into the kitchen and find my son drinking out of the juice carton. I missed that, I truly did. And now we're sitting down to eat together. My favorite way to start the day."

It was apparent the three of them were happy. That happiness chased off Kiera's concern over Tally's stimulated emotions. She walked over to Wendell and slid her arms around his waist.

"My favorite way, too," she said and deposited a kiss on his cheek.

Chapter 20

It was a good breakfast with plenty of conversation. Bright and laughing conversation, the kind Kiera had missed. When the meal was over Wendell and Rory ventured outside to take care of the goats and chickens while Tally, surprisingly, stayed in the house to wash the morning dishes. After throwing on a pair of old jeans and a t-shirt, Kiera tended to her horses. When she returned to the house she found Tally was finished in the kitchen and had gone to her room. Kiera busied herself by making her and Wendell's bed. With this done, she proceeded to make Rory's bed as well. As she draped his bedspread in place she made a mental note to call Skylar in a short while. Even if her youngest had plans with her precious Felix, surely she would postpone them to come by and see her brother.

Once Kiera was satisfied with Rory's bed she returned to the kitchen. She found a whole frozen chicken in the freezer and placed it in the fridge to thaw. Next she poured herself another cup of coffee. As she pulled out a chair at the table she heard the sound of a car motor coming up the long drive.

From the window over the sink she saw Rory and Wendell out in the yard. They were unhooking the horse trailer from Rory's truck. A metallic gray compact hatchback sedan emerged at the crest of the drive. It was not a vehicle Kiera recognized and she watched with interest. Rory and Wendell moved away a little as the driver rolled into the patch of lawn at the other side of Rory's truck. There the sedan stopped and her husband and son approached.

As Kiera squinted to see the driver, she was distracted by the sound of muffled music just behind her. She turned to find Tally standing there. Her daughter's small portable CD player was looped about her neck by a plastic bead cord.

"You spooked me," Kiera said.

Tally turned off the music and joined her in looking out the window.

"Who is that, Mom?"

Kiera's attention returned to the unknown car. As the driver's door opened, Kiera was nearly startled to see Rory move quickly forward to offer a hand to the driver.

A young African-American woman stepped out of the car. Not just any young African American woman, either, but a very pretty one, with a lithe figure complimented by a soft yellow jumpsuit with what appeared to be satin shoulder straps. The young woman had a long, very elegant throat and her hair was pulled back and weaved into a thick braid that reached her hips. She wore on her feet a pair of sandals with high wedge heels.

Kiera might have laughed derisively over the woman's chic –and so overtly feminine—taste in wardrobe. But then she saw Rory lace his arms about her narrow waist and pull her into an embrace. Kiera knew this was that Jacey he'd spoken of. Her scorn for the clothing was forgotten at once. The only thing Kiera cared to see now was for this woman to get back in the sedan and leave.

She heard Tally observe, "Must be the girlfriend Rory talked about."

Kiera felt building rage. Yet, it was a torn rage, for she hadn't expected a black woman. The politically correct defender inside her knew it wouldn't be easy to show her true feelings without the chance they could be misconstrued as bigotry.

"You're going to have your work cut out this time," said Tally.

"What do you mean?"

"She's black. You can't be rude to a black girl. That might come across as racist."

Kiera tried to ignore the possibility Tally had guessed her concern. "What a silly thing to say. What makes you think I'd want to be rude to her?"

Tally gave a wry smile. "Because she's dating your Rory."

Kiera summoned a confused look. "So? You have your dates, too."

"Yeah, but I'm not Rory. It wasn't me or Skylar you nursed at the tit for ten years. We only rated four years."

Kiera sniffed at the insinuation. Before she knew what to say, however, Tally added, "I'm not jealous, Mom, I know by the time I came along, Dad was giving you grief over all the breastfeeding. But still, Rory is your little boy. And I also know there is no woman on earth that can ever hope to measure up to his mother."

To Kiera's dismay, she noticed Rory kiss the young woman. Then he gestured an introduction to his father. Wendell shook the young woman's hand and the jovial expression on his face was almost too much for Kiera to bear.

That conniving slut!

At her side, Tally mused quietly, "I'm just saying it won't be as easy as coming between Rory and the other women he dated. I can tell just by the way Rory is looking at this one it'll be trickier this time."

Before heading back to her room Tally said she'd make a point of meeting Rory's girlfriend in a little while. Kiera was exasperated at the idea of meeting this Jacey. Yet she knew it was inevitable. She reminded herself to be composed and polite, and most importantly, to observe and listen to the things Jacey revealed in conversation. In this way she could glean what was needed to know about the woman's vulnerabilities and shortcomings.

Kiera drew a deep breath. She put on a pleasant expression, stepped outside and joined the little group by the vehicles.

"Oh, hey there," Rory greeted her. "Mom, this is Jacey." He glanced at Jacey and said, "This is my Mom."

The young woman looked at Kiera with a pleasant smile and extended a hand. "It's nice to meet you, Mrs. Scruggs. Rory has talked so much about you!"

By the bloom of youth in Jacey's face, Kiera knew she wasn't that much older than Rory. No more than a few years, surely. Kiera also noted Jacey had applied her make-up lightly but meticulously, and her cologne –some floral scent–wafted delicately in the air. There was also a wide yellow lacy ribbon pleated throughout her braid and her fingernails were long (professionally manicured, Kiera surmised). These were, like her toenails, painted the same shade of buff pink as her lipstick. To Kiera, these details denoted a shallow dumbbell in every way. She reasoned that all the young woman needed was blonde hair to be complete.

No doubt she shaves her legs and armpits, too! Kiera thought with animosity.

Kiera accepted the handshake. "Nice to meet you, too, Jacey. We've heard many good things about you."

"Oh, thank you," Jacey replied. "I was just telling your husband that you all have some beautiful property. And your house is so pretty. Rory told me you two built it yourselves?"

"Primarily Wendell," Kiera said. "He's a very hands-on man."

Wendell stepped over to Kiera and stretched an arm across her shoulders. "It was a mutual labor of love, Jacey. While I pride myself on being able to hammer and nail almost anything and I do have an electrician's license, Kiera has an eye for design. We drew the blueprint ourselves. And I'm glad to say my wife has never been afraid of hard work. She tiled the bathroom and stained cabinets and did practically all the indoor painting herself."

Jacey's eyes widened a bit. "How impressive! I don't think I could paint a straight line on a wall to save my life."

Weakling, Kiera thought, *Pampered little diva!*

But she did not express this. Instead, she suggested she should bring out some iced tea for everyone.

"That'd be nice," Wendell said. "Rory and I can gather up a few more lawn chairs from the storage building and set them up next to the chaise loungers. Unless you need me to help bring out the tea?"

"I got it," she assured him. "And while I'm inside, I will ask Tally if she'd like to join us."

Kiera noticed Jacey touch a finger to her pretty powdered chin. A puzzled glint sparkled in the young woman's eyes as she said, "I guess it's because Rory has spoken so much about you, Mrs. Scruggs, but it almost feels like we have met before. But that can't be, can it?"

Kiera nearly laughed. "I am sure I would remember if we had, my dear."

Kiera brought out a jug filled with iced tea and several plastic cups. Tally had indeed decided to join everyone. She had even taken a shower and changed into a voluminous thin denim dress (it was the olive-and-yellow tie-dyed one Kiera had made for her some years before) and a pair of flip-flops. Her hair was pinned back in a loose bun. It was obvious that Tally's mood was much less frenetic than it had been at breakfast.

Kiera noticed that while she'd gone for the tea, Rory and Jacey had set their chairs practically side by side. Conspicuously close, she deemed, and suspected Jacey had decided on this closeness just to send Kiera a visual message.

Wendell asked Jacey about her drive from Kentucky and if she'd ever been this far from home.

"My job takes me all over the south," Jacey said. "Though I must say, I doubt I've seen a much prettier region than here."

Tally asked Jacey what kind of work she did.

"I am a representative for a veterinarian medical supply company. Vet Bio-Sup. Maybe you've heard of them?"

Wendell nodded. "Ah yes. Out of Atlanta, aren't they?"

Kiera listened as Wendell and Jacey talked at length about the young woman's life and family back in Kentucky. Although Kiera made all the polite facial gestures necessary to feign interest, she found the conversation tedious and several times had to suppress a yawn. She also saw she wasn't the only one not impressed, for Tally looked even more bored. At one point Tally kicked the flip-flops off her feet and used her toes to pluck blades of grass out of the soil.

"So after my mother died," Jacey was saying, "I went to live with her mother. My Granddad died when my mother was quite young. And then, after Grandmom married again—to Mr. Geelen—the two of them adopted me."

Wendell made an empathetic sound. "I'm so sorry you lost your mother, Jacey."

Jacey's mouth turned up in a smile that struck Kiera as nothing less than ingratiating. "Thank you, Mr. Scruggs. But I was lucky. Grandmom and Grandpa were wonderful to me. And I'm lucky to still have Grandpa. We're very close."

"I know my son thinks the world of the man," Wendell said. "And it was very generous of him to give Rory a job and a place to stay during his sojourn."

Jacey gave another smile and said she was grateful Rory had been there for her grandfather while she was away.

"The job with Vet Bio-Sup pays well," she admitted, "but I don't see making a career of it. I want to move back home soon or at least close to home. Grandpa is getting up there in years. He needs me. And there are other things I'd rather do with the rest of my life besides selling veterinarian medications."

Kiera knew she needed to rouse out of her stupor and at least once give the impression she was interested in Jacey's life.

"Oh?" she asked, "Do you have a game plan, Jacey?"

Jacey sipped from her cup and told her, "Grandpa owns some residential property in Raywick and he always said I can take over as manager whenever I want. I might do that. But whatever I do, most importantly, I want to be close to him. And I want to make time for a family. Family should mean everything, you know?"

This struck Kiera as an unusual way to put the sentiment. As she pondered over this, she saw Rory reach for Jacey's hand and bring it to his lips. The endearing glance they cast one another sickened Kiera. Her son was smitten, truly smitten.

"Agreed," Wendell observed in a sage-like voice. "In the end, family matters most."

The comment didn't sound overly typical of Wendell and Kiera wondered if he was just being condescending.

"I don't know," Kiera offered. "There are responsibilities we all owe society. If we don't do our part, this world has no hope of seeing changes for the better."

"Responsibilities?" Jacey asked. "Like what, Mrs. Scruggs?"

"Mrs. Scruggs?" Kiera laughed. "No, no, call me Kiera. Mrs. Scruggs was my mother-in-law. But as an obviously intelligent young woman, Jacey, you surely understand we must all be stewards for a better world. Every person must start sustaining themselves as much as humanely possible. We have to stop the reliance on fossil fuels. We have to once and for all reject the artificial moralities of the old and decaying Western culture."

Jacey gave Rory an uncomfortable glance. "I suppose, Mrs. Scruggs – sorry, *Kiera*."

Rory chuckled. "You'll find my parents are very passionate on some topics."

"I recall you telling me," Jacey said.

It felt to Kiera as if the two were patronizing her. She reproached Rory, "These things are important, Rory, you know this."

Rory's jaw tightened, but he did not reply. Kiera eyed Jacey soberly and said, "You see, Jacey, for those of us who are educated and who are privileged with the financial means and opportunity, it is our ethical obligation to act as social stewards. Social stewards to set the example for those not so fortunate. It's all well and good to talk about the importance of family, but without the boldness it requires to help society meet its potential, humanity will continue to live in oppression."

Jacey looked at once uncertain. "If I may ask, how do you go about being social stewards?"

"That's probably a deep pool to dip into right now," Rory said. "What say we leave this discussion for another time, hm?"

Before Jacey could respond, Kiera chided her son, "But your girlfriend asks a good question. And I'll give her a succinct answer." Looking at Jacey, she explained, "My family and I have been very proactive about women's reproductive rights. In fact, we have invested years in defending and advocating the cause. And I hope anyone my son dates will be just as supportive."

"Ah," Jacey replied, "if you mean subsidized gynecological care for underprivileged women, most certainly."

Tally looked up and abruptly interjected, "Abortion. She means abortion."

A disquieted shadow passed over Jacey's face. It was short-lived, lasting no more than a second, but it scattered the clement glow from her pretty face. This elated Kiera. For if Jacey was repelled by abortion, it seemed the logical course of events would inevitably lead to contention over the subject between her and Rory.

Jacey replied, "Rory had mentioned his family are proponents of abortion. And that he used to help his family at a clinic here in your town."

The implication confused Kiera. She glanced at Rory. "What does she mean by *used to*?"

Rory seemed hesitant to respond. But at last, he said, "Mom, I told you I've always been impressed by your passion. This is true. But the abortion defender thing, I'm sorry, it is not for me anymore."

Kiera sucked in a startled breath. "You can't be serious?"

"I am, Mom. I told you I want to find work, real paying work. Besides, I've had a lot of time to think. And I realize I just don't share your and dad's passion for abortion."

Kiera felt the ire rise hot to her skin. Such a statement could not have been made her son! No, no, these had to be the words of the busybody stranger. She drew a slow inhale of air to calm herself. And once exhaled, she extended Jacey as benign a look as she could muster.

"So I can thank you for convincing my son women shouldn't have reproductive rights?"

Jacey answered with a ring of polite but noticeable exasperation, "To be perfectly honest, Kiera, I feel labeling the practice a *reproductive right* is expressly oxymoronic."

"Expressly oxymoronic!" Tally whispered, giggling softly as she enunciated each syllable.

Wendell threw Tally an admonishing look and brought a finger to his lips.

Tally ignored him. Instead she continued to giggle as she said, "What a shame you're okay with being a traitor to women."

That's my girl! Kiera thought proudly.

But Rory bristled. "Tally, that's uncalled for!"

Tally stuck her tongue out at him and mocked him, "Uncalled for! Uncalled for!"

Jacey looked shocked. In a shaking voice, she said to Tally, "Would you like to know what a real shame is? A real shame is that my younger sister died before she was born and my mother along with her. You see, they were killed; their lives ended by someone who thought they didn't deserve to live. Tally, you want to talk about being a traitor? It would be traitorous indeed for me, and more so downright cold-blooded callous, if I didn't care that every single day hundreds and thousands of other babies are denied their right to life— just like my little sister was denied."

The comment doused Tally's amusement. As a heavy quiet fell over the yard, Kiera felt almost remorseful about how the discussion had veered. Oh indeed, she was disgusted by Jacey's take on abortion and she would never quietly step aside to let another woman steal her son. The knowledge Jacey's mother had been murdered, however, was something that touched her as profoundly disturbing. As Kiera tried to think of the appropriate thing to say, she couldn't help but feel sorry for the young woman. And there was something about her wide, ingenuous eyes, even the way she sucked ever so lightly on her bottom lip, that Kiera seemed to recognize. Something that seemed sweetly, almost painfully, familiar.

Perhaps, she considered, *that as a mom, I just can't bear to see any child deprived of their own mother. Nor one so blinded because of a cruel loss.*

She wondered if it were fate that had brought Jacey and her son together. Had fate compelled this young woman to follow Rory all the way from Kentucky? Perhaps indeed fate decided Jacey just needed a proper role model, a woman with the knowledge to enlighten her about the world and the truths within it.

I can be that woman, Kiera thought. *I will be that woman! Enlightening her can only bear prolific fruit.*

"I had no idea," Kiera said. "I am so sorry you lost your mother, Jacey. Especially under such circumstances!"

Wendell, whose face was now creased with pity, chimed in with similar words.

Tally's mouth had twisted, her arms were crossed, and a dubious glint shone in her eyes as she regarded Jacey. But at last, she said, "That had to be rough. Really. Maybe we should just talk about something else?"

"You think?" Rory snapped.

"Geesh, how was I supposed to know?" Tally said defensively.

Jacey spoke diplomatically, "It's alright, Rory. What say we just put this particular conversation behind us?"

They all murmured agreement to this idea. Still, Kiera could see the conversation had left Jacey uneasy. Rory smartly suggested he take Jacey on a tour of the property. The proposal instantly brightened Jacey's face.

"If this is alright?" he asked Wendell and Kiera.

"Of course," Kiera answered for them both.

Jacey said she'd like a tour very much. They set their cups to the ground and got to their feet. Rory took her hand into his and together, they walked away and around the corner of the house.

With the pair out of sight Tally complained she couldn't believe her own brother could have ended up dating an *airhead*.

Wendell shook a scolding head. "Don't be so quick to judge, Tally. That isn't how you open somebody's mind. You must remember Jacey wasn't privileged to be born white. We have to be more understanding even while we are lucky enough to be more informed."

Tally groaned and threw Kiera an imploring look.

Kiera, though she couldn't care less about Jacey's ethnicity, advised similarly, "I'd wager there is still hope for Jacey. We just have to work on her. With finesse and patience, of course."

Chapter 21

While Rory and Jacey took their extensive walk Tally disappeared to her room and Kiera returned to the kitchen. From the fridge she took the chicken she'd set out earlier and used the microwave to finish defrosting it. She prepared the chicken for baking –with lemongrass and garlic seasoning—before placing it into the oven. She opened a jar of her canned green beans and poured them into a pot. Once the beans were at a boil, she set the temperature to simmer. After this she took plates, flatware and napkins to the dining room. The plates were part of her prettiest dinnerware set, eggshell white stoneware with scalloped rims. The flatware was from her rarely used gold layered collection. She set the table neatly, careful to lay the flatware out over the folded napkins as she remembered watching Dorothy do. The nicest of her glass tumblers she set in the appropriate spot above the plates.

A jug of lemonade she took to the table and then found a fresh loaf of sourdough bread in the pantry. The loaf she placed on a silver-plated tray before carrying it to the dining room table. Onto a butter dish from the same pattern as the plates, she put a cake of fresh butter. This, along with a bread carving knife, was carried to the table.

She brought in next two of her best fabric cozies. Atop one of these she put the serving bowl full of the beans. She washed a bunch of lovely red grapes as well and arranged these on the table in an old-style carnival glass bowl.

The oven timer went off shortly after the table was readied. Kiera removed the chicken from the oven and used a serving fork and carving knife to make a slice into the meat. Satisfied it was thoroughly baked, she used the fork to transfer it onto a serving dish that matched her dinnerware. She carried the dish of chicken to the dining room and placed it atop a second cozie on the table.

Kiera stood back to inspect her work. It had been a long while since she'd put so much effort into a meal. What she saw pleased her. Even if Rory's girlfriend didn't like her cooking, nobody could say his mother neglected to set an appealing table!

It crossed her mind suddenly that she'd forgotten to contact Skylar. Unless Tally had thought to text or call her sister that day, then Skylar still didn't know Rory was back. Kiera preferred to have her youngest at home for this dinner. But there had been much going on, she realized, and she could always get hold of Skylar that night.

On returning to the kitchen, she opened the door and shouted Wendell's name. He jogged up moments later. There was a lazy curl of a smile on his lips and his eyes were slightly but tellingly bloodshot.

"Time for dinner?" he asked hopefully.

"Yes," Kiera said. "Now if you will just find Rory and Jacey and bring them in? I'll get Tally."

As he walked off to find the pair Kiera made her way to the foot of the staircase and called for Tally.

"Time eat, Tally!"

A few minutes later the five of them were all gathered in the dining room. To Kiera's unspoken elation, Jacey admired the table.

"Everything is so lovely, Kiera," she said. "I hope you didn't put yourself out for my sake?"

Kiera made a dismissive gesture. "It was nothing!"

Tally chortled. "Nothing? I can't remember the last time I saw that dinnerware. And I didn't even know we had gold flatware."

No one responded to this, though Kiera caught the cross look Wendell shot their daughter. Tally snickered lightly but thankfully made no further quips. As the rest of them took a seat, Rory pulled out a chair for Jacey. This gesture certainly wasn't something either Wendell or Kiera had taught him. Oh, Rory had heard them laugh about such antiquated, so-called gallant practices, but it appalled Kiera to see him actually do such a thing.

So demeaning for both of them, she thought. But she was in a good mood and decided not to question Rory about it until she could be alone with him.

She barely thought of it again during dinner. The food was well-appreciated by all and Rory boasted about Kiera's cooking skills and also of her experience as a trained horsewoman. Jacey became animated over this topic as she had been raised around the horses her step-grandfather bred.

Wendell mentioned how Rory had been singing Mr. Geelen's praises just that morning.

"He sounds like a very nice man," Kiera added.

Jacey beamed. "Grandpa Waylon sure is. My mother's father died before I was born and I never got to meet him. But Grandpa Waylon has always treated me like I was his own blood kin."

Jacey showed a genuine inquisitiveness about Rory's childhood. She asked Wendell and Kiera what he was like as a child. Had he changed much over the years? Wendell and Kiera both enjoyed this subject. After a time the conversation drifted from this to that, all light and painless topics. By the end of the meal even Tally's demeanor had turned amiable.

The sun was beginning to set when Kiera remembered she had nothing fitting to serve for dessert. She apologized for this and asked if anyone wanted some cookies.

"Instead of that," Wendell suggested, "how about s'mores? I need an excuse to clean the winter clutter off our bonfire spot anyway. It won't take me long to get this done and then find some suitable branches to start a fire."

The idea was well-received. Rory offered to help.

"Nah, I need to work off some tryptophan," Wendell answered. "I stuffed myself on that chicken. You and Jacey just stay and chat with your Mom."

Tally smiled. "I guess that's a hint I should wash the dishes?"

Wendell winked at her. "Wouldn't hurt her feelings, I'm sure."

He got up from his chair and left the room. Seconds later the door leading outside was heard to open and close. Tally stood up and clasping her hands together over her head, twisted to her left so that a succession of *pops* rippled up her spine. With a swivel to her right, a few more of the vertebrae cracked.

"Okey dokey," she announced, taking up the bowls with the remaining beans and the grapes. "This scullery maid is off to the kitchen to scrub the pots and pans."

Rory chuckled. "Poor pitiful you, huh?"

After Tally carried the vessels to the kitchen, Rory rose and reached for the serving dish with the remaining chicken.

"I can take that," Kiera said.

Rory shook his head. "Sit, Mom. You've done enough. Besides, I remember how badly Tally scrubs pots. I'll give her a hand with them."

He blew a little kiss to Jacey as he passed with the serving dish. From the kitchen, he and Tally engaged in light-hearted chatter and Kiera heard Rory laugh over some jest Tally made.

"Rory is such a good son," Kiera murmured aloud.

Mindful of Jacey sitting in the chair opposite hers, she felt a self-conscious flush.

"Forgive me for boasting about my children," she told Jacey. "I can't help it. They are great kids."

"No need to apologize for that," Jacey said. "I look forward to meeting your other daughter, too. Skylar, is it?"

"Yes, Skylar." Kiera felt obligated to offer a white lie or two. "I tried giving her a call to let her know Rory is back, and to tell her you were coming for a visit. But she didn't pick up and her voicemail was full. I will try again tonight."

"I hope she can come by before I leave."

"How long do you plan on staying?"

"Just a few days," Jacey answered. "Grandpa will start worrying something fierce if I'm gone too long."

Kiera understood all too well worrying about one's children. And she felt a note of trepidation thinking Jacey might expect Rory to join her on a return trip to Kentucky.

"But you'll be coming back?" she asked.

The question brought a blush to Jacey's cheeks. "I imagine so, yes. And Rory has promised to visit me in Kentucky, too."

"So it'll be a long-distance relationship?"

"Maybe not for too long."

Kiera forced a smile she could not feel. "Are you two talking marriage already?"

Jacey blushed again. "Something like that."

"Ah." Kiera sensed she should make some comment about this uncertain answer, but she had no idea what to say. She didn't want to give false encouragement nor let Jacey assume she was the type of mother who would quietly sit back while some other woman sought to take away her son through marriage. At least not yet. That could wait until Kiera had time to fix the young woman's screwed-up ideas about abortion.

To her relief, Jacey started some small talk about the dining room. How nice the layout was, how she enjoyed the view of the purple and red setting sun through the bay window. How she looked forward to seeing the rest of the house when it was convenient for Kiera and Wendell.

Jacey's focus turned to the weathered bookcase where the family photos were displayed. "And that, now that is gorgeous! Look at all the family pictures!"

Jacey got up from her seat and walked to the bookcase. Kiera watched as the young woman smoothed a fingertip over the frame of one of Rory's baby photographs. Rory had been almost 18 months old when Kiera snapped this particular picture. It had been morning and they were in the kitchen; he'd been wearing a little tie-dyed tee shirt and a straw hat Kiera had made for him. Kiera loved this photograph, for it had perfectly captured Rory's cheerful, cherubic toddler smile.

Jacey mused, "I can tell this was Rory by that beautiful smile. And oh," she touched the photo of Kiera sitting out on the old metal rocking bench with Rory in her arms. "This was Rory, too?"

Kiera smiled. "He was about three weeks old there."

"So sweet!"

Jacey admired the other photos with sincere interest. As she asked about each photo, Kiera was only too happy to tell her about them.

Yes, that couple is Wendell and me. It was taken during our honeymoon at Linville Falls. A woman rooming at the same inn we stayed at was kind of enough to take the photo.

That little rascallion straddling the tricycle, her hair in braids? Why that is Tally. Yes, that's Skylar in that one, kneeling under a tree at the age of seven. The calico cat at her side was named Miss Smoke. It broke poor Sky's heart when she ran off.

The old couple there? That's Wendell's parents, Edith and Hanson. No, they're both gone now. They had him when they were already middle-aged. That pretty woman with the long hair and mod 60's miniskirt? That was my Grandma Lucinda, my father's mother. Yes, she was quite fetching, thank you. A horse of a different color, that one! The little boy and girl? That's me with my brother Daniel. No, you're right, we never favored very much. Oh, and the picture there, that's Wendell with his plow and mule. That was the first garden we had here. The mule's name was Elvira. Poor thing died only last year.

Jacey smiled and she touched a frame on the fourth shelf. It was a photo of some of the women Kiera had worked with back when she was still a member of the Avonport La Leche League. She waited for Jacey to ask about it when the young woman's attention was drawn to the frame standing to its right. This was the photo of Anthony Leyton Johnson. Jacey blinked. She lifted the frame and stared at Anthony's picture. The good humor in her expression dissolved.

"Jacey? Is something wrong?"

The moments waiting for Jacey to answer seemed to stretch into silent years. Kiera heard from the distance the sound of a pot clang against the kitchen sink, followed by Tally fussing and Rory teasing her about whatever had happened. Soon they were both laughing, and whatever they said betwixt one another Kiera found impossible to heed. All she knew was that this look on Jacey's face made her uncomfortable. She felt like snatching the photograph out of the young woman's hands.

Jacey looked at Kiera. Her eyes were wide with distress and her voice chary as she stammered, "Oh, oh my god...you are Kiera Phillipa Hambrick!"

Each uttered syllable of Kiera's maiden name felt as if they had been pummeled into her head. She had never expected to hear the name spoken aloud again. She'd stopped using her middle name years ago. Her kids didn't even know it. As far as her father's surname went, once she was married she was relieved to put *Hambrick* in the past. She had gone so far as to swear Wendell into never mentioning the old name to anyone.

How could this young woman know her full name? Certainly, there were plenty of pay-for-detective agencies online that one might use to forage personal information. Yet Kiera suspected one had to know the person's complete identity for any of these services to be worth using. She realized Rory must have told his girlfriend enough about his family that Jacey, for whatever reason, had hired someone to dig into her past. This thought was devastating. If Jacey had used a detective service, then she already knew her boyfriend's mother had been involved in a controversial Kentucky crime case. A case that happened in the very county Jacey lived in.

Kiera felt sick. If all this were true then it was also likely Jacey had taken whatever information she'd got and hunted Kiera up on the Kentucky State corrections department website!

But why, Kiera wondered fearfully, *what's it to her?*

"Why," she forced herself to ask, her mouth feeling arid now, "do you ask me this?"

Jacey tried returning the photograph of Anthony back to the shelf, but her hands trembled so much that the frame dropped out of her grasp and to the floor. Kiera instinctively stooped to snatch it up. As she rose to her feet and hugged the frame to her breast, her distrust of Jacey was now mixed with ire. She was just about to demand again Jacey tell her the reason for her question, but she was silenced by the strange glower in Jacey's wide eyes.

A gasp quivered in Jacey's throat. "I knew there was something familiar about you." She wagged a finger at Kiera's shocked face. "I just never made the connection until…" Jacey glared at the frame Kiera held so fiercely. "My father told me you were a friend. 'Miss Philly' as he called you."

Miss Philly. Hearing the pet name turned Kiera's feet to lead. It was a name she had not heard in decades. Not since the last time she had seen Anthony; on the morning of the day the police came and arrested them both. It had been the last time the two of them had shared a private conversation. The last time Kiera had felt Anthony's arms around her. The arrival of the police had been a shock, and she remembered how they had torn Anthony out of her arms. She could still hear herself screaming at them, calling them pigs, telling them to go to hell. Fresh in her memory was the tinny clang of the handcuffs as they were snapped around her wrists. She and Anthony never shared a private moment together after this. For after all the respective charges had been filed and after she had been bailed out by her father's attorney Charles Rogers, the only time Kiera laid eyes on Anthony again was the day she was compelled to testify in court against him.

Kiera suddenly remembered something else about the last day Anthony and she were together: the sound of his little daughter Jacqueline crying from the kitchen. She had sat at the table eating cereal when the officers' knock sounded at the door. In being torn apart from Anthony, Kiera had forgotten all about the girl. She did not think about her much afterward, no, it was too painful, because she had liked little Jacqueline. She had entertained fantasies of being a new mother to the little girl, of building a relationship with her after her mother was buried and forgotten, once Kiera and Anthony were wed.

And now Kiera recognized trusting, pretty little Jacqueline in the face of the woman who stood before her.

I must be mistaken, Kiera screamed silently. *This surely can't be!*

"Yes, something familiar about you," Jacey repeated, her voice thick with rancor. "I remember he took me to that trailer you lived in, Miss Philly, the one just outside of town. I had never met you before, but he said you were going to babysit me for a while. Babysit me, because Mama wasn't feeling well and he had to go visit his great Aunt Martha. He said the old lady was very sick. And here I had never even met this Aunt Martha! I wasn't more than five years old at the time, was I? But I remember you heating me up a TV dinner and giving me a big glass of lemonade. You played Old Maid with me. Later you brought me a pillow and covered me up with a yellow robe because you had only one blanket for your own bed. I remember that robe. It was silky, real soft. And I fell asleep and didn't see Daddy again till the next day. He stayed there with us, too, in those couple of days afterward. Until the police came. After they arrested him, they turned me over to child services until my grandmother could take me. I never saw you again. But I learned your full name. After it hit the news, everybody in the neighborhood knew your full name. Everybody in the whole damned county. My grandmother kept all those articles, you know? I read them when I was about twelve years old. And there in several of those newspaper clippings was your photo, right next to his and those two awful men he hired to put a bullet through her head. I tried not to think about you after reading those articles. I truly did. Yes, I'd heard some people say you and my father met when you enrolled in the riding school in town where he worked. But I didn't like to think about you. Of course, I didn't like to think about him either. And I never made the connection with the name after meeting Rory. But who would? It's not like Kiera is that uncommon, is it? There have to be many women named Kiera, right?"

Kiera realized she was hyperventilating. She steadied herself by grasping the back of the chair Jacey had occupied only minutes before.

She heard Jacqueline observe, "As hard as it is to believe, I think you're every bit as surprised as I am."

Kiera struggled to breathe evenly. "Yes. Yes, of course. Jacqueline, please. You have no idea how I have regretted what happened. Can we please speak of this..." She lowered her urgent voice to a whisper, "Somewhere else?"

Jacqueline's face blanched. "Somewhere else? Oh my god, Rory doesn't know, does he? You babysat me while hired killers murdered my mama. You allowed my sister to die in Mama's womb. Do you know those killers even took the life of my little dog Roscoe? That you allowed too! With your own hands you turned over to those murdering thugs the three thousand dollars my father left for their payment. And when my useless, self-centered father thought it was safe to come back to town, you welcomed him into your bed. Here you are telling me how you have regretted it. And yet, you never once told your own son what you did!"

The air constricted in Kiera's throat. For a terrifying moment she feared the walls of the house would implode upon her. Beyond this irrational fear, she was aware her relationship with her children was now in real jeopardy. She had lied to them about why she had been on parole when she and Wendell met. She had concocted the story told to all three children about being incarcerated in a Kentucky prison over a charge for buying weed. Wendell did know the truth, but he'd promised to never discuss it with anyone. Charles Rogers had died almost a year after Kiera began the sentence for conspiracy to commit murder. Her father, who had fought for her early release, was dead now, too. Aside from Wendell, the only people who knew the details of the crime and her prison time were Daniel and their mother. And those two were too ashamed to ever discuss it.

But Jacqueline will speak of it. She will speak of it to Rory!

Kiera ignored the wail that threatened to rip from her vocal cords. "You're absolutely right, Jacqueline," she said with all the calmness she could rally. "Rory doesn't know. And I beg you please don't tell him. Not now, not like this!"

"I suppose you think I owe you my silence?" Jacqueline asked sharply. "Think I owe you for watching over me while my father lay low and those brutish, clumsy thugs he hired left their footprints in my mother's blood? You really, really are delusional, aren't you?"

Kiera gently laid Anthony's photo face down on the tabletop. She started to take a step toward Jacqueline but stopped when the girl shuddered. Whether it was a shudder that came out of fear or anger or pure hatred, Kiera could not determine.

"No, you misunderstand, Jacqueline! It's just you're right. Rory does not know. None of my children know. For them to find out like this...oh, it would hurt them so very much."

Jacqueline blenched. Heavy tears fell from her eyes. "I would never set out to hurt Rory. Nor do I seek to hurt your family. I am not you, Kiera."

Somewhere in the overbearing terror that hung over Kiera, she knew a glister of hope. She regarded Jacqueline with imploring eyes. "Does this mean you won't speak of this to Rory then?"

In the next moment, she was aware of someone at the doorway. Her heart sank to see it was her son. It was obvious he was perplexed by the conversation he'd interrupted. And there, just a few paces behind him, stood Tally, peeking around his shoulder, her face animated with curiosity.

"Speak of what to me?" Rory asked Kiera. Seeing that Jacqueline was crying, he went to her and asked why she was upset.

Jacqueline pressed her palms over her eyes. When she drew her hands away, she wiped her face and shook her head.

"Rory, I have to leave," she declared.

"Leave?" Rory glanced at his mother. "What the hell's going on?"

Kiera could not have answered if she wanted. Her knees felt weak again and it was all she could do not to collapse.

"She can tell you," Jacqueline answered. "But I have to go."

"Do you mean the motel? Tell me you're not going back to Kentucky!"

Jacqueline assured him she meant only to the motel. She threw a baleful look at Kiera. "I'll be in the car. But I cannot stay in this house a second longer!"

She fled from the room, past Tally and into the kitchen. They all heard the door open and close.

Rory's eyes widened with uncertainty. He demanded Kiera tell him what had happened to send Jacey running out of the house.

The panic in Kiera's breast made her heart beat so rapidly that she felt dizzy. She was dimly aware that she was gasping for air. Rory, noticing she was encumbered somehow, helped her to sit down.

"Are you sick or something?" he asked. "I can't imagine Jacey would just up and run out because somebody doesn't feel well."

Tally entered the room and crouched at her mother's feet. She covered Kiera's hands with her own. "Your skin is so hot, Mom," she said with concern. "Are you sure you're okay?"

Kiera took several deep breaths. At last her head stopped spinning.

"I'm fine," she told them hoarsely. She felt their curious eyes on her and sensed Rory's anxiety. Her own sense of panic was not gone entirely because she knew the moment Jacey told him the truth then her relationship with her son would be forever altered. Altered and ruined.

For a moment, Kiera considered lying to him again, to discredit Jacey before she had the chance to tell him. But this was the age when it took only a few dollars to hire the services of a people finder site. They could trawl her information as surely, and probably more thoroughly, than when she herself had trawled for personal info on this or that anti. Rory would then discover confirmation to support Jacqueline's story. If Kiera continued to deny that which was so provable, the result would be Rory would feel she was a committed liar. He would doubt everything she had ever told him. He would turn away from her, and this she could not bear.

There was a look in Rory's eyes that bordered on suspicion. It broke Kiera's heart.

"Mom," he asked uneasily, "you can tell me why Jacey doesn't want to stay, can't you?"

Kiera could no longer look him in the eye. She turned and wrung her face in her hands.

"Alright," he said. "I'll just find out myself."

Kiera heard his footfalls as he left the room and took the same path Jacey had made to the kitchen door and out of the house. His departure brought Kiera only minimal relief. Very soon, he would know everything from Jacey.

She felt a light touch at her elbow. Her eyes opened again and she saw Tally was still crouched there, with worry shining in her regard.

"Whatever it is, it will be alright," Tally consoled her. "It wasn't nice of Rory to act like you had done something to that awful woman."

As endearingly loyal these words were to Kiera's ears, they only made her weep. How was she to explain to Tally that it wasn't Jacey who was the awful woman but her own mother? How, oh how, was she to explain all the years of lies and yet retain the respect of any of her children?

It was seconds later that Wendell returned. As he stepped into the dining room, he announced the bonfire was ready to be lit. But his words ended as soon as he saw Kiera's despair and Tally offering comfort.

"What's going on? I thought it odd Rory and Jacey were sitting out in her car."

As Kiera tried to speak Wendell noticed the picture frame lying photo-face down on the table. He approached quietly and lifted the frame. As he saw which photograph it was the color in his face drained away. He said nothing, but Kiera knew by his expression that, on some unconscious level, he had an idea of what had transpired.

Wendell returned Anthony's photo to its reserved spot in the bookcase. As he took a seat beside Kiera, he offered no words of condemnation. Instead, he reached over, stroked her arm and asked Tally to bring a glass of wine for her mother.

"It'll be okay, Kiera," he promised tenderly. "Everything will be okay."

Chapter 22

Wendell remained with Kiera as she drank the wine, and Tally retreated to the living room to watch television.

Kiera's nerves were still addled. She was glad Wendell didn't push her to talk about the conversation with Jacey right away.

At last, however, he did ask, "Can I guess? She knows your Anthony?"

Kiera drained the last sip of wine. "She's his daughter, Jacqueline."

"Ah," he said with a sigh. "Whoever came up with the idiom, *it's a small world* did not exaggerate, hm?"

She could have taken it as a blasé remark. But it was true.

"Oh Wendell! Rory will know I lied to him. That I lied to all of them. This will make him hate me!"

Wendell assured her that Rory wouldn't and couldn't, hold such a thing against her for long. "It was to protect Rory," he rationed, "to protect all of them. Besides, Rory is unable to hate you."

Kiera was about to exclaim she prayed this was true when they heard the kitchen door open and shut. Panic shot up Kiera's throat as heavy footfalls approached the dining room.

Rory stopped in the doorway. His eyes were wide and disbelieving. Kiera saw his jaw clench as he stuck his hands in his pockets.

When at last he spoke his voice was strained with emotion, "So Mom, the tale you told me and my sisters for all these years was that you served time in a Kentucky prison for dealing drugs. You made us believe that you were a victim of ignorant laws. *Red-neck laws*, that was your term for it. Not only did you tell us this, but you boasted about it. You credited this unfair stay in prison, spent at the mercy of cruel guards, as what opened your eyes to the injustices of this world. I remember you telling me how it made you mature into an independent, strong woman."

It felt to Kiera as if she and her son alone occupied the same room and yet were separated by an invisible and angry sea. She longed for the right words to comfort Rory, to explain she hadn't intended to hurt him.

Rory took a step toward the table and stared at the corner of it.

"*Mature. Independent,*" he scoffed. "I believed you, you know? Every word. And never in a million years would I have imagined you lied. Nor would I have imagined that in reality you're a cold-blooded murder conspirator."

Wendell's face turned florid. "This is no way to speak to your mother."

Rory's gaze flicked toward his father. "Don't get high and mighty *now*, Dad. You knew about this all along, didn't you? Went right along with Mom in perpetuating her fiction?"

Wendell could only shrug awkwardly. "You kids didn't need to hear the details."

Rory jerked his hands from his pockets and balled them into fists. "Then you should have just said nothing at all. But no, you two had to go and create a story to make Mom look like some damned martyr!"

He pointed a finger at Kiera now, his eyes gleaming with hostility. "What you did was anything but an act of martyrdom! You helped your lover kill his pregnant wife. The two of you plotted her murder, for god's sake! Your family was rich enough to get you off with a light sentence. Your depraved, wife-killing lover wasn't so lucky; he got the electric chair. But even now you keep his goddamned picture in our very dining room! Right next to photos of your kids and husband. This is the non-fiction version of the story, Mom. The *only story!*"

Kiera, too anxious to speak up before, knew she had to reach across the sea separating them or she would lose him forever.

"I am sorry, Rory. You're absolutely right. I should have told you the truth. Nothing less than the truth."

Rory nodded, but it was an agitated nod, as if he were trying to pluck a single thought out of a whirlwind of emotions.

"Yeah, okay. We'll talk about that later."

"What do you mean later?"

"Jacey wants to leave, get back to her motel room." Rory looked close to tears. "Naturally, she's extremely upset. I told her I'd join her."

Kiera felt a new panic needle her breast. "Are you saying goodbye? Leaving us for good? I said I am sorry, and I meant it!"

He combed the fingers of both hands through his hair. With the toe of one sneaker, he nudged the nearby table leg. "I don't know, Mom. All I know is Jacey is on her way back to the motel and she needs me right now."

He turned toward the door and told them not to wait up for him. Then he walked away and left the house. Kiera ran to the kitchen and through the window over the sink, watched as Rory got into the passenger side of Jacey's car.

"You have to come back," she sobbed softly. "Come back to me, please come back to me!"

She watched as the vehicle left. When at length she rejoined Wendell she brought a fresh bottle of wine for the two of them. Wendell drank half a glass before announcing he was ready to go to the bedroom and smoke a joint.

"I plan on calling it a night after that," he said. "Try putting this evening to rest, sweetheart. Rory might be at that motel for a while. You should get some rest."

She admitted that sleep sounded good and promised to brush her teeth and join him in bed. After he'd gone Kiera made her way to the living room. She was going to tell Tally goodnight, but the girl was curled up on the sofa under the throw blanket and appeared to be asleep.

By the time Kiera reached the bedroom Wendell was already asleep. The fragrance of recently smoked marijuana lingered in the air, and the sheets were welcomingly cool as she slid into bed beside her husband. But in the darkness Kiera's anxieties seemed to stand like specters all around the bed. Looming, ethereal monsters salivating in delight at the torture they inflicted. She was terrified Rory might turn against her. Not only him, but her daughters as well. Skylar, she was pretty sure, was already lost to her in many ways. She feared the possibility her dear Tally might decide she resented her mother's lie after all. Her oldest daughter might even grow disgusted in knowing Kiera's prison time came about over love for a man. Could Tally ever be able to accept her mother had once been young and headstrong and passionately, perhaps foolishly, in love?

The world remembered Anthony as a scheming and cold-hearted man. Kiera secretly knew now that she had been aware of his flaws all those years ago. Anthony had told her that Jacey's mother, Theresa, was the bane of his existence. He had claimed his wife came to suspect his affair with Kiera and had bitched about it for weeks. Kiera remembered Anthony explaining the details of his plan to get rid of Theresa. Where, when and how he wanted it to go down. The names of the people he was going to hire to get it done.

And despite the years she'd spent not dwelling on it, Kiera recalled the last thing Anthony had said to her the night of the murder: "The money I'll get from Theresa's life insurance will take care of us until we are married and have your parents' blessing."

It was with shame now Kiera understood that when Anthony had used the word *blessing*, what he really meant was monetary generosity from her affluent father.

She supposed Anthony had cared enough about little Jacqueline to get the child out of the house he shared with Theresa before the hired killers broke in. Jacqueline was, after all, Anthony's daughter and the same child whom, at the time, Kiera fantasized would come to love her.

But like Kiera, Anthony had not considered an unborn baby a real person. It was for this reason he had been unwilling to delay his scheme until after Theresa gave birth.

As much as it pained Kiera she wondered what Jacqueline's life might have been like if at least the baby had been allowed to live. Perhaps, the contrite possibility occurred, all the subsequent moments in Jacey's life would have been very different, so different she and Rory would have never even met.

Kiera needed the deluge of anxiety, guilt and questions to subside, to allow her sleep so that in the morning she would awaken renewed and capable of thinking clearly and hopefully with her enervating emotions calmed. So she prayed to Cailleach. It was a prayer as fervent as the one made when Lily had been sacrificed or when she asked the dark goddess to bring Rory home.

Mighty Cailleach, hear this prayer of your steadfast handmaiden. Return my only son home before the day is new. And cast aside and put asunder every circumstance or earthly concern that might tempt him to leave me again.

This prayer she repeated over and over, until the words stilled on her lips and resounded only in her brain. At last, her voice fell silent as her mind slowly sank into a semiconscious cocoon. In this twilight place her anxieties were pushed at arm's length. Their bites at her sentient mind transformed into only mild nibbles.

Kiera rested in the cocoon for an indeterminable space of time, until at last she felt herself drift toward sleep.

Chapter 23

At some point Kiera's repose was interrupted by what sounded like a distant fracas. The voices seemed to belong to Tally and Rory and the agitation in them roused her to full consciousness.

Her eyes opened to the soft darkness of the room. As she listened to the voices of her son and daughter, it was evident the two were arguing. She knew that wherever they were wasn't close by. The fracas continued for some seconds—seemingly from somewhere outdoors—before silence prevailed once more.

She felt truly drowsy by now and decided finding the cause of the argument could wait till the morning. Her eyes closed again.

A blast sounded from outdoors.

Kiera sat up, fully alert now. The blast had happened from far away and by its distinctive sound she knew it had come from the firing of a gun. Wendell lay on his back beside her. She shook his arm. He groaned sleepily and turned over with his back to her.

"Wendell, wake up!"

He gave a fussy groan. She shook him again. The only response he gave was the loud draw of a snore.

Kiera got out of bed. She stood listening for a few moments but heard nothing from inside or outside of the house. Everything was peaceful. Perhaps too peaceful. She padded to the dresser, where she found the incandescent flashlight kept on top. She picked it up and made her way out of the bedroom.

The lights in the house should have all been turned off for the night. Tally's and Rory's bedroom lights were indeed off, but when she clicked the switches for their respective overheads she discovered neither were in their beds. She proceeded through the house. No one occupied Skylar's old room or the downstairs bathroom. The living room light was on but Tally was not here. The dining room was likewise empty even as the light had been left on. She entered the kitchen to find it dark. But from the window over the sink she could see someone had switched on the porch light next to the door.

Kiera stepped outside. The porch light only canvassed a portion of the yard, but after clicking on the flashlight she was able to see that the truck was parked beside the family jeep. Rory would likely have taken the truck to follow Jacey to Kentucky. While seeing it still still there should have brought relief she couldn't forget what had drawn her out of bed. Kiera walked through the grass, looking this way and that for a sign of her children.

"Rory?" she called, "Tally? Where are you?"

A breeze drifted in from the north, and it carried with it the sound of a dog barking.

Not barking, she realized, but baying.

Kiera looked to the north. For a moment, she could see nothing except the dark landscape and the murky outline of the horse barn and pen. But as her eyes adjusted she noticed a faint swaying orb of light. When she reached the end of the yard she could tell this light appeared to emanate from some sort of lamp or lantern.

The continued baying had a resonance that suggested a canine more angry than anxious or afraid. She guessed it was the same little whip-tailed mongrel she'd seen before.

Perhaps Tally and Rory have gone for a late-night walk and encountered the dog?

That they'd be walking outdoors so late at night did make her wonder. But she was more concerned with the possibility some drunken or simply stupid opossum hunter had stumbled onto their property. That would account for the gunshot and possibly the light, too. If there was an inebriated, lost hunter out here, then her children definitely needed to get back indoors.

She started to cross the yard when a sharp pang of hesitance stopped her. It was the baying of the dog; something about the malevolent tone filled her with dread.

Don't be a mouse, she scolded herself. *This is your land, and if you're not going to take responsibility for your family, no one else will!*

Kiera followed the splay of radiance from her flashlight across the yard. She briskly took the path that led past the horse barn, with the strange swaying light seemingly straight ahead and the darned dog still baying. To let any potential trespassers know of her presence, she sang one of her favorite songs, Pete Seeger's "If I Had a Hammer."

The baying stopped just as Kiera reached the barn. She paused and shone the flashlight into the pen.

She stopped singing. "Tally? Rory? Are you out here?"

One of the horses gave a languid sigh from inside the barn. No other sound was heard from the building, and Kiera saw no sign of either Tally or Rory. She turned away, taking up the song again as she followed the path. As she passed the herb garden she saw the shades just up ahead. Her singing stopped, and as she scurried along the short distance she could tell the source of the orb of light issued from a lantern inside the little grove.

It appeared to be located some feet above the ground, and as she pressed forward the breeze caused the lantern handle to sway from the branch it hung. A sound issued from the grove, something between a thud and a deep scrape. Kiera was able to make out a hunched figure standing beneath the light. The figure appeared to push something that made a dull metallic flash. Through the low, thick branches, Kiera squinted for a clearer view.

"Rory?" she hailed. "Tally? Is that you two?"

The sound ceased at once and the figure stopped moving. As the silent seconds passed, Kiera's hunch it could be a hunter grew stronger.

"You better answer me now!" she exclaimed.

A few seconds passed and she heard Tally say, "You should go home, Mom."

Her daughter's terse tone made Kiera's skin tingle.

"What the hell are you doing out here?" she asked.

Tally's voice grew harsh, "I'll tell you later, Mom. But right now, just go home and get into bed."

Kiera knew something was amiss. She reached for the first branch and moved it aside. As she pushed away more branches she felt frustrated by whatever stupidity had compelled Tally and Rory to come out here.

"Is Rory out here with you?" Kiera asked sharply.

Her hands clutched a particularly thick Yew branch. The bristly green shoots stabbed her palm. Infuriated, she only clenched it harder and shoved it aside.

"Dear goddess, Tally, why don't you answer-"

The word *me* died on Kiera's tongue as she moved the very last branch. This branch blocked Tally from the flashlight's full illumination.

Tally stood in a little clearing at the center of the grove. The lantern hung from a nearby elm, and its light cascaded like milky fog over her and the ground. Tally's face was ruddy and damp with perspiration, her hair a tousled mess.

More alarming to Kiera, though, were the splatters of blood on her daughter's chin and across her shoulders. Even the front of her dress was speckled with blood. As Kiera glanced at the shovel in Tally's hands, she saw that they were reddened as well. Kiera recognized the tool at once as a round-point shovel from the horse barn. At her daughter's feet was a strip of upturned soil and Kiera saw the shovel blade was caked with fresh earth.

Kiera clicked off the flashlight. "What are you doing?"

Tally made a peevish little groan but did not answer. Kiera felt her patience run out. She shouted at Tally to explain why she was covered with blood.

After a moment, Tally said thickly, "Go home, Mom. Just go!"

"Where's your brother?" Kiera looked at the trees and low-growing shrubs behind Tally. "I know he's not at the house either. And you two shouldn't be out here! Didn't you hear that hunter fire a gun?"

As her gaze turned right, she saw a young pignut hickory standing at the very edge of the lantern light. It was evident the tree had struggled to establish itself; the trunk was lean and the branches had grown in an awkward fashion to accommodate other trees that grew so profusely around it.

Kiera forgot the struggling tree when she noticed something lying on the ground on the other side of it. This something was partially hidden by the leaves of sapling yews and elms.

Human legs.

The person wore jeans and there was a pair of gray canvas sneakers on their feet. Gray canvas sneakers that Kiera recognized as belonging to her son.

Her voice was shrill as she called his name.

The next instant Tally stepped forward and with both hands, thrust the length of the shovel in front of her mother. Kiera blinked with dismay at the almost menacing expression on her daughter's face.

Tally shook her head. "Don't, Mom. Just go home."

"What's wrong with Rory?" When Tally did not answer Kiera called out to him again. He did not reply nor did she hear anything to indicate he had heard her at all.

Kiera tried to skirt around the shovel blade but Tally leaped to block her.

"What's wrong with you?" Kiera screamed.

"He's fine, Mom. Now go home!"

The glower of Tally's eyes made the roots of Kiera's hair stand on end. She was fed up with whatever game her daughter was playing and she had to know what Rory was doing there on the ground and why he hadn't answered her!

Kiera grasped her flashlight with both hands and forcefully swung it against the shovel handle. The blow knocked the petite Tally off balance. As she teetered on her feet, Kiera seized the shovel handle with a hand and wrenched out of Tally's grasp. Tally fell on her butt. As she moved to get up Kiera kicked her in the hip.

It was a light kick, but Tally cried out in shock.

Kiera shook a finger at her. "You just sit and stay sitting!"

She stepped to the hickory and clicking the flashlight on again, directed the beam of light over her son's supine body. And there nearby, less than a quarter of a yard away, lay a rifle. It looked just like the one Wendell owned.

A gasp bled from Kiera's lips. She tried to blink away the image she saw but it refused to vanish. She stared, trembling, at her disfigured son. The top of his skull had been ripped apart. Blood still poured from the hideous wound and flowed onto the ground where lay his injured head. Bits and pieces of his brain were strewn everywhere. His beautiful face was barely recognizable.

As Kiera sank to her knees, the flashlight fell from her hands. It rolled a bit sideways where it landed, taking a portion of its glare off of the grisly, unthinkable sight. But Rory was still there, lying without moving, not making a sound, not even moaning. Kiera touched his shattered cheek beneath the caked blood and membrane. Seizing his arm, she found it heavy. She touched his throat and felt for a pulse. There was none.

"No, Rory! *No, no, no, no!*"

She clasped her son's body to her breast, rocked him, and kissed his mutilated brow.

"What happened?" she screamed at Tally. "What happened?"

Tally got to her feet and wiped old leaves and dirt from her arms. The expression on her face was one not of shock or sadness but of peevishness.

"Jacey brought Rory back home," Tally said churlishly. "But she told him she was driving straight away to Kentucky. Dumb thing wasn't even going to wait till morning. And Rory decided he was going to get in his truck and follow her. He woke me up when he came upstairs to pack."

None of this mattered to Kiera. "Tell me what happened to my son!"

"Your son," Tally murmured. "I told you. He was going to drive to Kentucky. To be with her. Leaving you and Dad, probably without as much as a goodbye. He had to be stopped."

Kiera shook her head. Her Tally surely couldn't have committed this abominable act!

"Tell me you didn't do this, Tally! You couldn't have!"

Tally grunted. "Oh my god, it's so simple, Mom. I couldn't see Rory putting you through another separation! Especially just to be with some shallow dumb tart like Jacey. I knew he had a key to the gun cabinet. I told him

I'd heard some kind of animal outside, that it had the horses spooked. So he opened the cabinet and came out here with me. He was going to get rid of the animal before he headed out." Tally inhaled deeply. "He owed me at least that much didn't he?"

"Jesus," Kiera gasped, feeling cold certainty creep over her. Tally had killed Rory. And her daughter was convinced she'd done it for a noble reason!

Kiera was conscious of Rory's blood soaking into her nightshirt. More was seeping onto the indifferent ground. It was thick and sweet smelling to her senses and it grew cooler by the moment. To her dismay, Tally just stood there with a smile on her face. A wide, self-satisfied smile, the mad brilliance of which threatened to send Kiera reeling from the rational world. For several moments, she felt like she was plummeting into a gaping abyss. Tumbling helplessly with her was every hope, plan and measure of happiness that was her life.

Tally's voice slithered into that awful chasm, "I know you love him, Mom. But Skylar abandoned us already. And I knew what that did to you. I just couldn't stand by and let you be put through it again."

The tenderness of these words struck Kiera as the most grotesque of paradoxes. For a second she was tempted to lay Rory's head down and reach for the rifle. To stand up and turn the murderous weapon on Tally. To wipe from the world of the living this awful girl who had forever taken away her beloved son.

But she loved Tally, too. She didn't know how this horrible act could ever be rectified, but no, she could not kill her daughter.

A shuffle sounded from the overgrowth behind Tally. A blinding light smarted Kiera's eyes, but she was able to discern a figure moving forward through the foliage. The light came from the flashlight in the figure's hand.

"What's going on?" she heard Wendell ask. "I heard you two yelling in my sleep!"

Tally had no reply.

"Kiera? What are you doing over there?"

She was sobbing too hard to answer. He came closer. The light he'd brought poured over her and the body of their son.

A dry choke rattled in Wendell's throat. He crumpled to the earth beside her. With trembling fingers he touched their son's shattered face. A piteous scream pealed from his lips.

The sound resounded through the grove and echoed across the whole property. Frightened birds flew from their nests and scattered to the sky. The crickets went silent in the fields and shrubs. The two horses inside the barn whinnied.

As Wendell knelt there in tears he asked who *has done this? Why, why would anybody do this?*

"Tally killed him," Kiera answered, her throat aching from her spent screams. And without thinking of what may come of it she told him what had transpired. She repeated to him every part of Tally's confession and disclosed Tally's insane motive for her actions. When she was through, Wendell raised his eyes to their daughter. Emotion burned in them as he demanded confirmation from her if it were true?

"Yes, Dad," Tally answered. "But I promise he didn't suffer. One shot in the back of the head and it was over."

Disbelief burnished Wendell's face. "Didn't suffer?"

Tally replied with a morally imperious timber, "One of Mom's children has to stay loyal."

"Loyal?" Wendell spat the word. A quick second later, he jumped to his feet and lunged at Tally, knocking her backward into a tree with such force that her head collided with a *clonk!* against the trunk. Her struck her forehead with the butt of his flashlight. As the flashlight fell from his grip he grasped Tally's arms and shook her like a rag doll. Tally's face whitened and her eyes grew wide with true fear. She yelled at him to stop; she screeched that he was hurting her.

"You vicious, vicious, stupid girl!" he seethed. "You had no right, no right at all!"

Kiera gasped. She had no doubt Wendell possessed the strength to shake their delicate and drug-wasted daughter to her very death if he chose. But at length he let go of Tally and jabbed an accusing finger at her face.

"This is not loyalty!" he roared. Tears pumped from his eyes now and he searched her face imploringly. "How could you possibly think this...this horrible thing you've done...is an act of loyalty?"

Wendell's arms raised and his hands clenched. With a roar he struck two fists against the trunk above the girl's head. Tally sidestepped away and watched mutely as her father pounded the trunk again and again. She folded her arms tightly about herself for comfort. She sucked her lips sullenly and anger, hurt and a measure of fear shone in her eyes. But Kiera noticed no measure of regret in Tally's expression.

Kiera could not bear seeing Wendell's pain. Gently, she laid Rory's head on the ground and moved to her feet. She wiped her tears away, and stepping to her husband's side, laid a consoling hand across his back. His arms lowered. Great tears streamed from his eyes and ran into his mustache and beard.

"Wendell, come with me to the house now," she pleaded. "Please."

Wendell let Kiera gather their flashlights and the rifle that lay close to Rory's body. As starkly wrong as it felt to Kiera to just leave her sweet boy in the grove, she knew there was nothing more she could do to protect him. Wendell was the one who needed her now.

Tally had quietly moved back to a space where her lantern's light blended into the shadows of the grove. After Kiera turned the rifle over to Wendell, she ordered Tally to give them Rory's key to the gun cabinet. She watched as Tally returned to Rory's body, and crouching, fished the key out of her brother's jeans.

Kiera gave her a glacial look as she handed over the key. "While we're gone, keep your hands off of our son. Is that clear?"

Tally shrugged and made the nonchalant statement that she'd just join them in walking back home.

"NO!" Wendell screamed, making Tally jolt where she stood. "You stay here. I can't, I just can't look at you right now!"

Tally said nothing as Kiera and Wendell made their way out of the grove.

Chapter 24

Wendell locked the rifle away in the gun cabinet in the dining room. He placed Rory's key for the cabinet into the pocket of his pajama bottoms and then turned to Kiera and asked her to get a phone so he could contact the police.

A blade of alarm skewered through Kiera's grief. She begged him not to call.

"We can't lose two children tonight!" she told him.

"My god, Kiera," he groaned, "Our oldest daughter murdered her brother!"

He stormed out. Terrified he'd locate a phone to make the call, Kiera followed him to the living room. He did not look for a phone, however, but instead sank into the sofa. His head fell into his hands and he cried with a bruised sound that reminded Kiera of the cry of a wounded animal.

Kiera took a seat beside him. She only stroked his back for she knew there were no words sufficient to console. He wept for a long time. Every moment or so he mumbled, "This is a dream, just a terrible dream!"

At last Wendell seemed to have no more tears to shed and he sat staring at his hands. Kiera laid her head against his shoulder now, her vision grown hazy from tears and unbidden visions of their mutilated son. In the otherwise silent room, so rank with sorrow, he told her they had no choice but to call the police.

Panic befell Kiera. In desperation, she tried to reason with him.

"It will serve no useful purpose!" she declared. "Tally needs help, not to be locked up in some god forsaken prison! Do you hate her so much now you would do this to our own child?"

He regarded her incredulously. "Do you really think I hate Tally, Kiera?"

Kiera regretted what she'd said and apologized. "No, of course not. But how, how could you even consider turning her in?"

He reached for her hand. "Look sweetheart, I agree she needs help. Tally has serious mental issues. But can you not see she won't get any better by not facing consequences? And we simply can't help her. That ship has sailed by. The truth is, we made Tally the way she is."

Kiera felt her jaw drop. "How can you possibly say such a thing?"

"What happened tonight is our fault," he said. "We invented the reason Rory felt he had to leave to be with Jacey. You and I created his assassin. It was you and I who gave that assassin motive to kill him. Just as badly, we nurtured the arrogance in her to carry through with it. Arrogance with no ability to feel regret. You saw her, you heard her! You know this is the truth."

The compassion Kiera had felt for Wendell only moments before threatened to evaporate. For even if he was right and they were responsible for Tally's state of mind, Kiera could not and would not allow him or anybody else to take her daughter away!

"Wendell! It's only that before tonight we didn't understand how frail her state of mind is," she argued. "Now that we do, we can guide her. We can teach her. We can help heal her, Wendell! We will do this, we will! And then, you'll see, things like what happened tonight will never, ever again happen!"

Wendell stared at her and she saw exasperation in his eyes.

Her voice rose to a hysterical, begging screech, "If you love me, truly love me, don't have my daughter sent away! Don't do this to me! Don't, please Wendell, don't!"

"And how would you explain Rory's disappearance?" he asked sharply. "To Jacey? To his friends? To his other sister, whom you almost seem to have forgotten? How do we explain to anybody why Rory's truck is parked in front of our house but by golly, Rory is not here?"

"Skylar doesn't know Rory came home," she assured him. "She doesn't know about Jacey either. And Rory has been out of contact with his old friends for a long while, I remember him mentioning this to me before he went to Kentucky! As for the truck..." Her mind searched for a logical course of action. The course came to her quickly. "We'll just get rid of it! Either by sinking it in the lake or having Shaun Wilcox crush it at his recycling lot. Oh Wendell, Shaun would do that for us, you know he would!"

"And what about Jacey? You don't think she won't call or text asking about him when he doesn't show up in Kentucky?"

"She will never know or have cause to ask," Kiera said confidently. "Because as far as we know Rory got in his truck tonight and drove back to Kentucky!"

Wendell looked at her for several long moments. Fresh tears welled in his reddened eyes. When he did speak again his voice was tinged with disdain, "You have it all figured out, don't you, Kiera? You want us to pretend our son is alive and well for the benefit of the world and you expect us to go on with our lives as if this never happened. All the while we have to act like his sister is not a murderous psychopath. Do you hear yourself? Do you have any idea how irrational and monstrously callous you sound? You revel in these fey impulses. I see it now, so clearly."

She could hardly believe the hostile accusation. Her first inclination was to react vehemently. But their daughter's very life depended on avoiding confrontation. She knew it would take all her guile to compel cooperation out of him.

So she clutched Wendell's arm –with imploring lightness—and let her emotions manifest in tears. She knew that at this moment she looked to suffer the kind of loathsome weakness she had always perceived in lesser women. But she needed him to be so touched by an exhibition he would consent to the only thing that could provide her comfort. Again she pleaded with him, her voice quivering, "Please, please Wendell! If you love me agree to this!"

The demonstration must have touched him for his expression softened. With a sigh and shake of his head he said at last, "I've devoted my life to supporting what you think is sensible. I guess I would not be the man you married if I stopped now."

Relief coursed through Kiera's body. His acquiescence would now allow her to grieve for Rory properly. This was the Wendell she loved: her complaisant partner, her best friend. The one person she had always been able to count on.

"Thank you, Wendell. You have no idea how much this means to me."

"But I do," he said, the ghost of a smile crossing his lips. "I do."

"It is the best thing for all of us, you'll see."

He lifted her hand and pressed her fingers to his cheek. "I need to do something that will relax me. You stay here and rest while I go do this, alright?"

She nodded and watched as Wendell walked out of the room. Alone now, she felt the physical toll that the night's horror had taken on her. All she wanted to do was close her eyes, visit a place without care, and forget, if just for even a few minutes, before she had to fully accept the fact she would never speak with her cherished Rory again. An emotional respite before she had to think about the next steps to conceal from the world what their foolish daughter had done.

Kiera's eyelids shut. Her body ached with fatigue and she had to fight to keep from crying again. She forced the image of Rory's face away, and directed her weary mind to look for that transient peaceful place.

But then she heard a sharp howl.

For the love of decency, not now! she thought.

Kiera opened her eyes. She listened as the howl changed into agitated barking. It seemed to manifest from somewhere outside the kitchen. The last thing she wanted right now was for Wendell to deal with a dog. So she got up from the sofa and padded from the living room into the kitchen.

From the window she saw that night's darkness was growing softer. And to her relief, the barking ceased. She listened for any more noises from the dog, hopeful the little beast had gone on along as it had always done before. Several seconds passed and the only sound she heard was that of her own breathing.

But as she turned to exit the kitchen a blast erupted from the dining room. The violent sound glued her feet to the floor.

"Wendell?" she shouted.

The whole house stood silent beneath the approaching dawn. Kiera's heart pounded in her breast and she felt nauseous with foreboding. She had to force herself to go to the dining room. The overhead light was still burning here.

There under its warm and cozy illumination she found her husband.

He was seated in a chair pulled away from the table. But his upper torso was slumped back and his arms hung limply. His head had fallen over the back of the chair. His hanging jaw, his mustache and part of his beard were saturated with blood. Even more blood, along with brain tissue and bone had splattered the floorboards behind the chair. And on the floor below Wendell's dangling right hand lay his Glock pistol.

Kiera heard herself scream as the place without care descended upon her without further bidding.

As the muted morning light made its appearance throughout the house windows Kiera's consciousness returned. Bile was creeping thickly up her throat and her head throbbed. When she sat up and saw Wendell's body still sitting upright in the chair her stomach almost revolted entirely.

On shaky legs she got to her feet. She fled from the dining room into the kitchen. To remove the taste of bile from her mouth she turned on the sink faucet and drank straight from the flowing water. As she spit the foul mess into the sink, visions of her dead son and husband saturated her vision and a mindless sense of utter desolation came over her.

This feeling drove her outdoors. The vermilion light of dawn stung her eyes, the sweetly indifferent air felt like a mockery.

Tally was just coming down the path from the shades. Kiera wanted desperately to hate her. Wendell would surely not have shot himself if it wasn't for this mad, vile girl. And yet she needed Tally now more than ever.

Kiera screamed and fell to her knees. Tally came running. In moments the girl was with her. Kiera managed to sob out that Wendell was dead. Tally fell to her knees, too, and drew Kiera into an embrace.

"Shh, Mother," she said, rocking Kiera against her small hard bosom. "I am here for you. I promise."

Chapter 25

In less than twenty minutes Kiera began implementing the plan she had hoped to carry out with Wendell.

On her instructions Tally returned to the shades and to Rory's body. There Tally retrieved Rory's personal keys, wallet and cell phone from his clothing. These things she brought to her mother.

She drove the truck, with Tally following in the jeep, to the lake. They took one of the winding back roads that led them to the abandoned and decaying old Malone & Sons mill house. The property was thick with ancient willow trees and blackberry shrubs, but it was positioned right on the lake shore and the nearest neighbors lived at least three miles away.

Kiera parked the truck with its front facing the water's edge. She took Rory's cell phone from where it lay on the passenger seat. It had been some months since Kiera had gone through any of her children's private correspondence. The times she had had resulted in arguments from all three kids. But she felt there was no choice now but to go through Rory's messages. She had to know if he'd shared his plans to come home with anybody or if any of his friends knew that Jacey had visited. If there was any indication of either of these scenarios Kiera would have to adapt her plans accordingly.

Determining this required her to go over Rory's recent communications. Firstly, she checked his regular text app. Luckily, Rory only had a short list of contacts. She checked every one of these. To her relief, she found he'd made no mention regarding his return from Kentucky with anybody except Jacey. This single text exchange had taken place the evening of his arrival. It was a light conversation in which Rory informed Jacey he had arrived home and looked forward to seeing her soon. His other message text app was for a social network site he'd belonged to. Kiera scrolled through these messages, finding that her son hadn't used the program in over three weeks.

The last thing Kiera checked was his regular phone service. Jacey's number was of course among the contacts. Thankfully, however, no call or message had been sent to Jacey's number for over two days. Just to be safe Kiera checked the other contact numbers and discovered the last number he'd actually called was her own. A call that had been made the afternoon before his return home. Kiera realized she had missed this call since the app revealed a time stamp without any minutes marked.

Kiera transferred Rory's wallet and keys to the jeep and stuffed his phone into the front pocket of her pants. Then she exited the truck.

With the emergency tools from the jeep she and Tally removed Rory's tag. Kiera placed this into the jeep. She then returned to the truck and took it out of gear. With Tally's help they pushed the vehicle until all four wheels were in the water. Once the truck was completely submerged, they returned the emergency tools to the jeep. Then Kiera drove the both of them home.

It was a silent drive and Kiera was thankful Tally didn't try to start a conversation. The only thing they spoke about was the next steps in the plan.

Once they returned the jeep home Kiera instructed Tally to wait in the horse barn. When she was gone Kiera went to the house and walked to the eastern side. Two hydrangea bushes here flanked the sloped aluminum door that led to the small cellar. Grasping the handle, Kiera pulled the door up like a car trunk and proceeded down the steps. In the cellar she pulled the string that switched on the overhead light. She approached one of the four standing cases of shelves used for storing canned preserves. What she sought was one of the glass jars with homemade pickles on the bottom shelf.

Kiera sat down on the soft earthen floor. She selected one of the jars and pulled it from the shelf. The seal broke with a single curt twist of the canning band. She wrenched the band off completely and set it aside before likewise removing the tin plate. A little bit of the astringent pickle juice sloshed in her hands, so she set the jar between her thighs. She removed three of the pickles, careful not to disturb any more of the juice. Taking Rory's cell phone out of her pocket she dropped it into the jar. She watched as it floated down among the other pickles. Then placing the tin plate over the jar mouth, she screwed the band tightly back into place.

With the cell phone concealed in the corrosive liquid she left the cellar. From the jeep, she removed Rory's wallet and keys as well as the truck tag and carried these items into the house. In her and Wendell's bedroom she stuffed them in an old shoe box. The box she hid in the farthest recess of her closet.

Now she returned to the horse barn where Tally waited. Felicity and Little Crest were anxious for their breakfast and were already starting to paw their hooves against the floorboards. Tally stroked their muzzles to calm them while Kiera located another shovel among the tools. Once it was found the two of them left the hungry horses and headed for the shades.

Burying one of her children was not something Kiera had ever envisioned herself doing. And to have to bury Rory before his time and under such circumstances seemed darkly surreal. After ordering Tally to take up the shovel which had been left here, she uttered nothing more to her daughter except instructions on how deep, long and wide she wanted the grave.

After a time digging Tally grew agitated. In a whiny voice she asked exactly how deep Kiera expected they'd have to dig.

"I'll let you know," Kiera answered coldly.

Once Kiera was content with the dimensions, she and Tally carried Rory's body out of the scrubs. They lay him at the pit edge. Kiera directed Tally to sit down by a particular tree. Tally looked reluctant and offered to continue helping.

"I will finish this," Kiera told her. "You sit."

Tally complied and sat cross-legged beneath the tree branches. She was pouting and squirmed irritably, but she kept her silence.

Kiera knelt on her knees beside her son. Daylight was trying to break through the canopy overhead, and its bright glints fanned across Rory's poor damaged face. She kissed his brow and his blood-stained lips. Her fingers combed gingerly through his lovely dark hair.

"I love you, Rory," she whispered.

Raw grief tore through her. Fresh tears spilled from her eyes and over Rory's once handsome face. Her voice trembled with misery, "And I am so very sorry. Please, please, forgive me."

It took all her strength to ignore the desire to clutch his body and never let it go. But she still had Tally to shield. For this reason and this reason alone was Kiera finally able to push his body forward and let it drop into the grave.

She filled the pit herself. When this was finished she packed the earth firmly. Just leaving him out here, so far from their home, was painful enough. The thought of some animal rooting at his remains was appalling.

Kiera and Tally walked out of the shades with the shovels. These they put back in the horse barn. It was here that Tally was told to wait until after Kiera dealt with the authorities.

Before Kiera started for the door Tally's lips puckered again into a pout. She looked close to crying. "You blame me for all this, don't you, Mom? Go ahead and say it, you hate me. You hate me!"

Kiera harbored rage at her oldest daughter, yes. The last thing she wanted to do was to offer her comfort. Not now, not yet. But she still could not hate her.

"I just buried my son so nobody will suspect you killed him," she said. "If this isn't love, I don't know what is."

In the bathroom Kiera took a sponge bath. Next she threw her dirty clothes into the hamper and put on a fresh pair of pajama bottoms and clean tee shirt. Dressed and ready, she found her cell phone and placed a call to the county sheriff's department.

The call was responded to in less than fifteen minutes. Kiera was watching from the kitchen window when two squad cars pulled up the driveway. Altogether four deputies stepped out of the vehicles. The sight of their uniforms sent an instinctive chill up Kiera's spine. But she pushed her feelings aside to open the door to them. At that moment, another car rolled up. The man who stepped out and entered the house introduced himself as Detective Jason Harris.

She declined to enter the living room with them, though she was certain nothing had been touched since she'd awoken from the faint. While they inspected the scene she remained in the kitchen. She stood by the stove, hugging herself as she listened to their low but dismayed voices while they talked among themselves. Detective Harris got on his cell phone and placed a call to one of his colleagues. Meanwhile one of the deputies called the coroner's office and asked for a van. Some minutes later another deputy walked into the kitchen. The name on his badge read *Deputy Canton*. He offered Kiera his condolences and asked her if she wouldn't prefer to sit down.

She nodded and took a chair at the table. He brought her a glass of water. *Are you alright, Mrs. Scruggs?* She drank a little of the water and nodded again. *I am so sorry,* he said. For the first time in her adult life Kiera found herself not resenting the presence of police. The sympathy in this deputy's face was genuine, his kindness not pretense. When Harris entered a few minutes later, his demeanor could not be more compassionate. He even apologized for the questions he said he must ask of her.

These questions were naturally numerous. But they were practically the very ones Kiera had expected to hear, so she had little problem answering.

What time did you find your husband? *I believe it was a little after six. I really don't know as I didn't look at the clock.*

Were you already awake when this happened or were you awakened by the shot? *I was sleeping. I remember what I thought was a loud sound in a dream right before I woke up and came downstairs.*

Was anyone else home at the time? *No, no. My youngest daughter lives with her boyfriend. My oldest had spent the night with hers. Our son, he is away on travels.*

Had there been domestic issues? *No, none at all.*

Have you noticed any indication your husband was not alone when this occurred? *No, I haven't.*

Had your husband been under the care of a doctor? Do you know if he was stressed or suffering from depression? *Well, to be honest, he had been quite distressed about our youngest daughter having moved out. They were so close at one time, you know?*

Do you know if your husband left behind a letter or note, perhaps even a text message? The kind that, you may not have realized until now, sounded out of character? Or one that may have been a hint he was considering harming himself? *Wendell never sent texts; he was not a huge fan of technology. But no letters, no note either. I suppose the closest to a hint I had was he was unusually tender the last time we spoke. But, dear god, I never suspected he was thinking of ending his life!*

Kiera had answered truthfully or at least given as much of the truth as she felt the detective needed to know. He seemed satisfied with her information, and he and the officers remained commiserative toward her. The coroner's and forensics team arrived soon. She did not wish to know what all they were doing and was relieved by Deputy Canton's offer to make her a pot of coffee.

Well over an hour later one of the other deputies came in to suggest that Kiera wait in another room. The coroner's team would be bringing her husband's body through, he explained, to take him to the van. She nodded and moved to the living room.

This process went by quickly. Minutes later Detective Harris and Deputy Canton again offered condolences.

They asked if she needed them to stay while she contacted a friend or relative to come to the house.

She shook her head. "No, no thank you. My oldest daughter is due back later today. I'd prefer telling her myself."

Deputy Canton took a card from his wallet and handed it to Kiera. She read the print on the card: Avonport County Grief Assistance. There was a phone number as well.

"These folks offer counseling to county residents who have lost loved ones to suicide," Canton told her gently. "If you need to talk to someone in this time of grief, they'll be there to listen. If you need assistance making funeral arrangements, they have all the contacts for county resources. They can also get you and/or your children in touch with therapists that offer long-term counseling. These therapists work on sliding scale fees, depending on your income." His face pinched uneasily. "Not that I want to imply any of you have emotional issues. But from personal experience –one of my wife's relatives killed herself—I know the emotional effect a suicide can have on family members. It isn't easy."

Kiera was eager to see them gone. All the same, she expressed her gratitude for their kindness and even saw them out the door. The coroner's and forensics teams and the other deputies were standing outside talking among themselves. Kiera stood just outside the door as they all piled into their respective vehicles. The coroner's van led the way in the lengthy drive down the driveway with the other vehicles following right behind.

Once they were gone Kiera went inside. With a weary sigh she leaned against the door. She craved something to eat and definitely some sleep. As much as she wanted to rest, she still needed to fetch Tally from the horse barn. They would tell everyone Tally had been out all night with a friend, and that she hadn't returned home until after the authorities had left. And before telling anyone else, of course, Skylar would have to be contacted.

Even as there was no way around telling Skylar her father was dead, Kiera dreaded it.

Before she could do any of these things Kiera found herself drawn to the dining room. She did not want to see where Wendell had died, but she couldn't stop herself. To her surprise she discovered the teams had tidied the room quite a bit after all their picture-taking and documentation of evidence. The area where Wendell had sat in the chair was draped over with two large bolts of white canvas. There were only a couple of splotches of dried blood otherwise discernible on the floor. The teams had even wiped down Wendell's chair and placed it back at the table. A faint anesthetic smell, like some kind of cleaner, infused the air.

Beneath this odor was the familiar scent of her husband. And the smell of death. The two mingled in an unseemly fragrance that threatened to quake Kiera to her very core, to splinter and rip apart the determination which had always been her fundamental strength.

With tears stinging her eyes, Kiera turned away from the room.

****

Kiera expected the police inquiry and coroner's work to cause a lengthy delay for Wendell's funeral service. The official autopsy report, however, was released only four days after his death. The verdict was *Suicide by handgun.* Wendell's body was given over to her that afternoon, and Kiera requested its transference to the Bay Family Funeral Home for cremation.

It was in the afternoon two days later that Kiera and Tally took the drive down Clanton Valley Hollow to get to the service in Avonport. Kiera had dressed in a simple ankle-length dark blue cotton dress (the closest thing to formal spring wear as she cared to own), along with a pair of sensible black loafers. Tally was dressed similarly.

Kiera had noticed a change in Tally over the last couple of days. Her oldest daughter had started washing dishes and doing the laundry without being asked. She had even been feeding the horses and livestock. Her tendency for blathering had practically vanished. Kiera couldn't even remember the last time Tally had made an inappropriate or awkward comment. By contrast, Kiera found herself often impatient and snappy with the girl. Yet Tally had offered no complaint.

Tally hadn't broken down crying over Wendell but Kiera could see she missed him. This was especially evident whenever they took their meals. Tally would gaze forlornly at the empty chair her father once occupied. Sometimes her eyes even misted over.

And though Tally hadn't spoken Rory's name once since they had buried him, Kiera was sure she missed him as well. How could she not? Rory had loved Tally so much and she had typically acted as being very fond of her brother.

She has to mourn for him, Kiera told herself time and again. *She regrets what she did, she knows how over-the-top she went.*

Even now while she drove this thought replayed like an affirmation in Kiera's head.

Tally piped up suddenly, saying she was thirsty and asking if they could stop by The Woodsman to buy a drink.

Kiera hadn't been back to the place since the day she had seen Micky. She'd told no one about the visit to the fortune teller and so far she had managed to stay completely clear of a need to stop by The Woodsman. Before Wendell died she made sure the jeep was always recharged in Avonport. Anything else she might have bought there she simply purchased somewhere else. Since losing her son and husband the jeep had needed recharging only once and she'd sent Tally to do it. The very idea of stopping there now was an odious one for her.

Kiera answered Tally, "The director is waiting for us at the funeral home. You should have brought a soda or water."

For the first time in two days Tally grumbled, "Sorry I forgot! But it'll only take, what two or three minutes of time? I'm *thirsty*, Mom."

Kiera's knuckles tightened as she gripped the steering wheel. Her inclination was to just tell Tally she'd have to wait until they reached Avonport. It was clear, though, that Tally still didn't know how to deal maturely with temporary discomfort. The last thing Kiera needed was an argument right before the funeral service.

The jeep rounded a curve and just up ahead was The Woodsman by the side of the road. Kiera pulled the jeep into the graveled lot. Business was obviously good today as there were many vehicles parked here. Kiera had to take a space practically right in front of the building. She saw Doreen and her elder daughter seated in rockers on the front porch. They were invested in their own conversation and did not even glance at the jeep. Kiera noticed the daughter must have given birth for her belly was no longer swollen.

Tally grabbed her little cell phone wallet that lay on the storage console and opened the door. She asked if Kiera wanted anything.

Kiera shook her head. "Just hurry up, okay?"

Tally promised and exited the jeep. Kiera watched as she skipped up the front steps of the building and onto the porch. As Tally started inside she held the door for someone to come out. Kiera was alarmed to see this was Micky. Cradled in her arms was a newborn wrapped in a gauzy green receiving blanket. As she walked out on the porch Doreen rose to her feet and pulled another rocker up closer to her own. Micky sat in it with the baby.

Kiera grabbed her sunglasses from the visor and put them on. She hoped Micky hadn't recognized Tally. She could hear the women's voices through the window pane, though the glass garbled most of their words.

She saw Micky rock the baby gently, making little kisses to its brow, fussing over it as any great-grandmother probably would. The three women laughed and talked, not once looking Kiera's way. They were centered in each other and in the baby and the rest of the world didn't seem to matter. The store's front door opened again and Doreen's two younger children with their sleekly shining black hair ran out. The little boy plopped himself in Doreen's lap while the girl stood beside Micky. Kiera watched as the girl made little kisses at the baby.

Kiera felt Cailleach's presence close by. The goddess's voice whispered in her ear, reminding her how stupid Sam Downie was to have turned his back on his native heritage and married a piece of white trash like Doreen. And how utterly selfish it was for the couple's daughter to burden the world by bringing another child into the populace.

Ask Me to end the fortune teller's happiness! The Dark Lady implored Kiera. *Invoke Me and let Us together cleanse the world of these soft and unlearned yokels!*

Kiera dearly wanted to ignore the women and children. But try as she did, she couldn't turn her eyes away from them. She wasn't able to feel hatred for them and the lens of Neo-Fabianism reason, which once served her so loyally, seemed suddenly a concept beyond her grasp. Instead, she felt only sadness. It was a sadness incomprehensible to her reason and crushing in its weight.

"Oh Cailleach," she whispered, "I cannot bear to look at them!"

In a few moments Tally exited the store with a bottle of tea in hand. Kiera was relieved when she got into the jeep. As Kiera turned around in the parking lot Tally mentioned Sam Downie had been minding the store counter.

"That plump woman was holding his grandson," Tally said, making a distasteful expression. "They were both making goo-goo eyes over it when I went inside. Sam asked if I wanted a peek. I tried to be polite, but geesh. I guess for grandparents those things are cute enough, but yuck, it looked like some troll with that big ole head and teeny tiny hands. Downright ugly if you ask me."

Kiera didn't want to hear about Sam's grandchild or any other baby. She pulled the jeep onto the road, hopeful this was the last time she would ever lay eyes on The Woodsman or any member of the Downie family.

Chapter 26

The sun had just began to lay low in the western horizon as Wendell's service started, making for an apricot burst of flame through the dimpled glass windows of the chapel. The funeral director had seen to it Wendell's urn was placed on a marble pedestal at the front of the wooden pews. A wreath of ivy and wildflowers encircled the urn. Two lengthy rows of baskets and pots of flowers sent by acquaintances, old and new, as well as distant relatives, flanked the pedestal. It was a lovely showcase, one Kiera hoped Wendell would have approved.

Dozens of people showed up. Among these were Wendell's closest cousins, aunts and uncles. Also in attendance were his old friends and a number of his like-minded acquaintances. Several of the Pink Escorts showed up as well. Braeden came, too, and he stuck close to Tally. As he gave Kiera his condolences she noticed that his pupils were as small as pinheads. His suit and dress shirt, even his hair, reeked of perspiration and chemicals. Although Kiera didn't comment on this to Tally, she knew now Skylar had been right about the young man all along.

Daniel and his wife Emma put in an appearance. To Kiera's surprise, they brought Dorothy with them. Daniel was dressed in a stiff dark suit, while Emma wore an expensive dress and shoes that Kiera thought looked very out of place among the other mourners. It was obvious to anyone that Kiera's brother and sister-in-law had nothing in common with most of the other mourners. But the couple was very polite and offered their condolences to Kiera and their nieces.

Dorothy looked even more frail and sickly than when Kiera had visited her.

"I am so very sorry for your loss, sweetheart," she told Kiera. "So very, very sorry."

Kiera found herself thanking her mother. It had to be painful for the dying woman to get out.

Tally had compiled a DVD video of photographs of Wendell consisting of pictures taken throughout his lifetime. Accompanying this collage was a recording of some of his favorite songs. As Wendell would have wished, Kiera made sure the service was absent of any religious overtones. She instead invited the mourners to share their memories of her husband. Some of these were admiring appraisals of Wendell's intellectualism and social passions. Others were recounts of the days of his wild youth and were related with humor and sometimes, shameless irreverence. But all were given with telling affection.

Where beforehand Kiera feared she would end up weeping, she found herself simply moved by the regard the others held for Wendell. After everyone had shared their memories Wendell's like-minded friends gathered together to talk among themselves. Kiera heard them exchange stories about Wendell when he was young and talking about subjects that had been dear to him. Kiera observed how Tally was drawn to sit with these people. She was obviously amused at their recounting of the many rebellious things her father had done in his younger days. And they encouraged her to share her two cents worth on subjects Wendell had cared about like social justice, homesteading and Marxism. They patted her on the back several times. Kiera heard praises for her like, *"Here's definitely a fruit off the same vine!"* and *"You must have made your father so proud!"*

If there was a morose cloud over the event it came from Skylar. She stiffened when Kiera attempted to embrace her, and would not even sit on the family bench alongside her. Instead she kept close to Felix at all times. Kiera noticed her youngest dab her reddened eyes several times as she watched the video. Eventually Skylar approached the pedestal. She bowed her head and Kiera saw her lips move. Whatever Skylar was saying was spoken too softly for Kiera to make out. Afterward Skylar joined Felix at a bench near the very back of the chapel. Daniel, Emma and Dorothy made their way to where she sat, and Kiera saw how readily and easily Skylar accepted their consoling words. She even cried in Dorothy's embrace. But Skylar notably turned her head every time she noticed Kiera look her way.

Kiera longed to extend comfort to the girl but she knew Skylar might make a scene. The last time they'd spoken was after Kiera called to tell her Wendell had died. Felix had immediately driven Skylar to the house. Skylar was unwilling to believe the news. This was until she saw the canvas bolts on the floor. Then she sank to the floor in the dining room and cried hysterically.

After Kiera had taken a needed nap, she found Skylar and Felix scrubbing the dining room floor with a brush and pail of soapy water. Only when Skylar was satisfied every last trace of blood was removed did she consent to sit down and drink the coffee Kiera offered.

"Why, Mom?" Skylar had asked. *"Why would Dad do this? Was he ill?"*

Kiera told her gently that Wendell had been depressed.

"Depressed? No, I find this seriously hard to believe."

It was this moment Kiera had dreaded the most. For she knew she'd have to lie to this daughter in order to shield her other one.

"You know how dearly family meant to your father," Kiera had said. *"But Rory was gone, and you had left. It was harder for Wendell than any of us could have predicted."*

Skylar shook her head. *"He knew I hadn't abandoned my family! If he wanted to talk with me all he had to do was pick up a phone. And as for Rory, he's coming back soon. This was what you told us at least, and Dad knew it!"*

Kiera tried telling her that depression wasn't always logical. But Skylar only eyed her suspiciously.

"You're right, family was dear to Dad. He wouldn't have just gone and shot himself without leaving a note or a letter. He would have given some explanation! Unless there was some other reason for him to do this! And you would know this reason, Mom, I know you do."

At that instant Kiera knew she had to act offended if there was hope to silence the girl's accusations. So she sniffed and told Skylar that her insinuations hurt.

"I've lost my husband. My best friend. My lover. And here you sit accusing me? Oh Sky, how could you be so cruel?"

A grave and pensive expression had crept to Skylar's face.

"I know how your mind works, Mom," she countered. *"Oh, you tell yourself you have the most ethical reasons for everything you do. Yet here you are, trying to make me carry the responsibility for Dad's so-called depression. And not just me, but Rory, too! I don't understand what your reason is, but I do know you prefer people not knowing your little world isn't as perfect as you would have them all believe. And how dare you? My brother has to be brokenhearted over this news and he has that long drive to make from Kentucky to get here! Have you stopped and thought about that even once?"*

The reminder that Skylar assumed Rory was still alive made Kiera nearly panic. She told Skylar she had not yet informed Rory. It was proving impossible to reach him, she said; he wasn't answering her phone calls and her messages had all gone directly to voice mail.

"*Then I'll contact Rory myself,*" Skylar vowed stiffly. "*I will tell him what has happened. And when I reach him, I won't be crediting his absence for Dad's death!*"

This had made Kiera chuckle nervously. "*I wasn't blaming you directly, but you asked why your father was depressed. Now you're just being overly sensitive! You aren't the only one hurting, you know?*"

Skylar expression grew bitter at this. "*What I know is Wendell Scruggs didn't fall into sudden depression because his son and youngest daughter left home. He would have called us before even considering taking his own life. I know this and you know it, too.*"

It was at this point they both noticed Tally standing in the doorway. Kiera could only guess how long she'd been there or how much she had overheard. But the tone as she spoke to her sister was jeering.

"*You abandoned us, Skylar, remember? In making that choice you gave up any right to know what happens in this household. You go on along now with your precious Felix. Mom and I don't need you here.*"

Skylar had reacted with a look at once disgusted and pitying. However, the conversation was quite over. She and Felix left immediately. Since that day Skylar had not called or returned any of Kiera's calls, nor had she responded to the text messages Kiera left regarding the autopsy report or about the details of the service. Kiera was left to wonder if Skylar had indeed tried to contact Rory. And if she had, what was going through her mind when she could get no answer from him?

Even now, while Kiera worried their relationship might be severed beyond hope of repair, she could not tell Skylar the truth. Not without incriminating Tally. Kiera knew Skylar would expect Tally to face criminal charges or, more likely, insist her sister be cast away into some mental facility.

It was dark by the time the service ended. Kiera and Tally thanked everyone for coming. Afterward, Tally walked with Braeden out to the parking lot to see him off. Kiera stayed behind for a few minutes to thank the funeral director and to take Wendell's urn.

With all the others gone she stood alone at the pedestal. She and Tally had decided to release Wendell's ashes over the vegetable garden where he had tilled and plowed the earth so many times. She could think of no more appropriate place for his remains to be set free.

Footsteps sounded behind Kiera and she heard Daniel speak gently.

"How are you doing, sis?"

He gave Kiera a warm squeeze as she turned. She knew she should be appreciative her brother and his wife had come to the service. But it still stung that Daniel had forbidden her from the Pink Escort work. At the moment, though, the hardest emotion she could muster for him was mild disdain.

She thanked him for coming and for bringing Dorothy. With a little sadness she mentioned that it must be growing harder for their mother to get out and about.

"It is," he conceded. "Mom is steadily going downhill." He sighed and offered an encouraging look. "I want to let you know Emma and I are here for you. Anything we can do, hm?"

Kiera eyed him suspiciously. She was unable to believe her brother could ever really care about her.

He changed the subject abruptly, saying he had some news that might lighten some of her stress.

"And what's that, Daniel?"

"About the abortion bill just made into state law," he said. "I guess you've kept up with the issues, haven't you?"

"No, sorry," she answered with an undercurrent of sarcasm. "I've had other things on my mind."

"Of course. I'm sorry. Well, this state law has entirely banned abortion after the tenth week of pregnancy. Except in cases of saving the mother's life, anyway."

Kiera felt a ghost of the fury such news would have once sent coursing through her veins.

"Well, dear brother, I guess we can't be surprised. It was probably inevitable in a stupid red state like ours." She regarded him curiously. "So what does this have to do with me?"

An awkward smile came to his face. "Two things, really. The Board has decided to open a new clinic just across the state line. In fact, just today, we signed the lease for a building in the city of Bridgeville, located less than five miles away from here. The place was used as a family dental practice group but it became open after all three dentists retired. The complex is small, yet ideal for use as an abortion facility. We'll keep the old clinic building open in Avonport, though, since some of our doctors want to continue offering other health services. We have also had an offer from a major hospital chain. They're interested in acquiring what they call our brand. This will have to be brought up in the next stockholders meeting, of course."

A derisive grin spread over Kiera's lips. She told him she hoped he and the Board would be very happy moving up in the big corporate world.

"But Kiera," he said, "I thought you'd be happy to know our father's legacy of providing abortion access will continue in Bridgeville."

"Of course I am, Daniel. But you've seen to it I'm not involved. So the legacy is all yours to laud."

Daniel cleared his throat and said, "It is the second thing I wanted to share that you may be most interested in. You remember that patriot website I told you about, The National Constitutionalist? The one that hosted those videos we were concerned about?"

"*You* were concerned about," she replied thickly.

"Okay, *I was concerned about*. Anyway, it is gone. The owner died and his wife has pulled the site offline. Seems they were in the middle of a nasty estrangement when he passed from a stroke. Good news for us. With the website gone so are those videos. The establishment video forums refuse to host them. And we've heard absolutely nothing from lawyers representing any people that appeared in them."

She lifted an eyebrow. "Then your dear colleagues on the Board have stopped living in fear of lawsuits?"

"So far it appears that way. Because of this I see no reason you shouldn't come back to help out with the new facility. And the other Board members agree with me."

The idea was tempting for Kiera, though she knew Bridgeville was already a much more liberal city than Avonport. She could imagine how boring serving as a Pink Escort might prove to be without encounters with pro-life people. But in truth, the last thing she needed was to see Tally involved in any more confrontations.

Daniel went on to say, "We don't foresee needing more than just a few Pink Escorts in Bridgeville. Only enough to have a presence, an optics for the media. What we could use is a frontman, if you will, to interact on our behalf with the media. Somebody passionate about abortion, who will be our representative on social media. To show the public ours isn't just some abortion mill, but a place that cares about women's reproductive health care. Ideally, too, this person would have a history of working with Campaign Parenthood. They have confidential lists of potential local benefactors, you know? It would be a benefit if they shared those lists. More than this, what we need is somebody with experience in social outreach."

"Outreach?" Kiera asked. "Like what?"

"A person to represent the Clinic in social forums. Like you did with the original PCKC Facebook page." Daniel gave the room a furtive glance and lowered his voice, "Somebody willing to provide links to our paid sponsors among the abortion pill makers. For the sake of women living in states who will be impacted by the new laws and prefer not to cross state lines for abortions. The manufacturers are very generous in kickbacks to the right people. And I know your posts were always passionate and a lot of people trusted your opinion. I have no doubt you can help a great many women by convincing them to order the medical aid they require."

Kiera was surprised. "You're offering me a job? Don't you figure Dad is rolling in his grave to hear this?"

"I don't care anymore," Daniel said. "I think you possess exactly the skills we need. There's no reason for you to be left behind in this expansion. And a salary comes with the job. It would be a recognized position within the facility, Kiera."

This was definitely a position Kiera felt she could take on! But she had to ask if there was a place for Tally in such an expansion? Kiera explained her daughter would be crushed to be left out. To this Daniel promised that if Kiera did decide to take the position then she would have the liberty of choosing her own assistant.

"Whoever you want," he said. With a cautionary timbre, he added, "As long as he or she understands being an assistant doesn't mean making a visual spectacle of themselves. The less confrontation we can give conservative media to see, the better."

Kiera drew a thoughtful breath. "I feel I should take it up with Tally. But I'll definitely think this over and let you know."

"You need something to put your mind to, Kiera. I don't want to see you turn into a recluse on that mountain."

Kiera still resented the fact Daniel wielded all the power over their father's legacy. But it was clear he cared about her. She couldn't help but feel a measure of gratitude. And she was excited by the prospect of returning to proactive work for the cause she loved.

"Thank you, Daniel."

"Of course. Just do me one favor, sis?"

"What's that?"

"Don't tell any of this to Mom. She knows the Clinic will no longer be performing abortions, which makes her extremely happy. But she doesn't know about the plans for Bridgeville. With her health as it is, I don't want to upset her."

It seemed almost karmic that even her perfect brother wasn't above keeping secrets. Nevertheless, Kiera promised to say nothing about the new facility to Dorothy.

"It's a strange thing," she observed. "Our mother always disproved of abortion, yet it is in part what paid for those juicy alimony payments she got from dad every month."

"Emma and I now keep up with Mom's finances," Daniel told her. "We have her records, the newer and the older. Turns out our mother provided for herself by knitting blankets and making cloth dolls. She actually operated a profitable little business out of her sewing room. She never held onto the money Dad sent her. She cashed the checks, and then handed the money over to charities.

Among those charities were pro-life groups. Our mother may be ignorant, but we can't accuse her of hypocrisy."

Stunned, Kiera admitted that she had not been aware of any of this.

"I'll never understand the woman," Daniel said. "The pro-life thing, that is. Mom has never been an extremist when it comes to religion. But I suppose her upbringing prevents her from appreciating the lucrative aspect of abortion."

"Lucrative?" Kiera asked defensively. But she remembered that her brother's views always stemmed from entrepreneurial ambitions. And she had to admit, such ambitions were what promoted the medical virtues of abortion to the public. "I suppose so, Daniel."

He smiled wanly. "I know the financial benefits were never the driving force behind your support."

His words were spoken kindly. Yet they made her suddenly think of Anthony. Out of seemingly nowhere Jacey's words echoed in her head: *"With your own hands you turned over to those murdering thugs the three thousand dollars my father left for their payment."*

Kiera shuddered. Daniel must have mistaken it for grief for he gingerly pressed her hands between his palms.

"You look exhausted, sis." He said, kissing her brow. "You and Tally should go home. Get some rest. If you need me, just call."

Epilogue

It was dark by the time Kiera was on the road. In the front passenger seat Tally sat with Wendell's urn clutched between her knees. Tally was chattier now than she had been before the service. Kiera tried telling herself this was because her daughter's spirits had been animated by the time spent talking with Wendell's friends. Still, it was Braeden—with his miotic pupils and chemically stinking clothes—Kiera had found waiting with Tally in the funeral home parking lot after most of the other mourners had left.

As the drive continued Tally's mood grew more ebullient. She talked non-stop, to the point Kiera tried to ignore her blathering in order to keep her attention on the road.

"Mom? Mom, are you listening?"

Kiera sighed and told her she was.

"Sorry," Tally said, "I thought you zoned out there. Anyway, I was saying that friend of Dad's—Zane, I think his name is—wants to give me some Antifa literature. And Brenda—Brenda Joyce—mentioned her son and daughter both belong. She said I'd be a good fit in the organization. I hate fascists, so I have to agree."

As Tally talked Kiera felt the weariness which the events of the last few days had taken. It was more than weariness, really, it was utter exhaustion from trying to hold herself together and present to the world the perception of a simple grieving widow. A widow who had no secrets to hide, no daughter to shield, no son she had buried with her own hands.

"-and a book by some guy named Ernst Bloch," she heard Tally say. "I have already read the Saul Alinsky book, of course, it was one of Dad's favorites. You've read it, too, right?"

Kiera smiled indulgently and assured her that yes, she had read the book.

"That's what I thought. But I wouldn't mind having a first edition, especially since this Veronica woman offered it."

As Tally rattled on about books and communism and her father's wonderful friends, Kiera yawned. It was such a hard yawn her eyes watered.

When Tally paused at last to take a breath Kiera tried to change the subject. In a blithe voice she told Tally about the offer Daniel had made. About the offer and the position which included her choice of an assistant.

The info was enough to make Tally say nothing for several moments.

"Oh my god!" Tally suddenly sputtered. "You working for Daniel of all people? And me working as your assistant?" She giggled. "A nice respectable nine-to-five job in a nice sanitary office? Under his watch all day and that of his stupid, stupid Board? Oh yeah, that's the life I've always dreamed of!"

Her giggle turned into a full-throated disparaging chortle. She was laughing so hard Kiera feared the urn might loosen from between her quaking knees and drop to the floorboard.

"It was only an offer," Kiera said, tightening her grip on the steering wheel. "If you don't want to do it this is fine."

"Jesus, Mom! Surely you're not really considering going to work for that crap-ass brother of yours? That's not you. Working for the corporate world isn't you, either. You are a domestic goddess. A self-efficient woman of the land. A foe of convention, remember? If you work for Daniel you will have no time for aggressive activism against the establishment! You'll be sitting back while others go into the trenches to do the real soldiering for social justice!"

Kiera shrugged. This gesture brought silence from Tally again, silence which this time seemed to thicken and sour the very air inside the jeep.

In an injured tone Tally said, "Look, I'll do whatever you want, even be your assistant at Uncle Daniel's new facility if this is what makes you happy. But just so Daniel and the rest of his precious Board know, this doesn't mean I will be a voiceless little serf. If I see any antis show up on the property, believe me I will be out there and in their faces. I will tell every one of them exactly where they can shove their stupid posters and anti-choice bullshit!"

Tally snapped her head toward the passenger window and folded her arms tightly across her chest. Kiera knew her daughter meant every word she had just said, and experience also warned that Tally's temper was starting to boil over. She braced for a tantrum.

Kiera sighed and took a soothing voice, "You're right. A job where I answer to anybody probably is *not* me. And I don't wish to do anything that will make you unhappy, Tally."

Out of the corner of her eye Kiera saw Tally turn her face from the window. She was smiling now.

"I appreciate this, Mom." Tally scrunched over in her seat belt to give Kiera's arm a little squeeze. "You don't need Uncle Daniel or his pity job. It would be a waste of your talents and passion. Besides, you have me and I have you. We're all either of us really need."

Kiera was greatly relieved Tally was satisfied. For the rest of the drive home Kiera managed to force a smile and listen to her daughter's rambling conversation.

The crickets were singing in the grass, the trees and shrubs by the time they drove up the driveway. Listless clouds drifted overhead, imbuing the air with the hint of coming rain and blocking out every bit of starlight above the Scruggs' mountain home. Kiera had left the porch light on, however, so she and Tally were able to see their way from the jeep to the house. As Kiera felt her clutch purse for the house keys she noticed a little figure curled up beside the front door. The figure's head lifted. On seeing her it got to its four feet.

It was the same dog Kiera had seen several times recently. The dog stood very still, its eyes set like two orbs of unblinking onyx in the starless night. Kiera knew it was staring at her, that it had been waiting for her.

Tally asked if something was wrong.

"That dog," Kiera said, "what's that dog doing here?"

Tally looked to where Kiera gestured. "What dog?"

"At the door. Right outside the door."

Tally squinted. "I don't see a dog, Mom. It must be a shadow playing tricks on your eyes."

They proceeded to the door where Kiera stuck the key in the keyhole. She gave the knob a turn and glanced down. The dog was right at her feet. When she opened the door it stood where it was without offering a sound. It made no sense that Tally did not see the thing for Kiera could plainly make out the red and black plaid of its collar, how its long ropey tail stood up without wagging. And she felt how its fathomless dark eyes bored into her.

On entering the house she decided to say nothing more about the dog. She told herself Tally was perhaps just too tired to have really looked.

After Tally had gone upstairs to her room Kiera was aware of the fatigue in her bones. It felt to be sinking straight into the very marrow. She was ready for a glass of wine or a joint before going to bed.

In the kitchen she opened a cabinet door to find a wine glass. She heard a squall of laughter from upstairs. Tally was probably on her computer, she reckoned, chatting with some friend. But a second squall erupted, this one even wilder than the first. Kiera was curious now so she ventured upstairs and tapped on her daughter's door. When Tally failed to answer Kiera pushed it open.

The room was dark except for the glare of the laptop positioned on the floor. Tally sat cross-legged in front of it with Wendell's urn cradled in her lap. Kiera was dismayed to see her firing a crack pipe with a lighter.

Noticing her mother now Tally choked back an inhale and flipped off the lighter. A wide grin lifted the corners of her mouth. But Kiera saw there was only the slightest embarrassment in the expression.

"Sorry, Mom," Tally offered. "If you knocked I didn't hear. I was reading a meme."

Kiera's first instinct was to demand an explanation. It wasn't as if Kiera had ever once given Tally a hint she was okay for her child to use destructive drugs. Wendell being gone didn't make it alright, nor did the fact only the two of them now occupied the house.

But these insights gave way to the recognition that it simply didn't matter. Kiera knew now Tally had been using drugs for a long while. She also realized that no matter what she might say Tally would find her own excuse for doing exactly what she wanted. Her oldest daughter possessed no concept for the meaning of self-restraint. This had been shown in Tally's aggression toward the antis. It was demonstrated in the drugs. It had been exemplified when she decided to kill Rory.

Kiera gave her daughter a tight smile and closed the door. She padded downstairs to the kitchen and poured the glass of wine. Strangely, she did not really want it now. But she carried the glass as she left the kitchen, swirling the liquid absently with one hand as she entered the dining room.

Here she flipped on the overhead light. She twirled the glass gently between her palms as she stood before the book case and regarded the picture frames. What tears she may have wept looking over her family photos had all been spent. This did not wipe away the misery, oh no. It did not quiet the yearning to have her husband at her side nor did it lessen the ache to clasp her son in her arms. She missed Skylar, too, and knew her youngest might well never step foot into the house again.

Her eyes turned from the images of her family to the frame with Anthony's photo. For the first time she understood it was completely out of place here. It had always been out of place here.

Kiera lifted the frame. She gazed at the handsome face looking back at her and pressed a finger pad against the glass. If Jacey hadn't seen this photograph Rory would probably still be alive. Why had she kept it? Most other women wouldn't even consider displaying an old lover's picture beside those of her family.

I have never been like most other women.

She didn't know she was shaking until the frame fell from her hands. It struck the floor front-side first with a tinkling implosion of glass. She knelt and turned the front over. A long gap forked across the glass. More broken glass lay in needle thin shards upon the floor. Worse, the shards had left tiny pockmarks in the picture. She was too weary to cry or feel anger. But the marred photograph meant something, this she knew. Exactly what she was not sure.

Kiera carefully lifted the picture frame out of the shards and laid it on the table.

Returning to the kitchen with the wine, she went to stand in front of the window. She gazed out across the lawn, her mind craving silent peace, when she heard something at the door. It was like a scratch—no, more of a shuffle, like something rubbing against the wood. She set the wine glass to the counter.

As she opened the door she felt no surprise to find the dog standing there. It was as if this dog nobody else could see had been waiting for her. She imagined that even if Jacey –who had loved the little thing—were here at this very moment, she would be unable to see the dog.

Roscoe, Kiera remembered. That had been the name of Jacey's dog. And she understood completely now Roscoe had started appearing either as a warning to her or as a harbinger of karma.

The little dog yelped at her. Just one yelp, before twitching its tail and bounding away. Kiera watched as it ran past the reach of the porch light and slinked into the shadows. It mattered not to her if the spectral dog were a warning or harbinger. She had prayed and sacrificed to Cailleach so she might be shielded from exposure and retribution from her enemies. The dark goddess had accepted her offerings and rewarded her with everything she'd asked for. Not in a way Kiera would have ever expected, no. But the antis' videos posed no more of an issue and the threat of lawsuit no longer barred her from enjoying pro-choice activities.

In Cailleach's uncanny sense of generosity she had seen to it Kiera was left with the one child who was almost a clone of herself. The one who acted with self-righteous purpose in her every dealing, the one who never shied away from hurting those who stood in her way. The daughter who, thanks to Kiera's own carelessness, could never give her grandchildren.

And now Kiera, dutiful and proud devotee that she was, was wracked by grief and guilt. All the same she knew these emotions were weaknesses. Weakness was intolerable to the crone.

Cailleach's whispers murmured close to Kiera's ear. Putrid odors imbued the air and unseen fingers teased and yanked at her hair. The demanding crone's summon to worship lashed in the breeze and rumbled in the floorboards of the house. It echoed in the unholy wail that rang out across the property.

"I am stronger than any ghost or harbinger of doom. But where is my slayer of the weak and the fecund? Where is she whose prayers I answered? Have you forsaken your dark Queen?"

Kiera sighed and rested her forehead against the door molding. Without her even willing it the future glowed clearly behind her closed eyelids. It was possible, Kiera thought, to live with the repercussions that came with Cailleach's gifts. The day might come when she could remember Wendell without grief. Or to walk across the property without thinking about how their son's forsaken bones lay buried in the shades. Perhaps someday even her relationship with Skylar might be mended.

And Tally would be there with her. Poor mad, drug-fueled Tally, who was already eager to take up her own causes. Tally expected Kiera to join her in righteous protests and demonstrations. In her own emotionally unstable way Tally exalted Cailleach on a level superior to any sacrifice or deed Kiera had ever committed.

Kiera knew she should be proud. But the truth was Tally threatened to best her. The risk of being bested was the one thing Kiera had never tolerated from anyone. She had not abided such risk when her sister Monica was born. It was for this intolerance she had happily helped Anthony in setting up the murder of his wife. Now she had one rival left, and this was the one who threatened to replace her in Cailleach's favor. The single person unimpeded by any capacity for remorse; the one whom—by Kiera's own dedicated teaching over the years—had been molded into a flawlessly merciless disciple of the Dark Mother. The one who already planned to dictate Kiera's activities from here on.

Grief could be lived with. Changes in lifestyle could be managed. To be supplanted in her goddess's favor, however, could not be endured. Especially not by one whom Kiera had worked so hard to shield.

I will not be bested! Especially not by a child whom I have gone to such lengths to protect!

The admission silenced the apprehension Kiera had felt all evening. It quelled the disquiet left over from Tally's rage in the jeep. It shoved out the images of Wendell's funeral and comforted the despair of losing Rory.

Softly Kiera closed the door. With a determined inhale she proceeded to the dining room. Here, Wendell's gun cabinet still stood. His key as well as Rory's copy hung from a chain around Kiera's neck. After the authorities came to remove Wendell's body she had removed the silly and useless pentagram and replaced it with the keys. Now she needed to unlock the cabinet again. Tally, addled by drugs in her dimly lit room, would not hear her mother enter.

As Kiera unfastened the chain she entertained a last charitable thought for her demented daughter: *I will wait until she has closed her eyes for the night.*

This, she conceded, was the least a good mother could do for their child.

THE END

About the Author

Penny Fairland is the pseudonym of a published author of multiple books and short stories. Adopted at a young age by a loving American couple, she credits the man who raised her for stimulating an early and abiding interest in literature and later, the desire to pursue a career in writing fiction. As a lifelong fan of gothic horror she has sought to harmonize the fundamental elements of the genre with contemporary backdrops. Penny is married to a Native American gentleman and they make their home close to the Cherokee National Forest.

www.ingramcontent.com/pod-product-compliance
Lightning Source LLC
Chambersburg PA
CBHW051247210726
48287CB00002B/390